The Wives of Lucifer

by

Caryn M. McGill

This is a work of fiction. Names, characters, places, and incidents are either the product of the author's imagination or are used fictitiously, and any resemblance to actual persons living or dead, business establishments, events, or locales, is entirely coincidental.

The Wives of Lucifer

COPYRIGHT © 2016 by Caryn M. McGill

All rights reserved. No part of this book may be used or reproduced in any manner whatsoever without written permission of the author or The Wild Rose Press, Inc. except in the case of brief quotations embodied in critical articles or reviews.
Contact Information: info@thewildrosepress.com

Cover Art by *Debbie Taylor*

The Wild Rose Press, Inc.
PO Box 708
Adams Basin, NY 14410-0708
Visit us at www.thewildrosepress.com

Publishing History
First Black Rose Edition, 2016
Print ISBN 978-1-5092-0669-8
Digital ISBN 978-1-5092-0670-4

Published in the United States of America

Dedication

To my little brother, Johnny.
Where did you go?

"Fairy tales do not tell people that dragons exist, children already know that dragons exist. Fairy tales tell children that dragons can be killed."

G.K. Chesterton

Prelude to the Storm

April 30, 1802

The boy's body tossed wildly on turbulent waters, his vacant eyes black as the sea. I couldn't save him. The pier's rickety wood pilings creaked and shifted under my feet. Merciless rain stung me. Needlelike droplets pelted the threadbare patch at my nape, my exposed hands, my frozen cheeks, slapped at me like my sister did.

I wanted to cry, not for myself. For the boy.

As I confronted my twin sister, her dark eyes flared with anger, the howling wind whipping our chestnut tresses hither-thither. Spying the bloody knife in her hand, I yelled, "You killed him!"

"He had it coming."

The calmness in her tone knotted my stomach. Fear and disgust polluted my veins. Once, I'd caught her torturing an emaciated tabby cat. I'd rushed her, and we'd tumbled to the ground. Rolling, kicking, biting. Somehow she always brought out the worst in me. The *hate*.

My sister said, "Stupid boy. He annoyed me. And you always take his side!"

Before I could respond, her gaze shifted, widened unnaturally. Reality vibrated, halted, then sped up. Was something behind me? Breathe, one thousand, breathe. I shivered, even as an inexplicable heat grazed my flesh.

Don't do it, don't turn around. Trembling, I pivoted. A lanky figure towered over us. Moonlight glinted off the golden chain from his pocket watch. His double-breasted frock coat, tailored breeches, and impeccable striped ascot signified wealth. His blue eyes radiated such malevolence I recoiled, unable to move, not one insignificant muscle.

The stranger lunged for my sister. His long gnarled fingers wrapped around her tiny arm like the hairy legs of a tarantula. She kicked his shins, tried to wrench herself away, but his claw-like nail sliced into her tender skin, branding her with…some…mark?

The stench of burning flesh hitched in my throat. My sister screamed. Primal instincts squeezed my guts, fusing my scattered thoughts into one goal: *survive.*

I fled. Running fast, faster toward all the closed stores on Washington Avenue. The tavern. The fishmonger's stand. A carriage parked next to the blacksmith's corner shop, no horse in sight. If only, if only. Stumbling onto wet cobblestones, I lost my footing. My hands and knees skidded across slick pavement, grit scraping against my teeth, my ragged petticoats flung nearly over my head.

Images strobed. Mother covered in gore, dying after giving birth to me and my sister. Father drunk, whoring around town, stealing anything he could get his hands on. Townsfolk bringing me and my twin bland porridge. A lady in the church choir surprising us earlier this very day with a days-old sponge cake disguised as birthday cake, minus ten sparkly candles—my pathetic life.

Gleaming black boots straddled my hips. I closed

my eyelids and braced for agony. The man grabbed the back of my dress and jerked me upright. My left shoe slipped off, my toes landing in a tiny pool of frigid water. He yanked me close, then turned my wrist to the night sky, his talon carving into my flesh.

Blood oozed. I waited for the pain. But...nothing.

He peered down. A smile quirked his lips, or was it a sneer? My heart galloped uncontrollably. I reached up, up, up to the heavens. Why? Why!

A bolt of luminosity blinded me. Thunder gnashed and roared. I shut my eyes and rage reverberated inside me like a caged beast. A lightning strike? Every bit of intuition I possessed shrieked that wasn't the case. Yet fire flamed my skin, frying me.

Once again, no pain?

A dreamlike stupor blanketed me, my inhalations slowed. I opened my eyes. My sister lay sprawled nearby, contorted into the awkward pose of a fresh corpse. Gazing over my body, I couldn't understand how I'd survived. Or had I?

Panic slammed in from every direction. I searched for the stranger. Gone, he was gone.

Struggling for breath, I tried to make sense of the impossible. I wiped at the reddish-black smudge on my wrist. A perfect crimson crescent branded my skin. What did it mean?

Familiar arms swept me off my feet. The sugary fragrance of maple syrup filled my head. I rocketed skyward in shards of rainbow hues. Home. I was going home! Except I couldn't recall where that was.

Traveling, traveling. My senses eroded into nothingness. Only emotion remained, amplified. Loneliness. Fear. Love. A veil of fog wrapped me in its

chilled embrace, and I spiraled into an abyss.
    And then I remembered.
    Dead.
    Again.

Chapter 1

Present Day

Ravana simmered in barely controlled rage, a fury buried for nearly a century and a half. Walking around the exercise yard at Upstate Women's Correctional Facility, she awaited Lilith's arrival. Ravana's dark hair hung over her left shoulder, bound in a tight ponytail. She mindlessly twisted it into a braid, then tugged on it, hard. Not painful enough. Pain empowered her, like the rush of heroin through a bloodstream.

Lilith was late, as usual.

"Am I interrupting a masochistic moment?" Lilith said, appearing at Ravana's back.

Ravana wheeled on her. Lilith embraced the Goth look, with cherry-red hair and entirely too many tattoos and face piercings for Ravana's taste. Ravana preferred something more dignified, more sophisticated. Her head held high, she looked down her long aristocratic nose at her sister-wife. Ravana stood at least four inches taller, but Lilith had a good twenty pounds on her. She narrowed her eyes and flashed red light at Lilith's face.

"What the blazes was that for?" Lilith said, feeling her cheeks.

"Darling, you can't walk around with all that metal in your face. It's against the rules. I'll put it back later." Ravana held her disgust at bay. Nothing would ever mar her immaculate ivory skin.

"You left that part out. I got the jumpsuit right though." Lilith huffed. "I think you like to see me screw up."

So true, Ravana thought. "Don't start with me, Lily. I'm in no mood." Together, they walked to the opposite end of the yard, and took a seat on a metal bench. An uncomfortable interlude dragged on, and Ravana sensed Lilith's annoyance as she watched her pick the cuticles surrounding her stubby, black-lacquered fingernails.

"Thou knowest what hath transpired?" said Lilith. "A woeful day hath descended upon us."

"You're lapsing into old-speak. I hate when you do that," Ravana scolded.

"My apologies, sister of the night. It happens when I'm stressed."

"Tell me," said Ravana.

"Why did you choose this place to meet?" Lilith muttered.

"I needed to be around my people. It soothes me." The prison housed many souls belonging to Ravana, and she gleefully anticipated a fine new crop to capture and torture.

"Well," Lilith said. She sighed heavily. "You've heard the news?"

"I heard. Why are they bringing her in ahead of schedule? I thought she wasn't due for another sixty years."

Lilith hesitated, shuffling her feet in the crusty soil. "I think they're getting nervous. After the night on the pier, they kept her hidden in Raphael's kingdom for nearly a hundred fifty years…we couldn't get near her."

Ravana inhaled sharply, and her right hand immediately wrapped around the red crescent mark on her wrist. She glanced down at the brand, rubbing her thumb across it in a soothing stroke. "I've told you a dozen times, Lily. I don't want to talk about that night. Ever!"

"My, my, little missy, don't get all cranky on me," Lilith crooned.

Ravana thought back to the stormy night, her last chance to enter the City of the Sun. The day the gates slammed shut in her face with no chance of a reprieve. She hadn't had a great track record during her lives on Earth. For some reason, she always picked the wrong path, yielding too easily to temptation. After each rebirth, she vowed to do better, yet never did. Eventually, she accepted the fact she was just a bad seed. No matter where she got planted, she always sprouted into lethal ivy, strangling everything in her way as her soul crept along the road to perdition.

Truthfully, Ravana didn't care anymore.

The glare from the eternal light burned her skin, and she found the darkness more comforting. And when Lucifer offered her another life, she jumped at the chance to walk the path that would finally define her destiny. With the benefit of hindsight, she understood: after the night on the pier, he would test her. Subject her to trials to prove her worth. He couldn't give her a *new* mortal life, only the Travelers could do that, but he gave her a new body, a beautiful young woman's. She passed into the female's flesh at her moment of death, a possession of sorts, and since Travelers mostly cared about souls and not bodies, she could begin her wicked work in earnest without fear of detection. She toiled hard at honing her evilness and lured hordes of souls to dwell permanently in Hell.

Lucifer loved her for it.

A squadron of six fighter jets screamed overhead. Ravana startled, distracted from her thoughts. "What the hell?"

"There's a military base only a few miles away," Lilith said. "Why so jumpy?

"Shut up."

Lilith stood. "I'm not about to waste any more time listening to you, bitch. Call me when you're not such a crank."

"I'm not cranky, I'm mad." Ravana struggled to keep her voice under control. "I thought we'd have more time to prepare for Olivia's arrival."

"You're mad? I'm pretty sure I literally have steam coming out of my ears."

A sudden hush surrounded them while Ravana considered their options. That damned Covenant forbade them from taking souls against their will. "Sit," Ravana ordered.

Lilith grunted, then complied. "You know what really riles me? His Highness thinks he's so goddamned sneaky and we don't know what he's up to."

"He's a man, Lily. Men always think they can get away with shit."

Lilith crossed her arms over her chest. "Having one sister-wife nearly sent me over the edge, but his obsession for Olivia is where I draw the line." She flared her nostrils and exhaled noisily. "I should be used to this crap by now, but sometimes I wonder if it's worth the effort. He's mine, and...?" Lilith frowned, obviously aware she'd stepped into sensitive territory.

Ravana glared. "Careful, Lily…"

"Okay, *ours*, I should say, and I fully intend to keep it that way. I've no intention of relinquishing my kingdom to anyone else. Hell, I can barely stand you."

Ravana knew jealousy consumed Lilith twenty-four, seven. The day Lucifer called Ravana to "come hither," Ravana had chuckled to herself. He'd actually said that. Seriously?

Upon Ravana's arrival Lucifer brought her to his bedchamber. Against the far wall sat a king-sized bed in an onyx frame dotted with shimmering black diamonds. Ravana gazed at the red satin sheeting and quickly surmised it would serve as her marriage bed. No ceremony was performed, no pomp and circumstance. Lucifer claimed her as his second wife, and it immediately became the law of the land. *Then*, she'd met Lilith.

Ravana marveled at her first day in Lucifer's Kingdom. She'd always imagined Hell as a fiery pit of unending agony, populated by horned creatures bearing pitchforks, where the screams of tortured souls would echo in smoldering chambers, begging for a release that would never come. However, the magnificent city he'd constructed beneath the surface of the Earth had been built from black ice and diamonds, the caverns and tunnels frigid.

Lilith kept at it. She got up and began to pace. "That bastard never could have built this damn kingdom without me, a simple fact that seems to have slipped his mind in the last millennium. And now, he does *this* to me?"

"Bitch, bitch, bitch. You complain too much, Lily, and I'm about out of patience with you."

Lilith froze in place and faced her sister-wife. "I was doing just fine until you came along!" They scrutinized each other, but Ravana held her tongue. Lilith sat down heavily, and grumbled. "And last night, well, blazes, he was in a vile mood, and I don't mean that in a good way. I have no idea what had his jockey shorts in a bunch. I couldn't wait to get out of there this morning." Lilith sighed, a loud whooshing sound.

Ravana smirked. "He doesn't wear jockey shorts, darling."

Lilith glowered. "I know that, it's just an expression, Vana."

"An expression? Really? Who says that, Lily?"

"Whatever." Lilith shook her head in annoyance. "He's getting on my last nerve."

Ravana suppressed a chuckle. Getting Lilith all hot and bothered gave her immense satisfaction. But lately, with all this whining, she could only endure Lilith in small doses.

Lilith obsessively bit at the skin around her fingernails, spitting the fragments onto the ground.

"You're ruining your lovely manicure," Ravana chided.

"Don't change the subject." Lilith shoved Ravana with her shoulder. Ravana shoved her back.

Lilith refused to look at her, and Ravana was glad. A confrontation with Lilith would summon the prison guards, and, although she had control of their minds and didn't fear reprisal, she needed an ideal place to talk without interruption.

"It can't be just what happened that night on the pier that's got them bringing Olivia in ahead of schedule," Ravana said. "It was too long ago, there has to be some other reason."

"I'll take credit for it. I've been working her boyfriend, Ryan, pretty hard at turning Olivia in our direction. But I think her damned guardian's onto us and alerted the Scepters. That's why they're bringing her in now."

Ravana knew exactly what Lilith had been up to and delighted in the fact she could sit back and just wait until Lilith screwed up. Then she'd make her move on Olivia, and she'd finally have victory. "All right. Let's focus on the task at hand."

"What are you thinking?" Lilith said, hopefulness coloring her voice.

Ravana leaned her forearms on her knees, glaring into the dirt. She turned her head toward Lilith. "I don't know. She has to come with us willingly."

"Let's just throw our weight around. Let the Travelers know we're paying attention, and we have our own intentions for Little Lightning Girl. Those Travelers are so arrogant. I want to rattle their cage a little."

"Done."

"Good. Put your best bitch face on. The one you usually use on me." Lilith narrowed one eye and grinned.

Ravana leaned back against the bench, and sighed heavily. "Don't go there." She had formulated a plan of her own, but she needed Lilith's help. And if her plan worked, then she'd be rid of both Olivia and Lilith and she would inherit the Kingdom of Hell.

Lilith sighed. "Look, Vana, I know we're not going to become BFFs or anything. Blazes! I never wanted you here in the first place, but I'm stuck with you and if we're going to get rid of Olivia, we're going to have to work together."

Here we go. That's the Lilith I know and love! Well, not really. But that's the girl I need in my corner. Ravana had to be careful around Lilith. If Lilith discovered her scheme, she'd rat her out in a New York minute, and then Ravana would suffer her husband's almighty wrath, not to mention Lilith would be overjoyed at the chance to be rid of her. Although Ravana didn't usually fear Lucifer, she'd never truly tested him, and the thought of being imprisoned in his *special place* forever sent an unwelcome chill down even her evil spine.

Lilith squinted up at the bright blue sky. The midday sun beamed down on them. "Blazes, it's too bright out here. Can't we go somewhere shadier?"

"I like it here," Ravana said.

Lilith grunted. "Fine." She paused and then added, "Tonight's the night. They're bringing her in at 8:07. On the road in front of her house. I plan to be there, and I suggest you back me up. I want to throw some serious shit her way and you know Thomas will be with her, and I wouldn't be surprised if John showed up, too."

"Count me in," Ravana said.

Lilith focused her intense gaze on Ravana. The excitement on her face heartened Ravana. She'd let Lilith take the lead while setting her up as the foil and keeping her own involvement under wraps.

"I'll meet you there at eight," said Lilith, getting to her feet.

The horn blared, announcing the end of yard time. Ravana got in line with the other inmates to return to their cells. Lilith narrowed her eyes. "You're going inside?"

"Yes," Ravana whispered. "Tonight's my night with His Highness, and I'm bringing him a horde of new souls as a token of my devotion." Lucifer had a powerful presence, his physique flaunting lean muscle and unbridled strength. Ravana considered him seriously hot and clearly dangerous, her attraction to him undeniable. Her veins pulsed with uninhibited lust.

"Come on, Lily, it'll be entertaining."

Lilith ran her fingers through her spikey red hair. She followed her sister-wife down the corridor lined with open-door cells as the mass of inmates trickled into their cubicles. "Make yourself imperceptible and wait," Ravana said, putting a hand on Lilith's arm. Another warning bell rang and a minute later the cell doors slammed shut.

"What do you have planned?" Lilith asked, excitement tingeing her voice.

The guards checked that each inmate had been secured and then exited. "Come on," Ravana urged again. She walked to the first cell in line and pointed her finger at the mattress under the woman reading a trashy romance novel. A beam of glowing red light sprang from her fingertip and ignited the thin mattress. The prisoner bolted upright and screamed.

"Blazes!" Lilith cried. "What fun!" The two evil princesses moved quickly down the aisle setting each mattress on fire. The terrified screams thrilled Ravana's dark soul. A wicked grin crossed her face as she glided through the flames and exited the prison.

Lucifer would be so…pleased. And she needed to keep him happy, for just a little while longer.

Chapter 2

The sound of crunching gravel made my heart skip erratically. Ryan was here! We'd met last year as freshmen at Columbia University. He lived in the next town over, near the military base where my stepsister, Carrie, was stationed as a test pilot.

I ran to my bedroom window to see him exiting his parents' black Audi. I knocked on the pane, and he looked up, flashing his devilish smile. I gave a pert little wave. He waved back.

I bolted down the stairs so fast I missed the last two steps and grabbed the banister to avoid a full face-plant on the green-and-white tiled floor. Ryan opened the unlocked door, and I threw myself at him, wrapping my arms and legs around him like one of those crazy characters I decorated my pencil with in first grade. His arms circled me in a tight hug.

"Hi," I said.

"Hey, babe." He kissed the side of my neck, and the heat radiating from his luscious lips sent my libido into high gear. I simply could never get enough of him.

We stayed that way for a minute, inhaling each other like we were starved for oxygen. I hadn't seen him for three whole days. I pulled my head back and gazed into his gorgeous blue eyes, then planted my lips on his.

Sliding down his body, our belt buckles hitched

together, and my feet failed to hit the ground. We laughed as he placed his hands on my ass and hoisted me up to untangle us, then returned me to the floor.

"Crappy trip home yesterday, huh?" he said.

"Yeah, if that bio test hadn't been scheduled so late I could've avoided the insane traffic. I made it home just in time for dinner."

Ryan smirked. "My last few days of classes were cancelled so I cut out early." I was pretty sure Ryan was lying, but nervousness kept me from calling him out on it. Abysmal grades had landed him on academic probation, jeopardizing his scholarship. A star player on both the soccer and lacrosse teams, he had extraordinary stamina and could outrun anyone on either team. I wound up tutoring him. Spending all those hours in each other's rooms quickly led to dating and, well, a lot more. Losing my virginity to Ryan was almost painless. He was experienced, and I was thankful. There wasn't even any blood. Ryan said it didn't seem like I'd never had sex before, but I said it was because of his exceptional sexpertise. It was the truth.

I got his grade up to a C, but it wasn't enough to keep him off probation. I found it difficult to understand how students playing a sport in college could pass at all; the number of road trips forced them to miss a good amount of class time.

"Give me your jacket," I said. He shrugged it off, and I hung it in the hall closet.

Ryan pulled me to his chest and draped his arms over my shoulders. "Is Mommy home?"

"Nope. She volunteers at the library today. She won't be back until three." I wiggled my eyebrows.

Ryan laughed.

"Mmm," he said. "A nap then?" He arched his eyebrows in return. "Nap" was Ryan's euphemism for sex.

I grabbed his hand and tugged him up the stairs to my bedroom. Ryan removed his wallet and keys from the pockets of his jeans, and placed them on my desk. He turned and leaned his cute bubble ass against the desktop and tucked his hands into his armpits. I took a seat on my bed and ran my gaze over his chiseled body. I couldn't wait to get my hands on him.

"Listen, Livy," he said. "I need to ask you something." His gaze turned serious and he came over and sat next to me on the bed. Our shoulders touched. Ryan focused on the floor, then turned to look at me. "You know I'm not the best student." He breathed a long, slow sigh. "I'll never pass Calc II on my own. I mean, you're a great tutor and all, but I just don't have the head for it. When you explain it to me it makes sense, but then I get that damned test paper in my hand and freeze."

"Then drop the course," I offered as a lame solution.

"You know I can't do that. I need it for my major, and I'm pretty sure no matter how many times I take it, I'll still fail."

I leaned back on my elbows and frowned. "I don't see what other options you have."

"It's easy. I'll sit behind you, and you just have to lean over and let me copy the dots. I don't see any other alternative. I won't have to do math when I'm in my real job. I'll get some flunky to do it for me."

Ryan's attitude annoyed me. Even with a sports

scholarship, he had to be a reasonably good student to get into Columbia University in the first place. I knew math was sort of his Achilles heel, but then he'd rather be on the field than in a classroom any day of the week. And I wasn't convinced he put forth enough effort.

I grumbled, stopped myself from rolling my eyes. "That's cheating, Ryan. It's wrong and besides, only half the test is on a scan sheet. There are still problems you have to work out. Then there's the issue of getting caught."

"We're too smart to let that happen."

I got up and walked to the window. I had awoken to sunshine, but now clouds filled the sky, matching my mood.

"I don't know," I said, and yet I wanted to please him, in every way. This worried me. Lately, it was like he had some strange hold over me. He was a bad boy, no doubt, and someone I'd never imagined I'd fall for. My parents didn't like him, and if they knew he was here in my bedroom, they'd be pissed.

Ryan followed me to the window and wrapped his arms around me from behind, trapping my breasts beneath his muscular arms. He nuzzled my neck and his tongue traced a trail down my neck. A delightful tingle made me shiver.

I let out a long, labored breath. He ran his hands across my belly and opened my belt, slipping his fingers down the front of my jeans. "Just think about it, okay?"

I turned around in his arms and landed my hands on his firm biceps. "Okay, I will."

In that moment, all I could think about was I wanted him so badly. He sealed his lips over mine and my back arched, my body curving into him. His fingers were in my hair, and he whispered, "I want you, babe."

He picked me up and tossed me on the bed with enough force I bounced. I giggled, and yet something dark and sinister seized me. Sometimes he was too forceful, too demanding. More than once his fingers grasped me in a chokehold, like some psychopath.

The breath in my lungs suddenly vanished. His gaze felt like lightning in the shadows, blinding, beautiful, and mysterious. "Let's get you out of these clothes," he said. Suddenly I felt flushed, feverish. The ache deep in my belly, a hunger I couldn't satisfy. Before I could reach for the hem of my T-shirt, he was on top of me and his kisses burned my neck.

Ryan rolled onto his back and dragged me onto his chest. He pulled my shirt over my head, tossing it on the floor, and unhitched the clasp of my bra with a single pinch of his fingers. He liked to brag about how he always got it on the first try.

My bra followed my shirt to the floor and within another minute we were both naked. He flipped me onto my back and straddled my hips. Taking my breasts in his hands, he kneaded them slowly, pinching my nipples into hard peaks.

"Close your eyes and keep them closed," he ordered. "Set your mind free and just let me please you." I did as instructed, and he slid his body down and knelt between my legs, then grabbed my ankles and spread them wide.

His kisses landed on my breasts, and I moaned. His hand pushed between my legs, fingers teasing me, taunting me, moving in an unhurried, steady rhythm. Two fingers slipped inside me and I cried out.

"That's it, let me hear you, babe."

I gripped the covers, and another moan escaped me. He had talented hands, confident. I felt like I'd spontaneously combust any second. Everything tightened, the tension building in response to his probing fingers. The explosion rolled through me like a river of sparkling light, and the aftershocks prickled my insides for long lingering moments.

"God," I said. "You're amazing!" I opened my eyes, his nose only an inch from mine. I couldn't look away. In that moment he owned me, and he damn well knew it.

"I need to be inside you," he hissed, pressing his body on top of me. In one quick motion he was, and all the breath whooshed out of me, as if I'd just taken a blow to the chest. He pushed my hands over my head and held them there. He pressed into me, burying himself deep, deeper. He nipped my lips with his teeth, then thrust his tongue in my mouth. He was eating me alive, and I feared I couldn't give enough, that I could never satiate his lust. It felt like crackling electricity, a blinding luminosity. His fingers were around my throat, pressing, choking. I opened my eyes and startled. I swore a red flash of light had passed across his irises. I must have imagined it because it was just Ryan.

A wash of heat spread over me, bringing a mist of perspiration to my skin. "I could do this for hours and hours with you, Livy. I'll never have enough. I need to own you, to have you like this forever."

The warning in his voice aroused me, lewd and dangerous, and yet it scared me, too. Ryan scared me. And I didn't like the idea of being possessed...by anyone.

"Ryan, your hand…it's too tight." His hold on my neck loosened, and he thrust into me violently again and again until I felt his release, explosive, primal. He collapsed on my chest, damp with sweat. As our breathing calmed, the syncopating rhythms of our hearts merged.

"Sorry, I got a little carried away," he said.

My arms circled his neck, and I fastened him to my chest.

Rolling onto his back, he intertwined his fingers with mine, then pulled my palm to his mouth and kissed it. "Look, babe, if I flunk out, everything will turn to shit. I'll lose my scholarship and my parents might even kick me out of the house. They've threatened to revoke my trust fund too. That will kill our plans to go to Europe after we graduate."

My chest tightened at the thought of saying no to Ryan. When I'd first met him, he was so sweet, but in recent months he'd developed a temper, one that I tried to avoid. I stared at the ceiling, considering my words carefully. "I don't understand why this scholarship is so important. Your parents are loaded. Why can't they just pay for school? You could go to community college for a semester and get your grades up. Then you could come back."

He grunted, then turned on his side to face me. "Because my father is a prick, Livy. He's old-school and expects me to prove myself before he bestows any of his hard-earned dollars on the likes of me. He's told me that every day of my fucking life."

My stomach knotted as I considered helping Ryan cheat on his test. Maybe…

"I can't believe you, Livy. I thought you loved me.

What I'm asking isn't that big a deal." He jumped out of bed and reached for his boxers and jeans. "I. Love. You. Plain and simple. I'd do anything to prove it."

He pulled on his pants, and I suddenly felt uncomfortable being naked and dragged the covers over me. What could I say in response to his declaration of undying love?

As Ryan struggled into his T-shirt, his escalating annoyance rumbled through the room like a thunderclap. "Maybe you're not the girl I thought you were."

I bounded out of bed, and threw my shirt on. "Ryan, are you threatening me? You'd break up with me over this?" I strode over to the other side of the bed and faced him.

I heard a yell from somewhere downstairs. "Livy?"

"Shit!" I said, scrambling to find my jeans. "My mom!"

Chapter 3

Ryan ran past my mother with a quick "Hi, Mrs. Miller...ah...sorry." He grabbed his coat from the closet and slammed the door behind him. Tires loudly spewing gravel marked his departure.

"I can't believe this, Livy!" my mother yelled. "You're still seeing that boy! And you bring him here?"

"I wasn't expecting you home early."

"Well, that's obvious, Livy!"

"Why *are* you home?"

"Perhaps because it's *my* house?" She exhaled noisily. "In case you haven't realized, tomorrow's Thanksgiving. I have a ton of things to do. And besides, your brothers have a half-day of school. What if they discovered you in bed with that boy?"

Damn. I was hoping she hadn't put two and two together. She was right, though. It would've been awkward if Keith and Tyler had found Ryan and me doing it. And I had no doubt that would've happened. Almost eight, Tyler still clung to me like ivy. Reading a bedtime story nearly every night of his life was our thing, and its absence caused him serious distress when I went off to college.

"Your father's going to be furious!" my mother screamed, trudging into the kitchen.

I followed her. "Not if you don't tell him."

She slammed her purse on the table. Her hands

landed on her hips. "Your father and I have no secrets from each other."

I walked around her rigid form and faced her. "Come on, Mom, it's not that big a deal. I'm nineteen, almost twenty. I can have sex with my boyfriend if I want."

My mother sighed, sounding weary. "You're too young to appreciate what it's like to really love someone. Sex is more meaningful with someone you love."

"I loathe having this conversation with you, Mom. But as long as we are, I should make it clear that I seriously don't think we have the same ideas when it comes to sex."

Okay, so I got that this was kind of a big deal, but my mother and I never discussed anything rationally. We knew how to push each other's buttons. Plus I was beginning to realize another horror: we were simply too alike. Not only on a physical level, as we both had matching brunette hair and brown eyes (although I'd inherited my five-foot-nine-inch frame from my grandmother Eden), we also had similar combustible personalities.

"Are you using protection?" she asked. "What about STDs?

"I'm on the pill. I'm not an idiot, Mom. And Ryan was tested. I'm not careless. You should know that."

"Honestly, Olivia, there's something sinister about that boy. It's like he's possessed you somehow. You're not yourself around him."

In some ways, I knew my mother was spot-on. I couldn't see anything but Ryan and what he wanted when I was with him.

"Livy, I don't want to talk about this anymore. Carrie has leave for Thanksgiving, so she'll be arriving later tonight. Maybe she can talk some sense into you." Carrie had a good ten years on me, and we'd never been close, although she had brought me to the base a few times and showed off her fancy F-22 Raptor. My Dad had her when he was only twenty, a result of an unplanned college pregnancy. He never married her mom, and Carrie spent the odd weekend or vacation with us.

Mom turned away from me and walked toward the refrigerator, pulling out the makings for Thanksgiving dinner. "I'm still calling your father, and you'll have to answer to him when he gets home. He's going to be very disappointed in you."

I adored my father, and her declaration hit me like a baseball hurled into my solar plexus. I ran upstairs to my room and slammed the door, throwing myself on my bed. My pillows smelled like Ryan and waterworks erupted. Next thing I knew, I awoke in darkness. Mouthwatering aromas wafting up from the kitchen made my stomach twitch.

I grabbed my phone and dialed Ryan. "What?" he mumbled into the speaker.

"Are you still mad at me?" Tears stung my eyes, and I struggled to keep my voice from betraying my misery.

"Depends on your answer." His voice came harsh, cold.

"You're using our relationship as ransom? I don't understand, Ryan. It's…it's…cruel." A sob escaped me, but Ryan said nothing in response.

"You'd really break up with me if I don't help you

cheat?"

"It's simple, Liv, you either love me enough to help me or you don't. I'm not going to be with someone who doesn't love me as much as I love them."

Now my voice broke, I couldn't hold back the tears. "So what...this is a test? What comes next? Would you expect me to lie for you, steal for you. Where does it end?"

"Don't be a drama queen, Livy. Just say yes or no, and if it's no, then we're done."

I pushed the end button, and threw my phone across the room. The tears flowed freely, and I wept into my pillow. How had things gotten so fucked up in just a few hours? I turned things over and over again in my mind, but just couldn't bring myself to give in, especially after his threat.

I sat on the edge of my bed and held my head in my hands. I didn't know what to do. My face was a mess. I'd never be able to face my father in this state. Why not go for a run? It would help me de-stress, maybe regain some remnants of sanity.

I donned a long-sleeved gray Columbia T-shirt and black running shorts, tied on my sneakers, grabbed my phone—which somehow had escaped unscathed—and slipped out the back door, thankfully avoiding my mother. As soon as I returned, I'd offer my help preparing food for tomorrow's festivities. Something I should have done earlier if I hadn't passed out on my bed. Maybe my parents were right. Perhaps Ryan wasn't such a good influence. Maybe he was corrupting my morals.

****

The sun had gone to sleep, the stars twinkling as

the moon held court. The perfect silver crescent hung low on the horizon—enormous. The streetlights cast white circles along the desolate roadway like spotlights. I counted how many steps it took, about five, to span the dark space between each shimmering pool as my feet pounded along the macadam.

Headlights flashed from behind, the cue to move farther off the road. I pulled my earbuds out, glanced over my shoulder. The semi's engine roared, and I fanned to the right to give it a wide berth. *What was a tractor-trailer doing on this road?* And traveling way too fast! From the other direction another set of headlights glared around the sharp curve. Both vehicles veered toward me in an attempt to avoid each other. Terror momentarily stole my breath. Beams intersected, trapping me in a hellish crossfire. I couldn't outrun them. I sprinted, my lungs burning, but stopped short, my running shoes melding with the asphalt. I fell onto my hands and knees, the grit from the cinder roadway biting into my flesh.

Everything. So fast. Shifting.

Screeching brakes, burning rubber, shattering glass. The gleaming grill of the giant behemoth smashed into the Porsche's side door, the night air exploding in a fiery holocaust. Gasoline fumes seared my eyes and nose, the acrid taste rammed down my throat. A tire crushed my foot, dislodging my shoe. The impact hurled me upward. Gravity yanked me down. My face hit asphalt, a sickening crunch echoing. Pain scorched me in blistering waves.

Everything went black.

I opened my eyelids and gazed into the blazing lights of the huge smoking truck. I stood on wobbly legs and brushed myself off. I was alive! How?

And then I saw him.

His dark silhouette emerged from between the headlights of the smoldering semi. Everything morphed into slow-mo. The familiar dread set in. Frantically, I felt my chest, my wrist. No heartbeat, no pulse. I gasped. The heart pounding in my chest merely a memory. Growing more distant with each passing second. This couldn't be happening. I was only nineteen.

"Goddammit!" I stomped my feet like a two-year-old. My eyes burned, and I wanted to cry, but no tears came.

He leveled a stern, disapproving look at me. "Nice mouth," he said. Dressed in a military-style jacket, flannel shirt, and jeans, he could easily be the guy next door. His longish, dark hair framed his chiseled face, alight with the glow of the lethal firelight. And there was no mistaking his scent, he always smelled of freshly made waffles smothered in warm maple syrup. If I had to hang out with a soul collector, it might as well be him.

He headed toward me with that swagger of his. He always led with his left shoulder when he walked. Gazing into his denim-blue eyes, I felt a tremble run through me and didn't know if it was because he was a harbinger of death, or I was just happy to see his handsome face again.

My anger returned quickly, and my hands balled into fists at my side, fingers biting into imaginary flesh. I so wanted to punch him. Hard. "Come on, Thomas! I'm only nineteen!"

"Tell me something I don't know," he said in his

usual calm tone.

"I'm not ready! I have a great life! I have a boyfriend who loves me, and well, my family is going to freak out."

"All the usual," he said. The diamond stud in his left ear flickered like a tiny flame.

"That's all you've got? No words of wisdom? Didn't they teach you any conversational skills in Spirit School?"

He chuckled. "That's funnier than you think."

"What is?" I said.

"Never mind." He sighed. "Let's get a move on."

I knew what would happen if I refused to go. He'd leave me here to ghost around. I'd tried it once, and it totally sucked. I waited a long time, and Thomas wasn't happy about having to come back a second time. That's when I'd first learned Thomas wasn't from some storybook heaven. "I don't have wings, and trust me, Olivia, I'm no angel."

"You definitely don't have a halo," I'd said sarcastically. He hadn't seen the humor. "How about the harp? Is that bullshit, too?"

That he'd found funny, and actually chuckled. "No, Olivia, I'm not particularly musically inclined." And then he'd gone and gotten all serious on me. Well, then what was he? I still had no idea.

The sound of screaming sirens caught my attention and pulled me from these random thoughts. Watching my parents come upon this horrific scene would be too much to bear, and I needed to heed Thomas's urging. The first few times I'd died, I'd hung around and watched, even attended my own funeral on several occasions. But I was done with that stuff…way too heavy.

The smoke billowing from the metal sculpture of death erased the waning moon from the sky. A violent fireball erupted as the mangled Porsche's gas tank exploded. I flinched. Thomas didn't.

But suddenly his face became rigid. He gazed past me, looking sort of spooked. He lurched toward me and grabbed my upper arm. "Hurry."

Air crackled. A brilliant flash of crimson light tore through an indigo sky. I broke free from Thomas and shielded my eyes, the quivering waves searing my ethereal skin. I tried to step backward, away from the intense heat when Thomas wrapped his arms around my waist and pushed me behind him. Was he protecting me? From what? I peeked over his shoulder.

Two towering women dressed in black velvet capes faced us. They were...so...*beautiful.*

"Holy shit," Thomas muttered under his breath. "This is going to get ugly."

The woman on the left spoke first. Her icy stare gave me the shivers. Unnaturally bright red hair spilled out from beneath the hood of her cape, her hands clenching and unclenching at her sides.

The flame-haired beauty spoke to Thomas but her eyes never left me. "Are you prepared to fight us for her?" she said in a sultry voice. "You know you're no match for us, Thomas. It's over, she must come with us."

Thomas groaned loudly. "Well, well, if it isn't Lucifer's two illustrious wives. I thought he kept you two on a pretty short leash these days."

The redhead scowled. She growled, her voice low. "We're not mere pets, Thomas. You underestimate us.

We have countless legions at our command. More than you have in your entire army."

Thomas snickered. "Lies."

I wrapped my arms around Thomas's waist and continued to peer over his shoulder at the two mysterious creatures. I whispered, "Did you just say 'Lucifer's wives'?"

"Keep your mouth shut, Olivia," Thomas said.

I tightened my grip on him, resting my chin on his broad shoulder. The other woman stood taller, as tall as me, with lips red as blood, hair black as midnight. Her hood lay across her shoulders, her shiny tresses cascading down her back. She took a step closer. "She bears our mark. She belongs to us."

"How many times are we going to do this, Ravana?" Thomas said wearily.

"Seventy times seven. As many times as it takes."

"You know that's against the agreement established between your boss and mine, at the beginning of time, no less. *No taking souls against their will.* Olivia chooses to come with me."

The dark-haired beauty smirked. "She's no ordinary soul, Thomas. We both know that."

A spectacle of white sparkle—grander than a thousand Fourth of Julys—momentarily distracted me. The redhead declared, "Oh, look, he's called in reinforcements."

"Do you really think John is enough to help you fight us off?" Ravana said, exploding in raucous laughter. "That's actually amusing."

Johnny was also a spirit guy and my guardian, but I never saw him until I reached the other side. Things were definitely not going according to the usual plan.

Johnny moved in close, taking a protective stance, but kept silent.

"There's no way you're taking her," Thomas insisted.

"Why do they want *me*?" I said.

He ignored me. "There isn't going to be a fight. You're bluffing. She has to choose to come with you and that's never going to happen. Not as long as John and I are around."

"Let's ask her then," the redhead said. The glare of her crystalline green eyes felt like I'd been hit with a mammoth wave of frigid seawater. "Olivia, you're playing for the wrong team. Come with us, we're kindred spirits. Family."

Johnny laughed out loud. "Family? I don't think so, if anyone is family it would be me."

Ravana glowered. The night air crackled. Her left hand shot out and fiery red sparks pummeled Thomas's feet. He jumped back, stepping on my toes and forcing me to hold him tightly to stay upright. Smoke wafted up from his blue and white Nike sneakers.

I gasped. *Holy crap! What the hell?*

"Cute," Thomas said. "But I'm in no mood for parlor tricks."

"Tread lightly, Thomas. We have the blackest of magic at our disposal, something you do not. In fact, our power is much greater than yours. That's why Olivia doesn't belong with you. She has the same magic in her. The darkness we both want. We will teach her how to channel it. And once she does, you and your almighty Scepters will be rendered powerless. We shall rule Earth and all the souls will be ours to command."

"Black magic?" I shouted into Thomas's ear. "This

can't end well."

"Keep quiet, Olivia. Don't listen to anything they say. Let me handle this," he said, his voice loud enough for everyone to hear.

The auburn-haired woman went on. "Olivia, if you come with us you will finally be in control of your destiny. You can have any life you want, an immortal life, a life of great wealth with any man you desire...as many men as you desire. Your every wish fulfilled with a simple wave of your hand. Just say the word and that world is yours."

"Don't answer her," Johnny said. "They're trying to trick you."

The redhead trembled. The ground beneath us shook. I tightened my arms around Thomas's waist, and Johnny moved in behind me. A feral screech filled the air, and I shut my eyes, fully expecting the ground to open up and swallow us whole. "Lilith!" Ravana yelled. "Not now!" Immediately the redhead calmed. The earth stilled.

I pressed Thomas again. "I have a right to know—"

"Just shut up, Olivia," Thomas snapped, shooting me a nasty glare over his shoulder. "Don't listen to anything they say. They're deranged."

"Let's beat it," Johnny said to Thomas. "We need to get her out of here. I don't trust them to abide by the Covenant." The tension in Johnny's voice unnerved me further. They grabbed me firmly by the upper arms and pulled me away from the two mysterious women standing against the fiery backdrop.

"Olivia," Thomas said. "We need to leave now. Ready?"

Like I had a choice.

"You can't guard her every minute!" Ravana yelled to our backs.

"Don't look back, Olivia," Thomas ordered. "Ever."

"Okay, okay!" I shrieked. My twisted body lay directly in front of me, and I had to step over it. Ick! I avoided looking into my vacant dead eyes.

Sweeping me into the safety of his muscular arms, Thomas focused his soft blue eyes on mine. "Try to stay calm," he said with sudden and unexpected tenderness. "I've got you."

Fear snaked its way through my ethereal body, and I clasped my arms around Thomas's neck. Burying my face in his strong shoulder, I inhaled his sweet scent and braced myself. At least I understood this part, what came next. Even if I always hated it.

My body went limp as a beam of light pointed toward the heavens. The ominous swirling tunnel would tear us apart. I just knew it. And yet, it never did. My mind drifted to my family. I loved them so much and thoughts of leaving them behind clutched at the memory of my heart. My two sweet little brothers and my mom, and even my stepsister, Carrie. I'd miss them so much. But mostly, my dad. I mourned over the idea I'd never grow up and prove to him I could do something good in the world, to make him proud. And...Ryan...what about him?

But my last thoughts were of the two mysterious women. Lucifer's two wives. Lilith and Ravana. They wanted me, why? Black magic? Ridiculous. I was just a nobody traveling back to the Astral Plane for the twelfth time. They must be mistaken. Yet they seemed so sure.

I shut my eyes against the stinging wind as Thomas lifted me off the ground. I felt lighter than the tiniest molecule and, without the aid of wings, we ascended into the vast abyss.

I couldn't believe it. Dead. Again. Geez.

Chapter 4

I awoke as Thomas gently placed me on the Astral Plane's ever-foggy ground, where I would be forced to wait, not so patiently, until I got recycled back to Earth once more.

Johnny knelt beside me. His warm brown eyes and generous smile gave me small degrees of comfort. "Hey, sunshine, welcome back."

A flood of emotion overtook me at the remembrance of our short life together. He'd been my little brother once…a long, long time ago, though that notion confused me. "Someday I'll explain," he'd always say. "Just won't be today."

I forced a grin onto my face, and propped myself on my elbows. "Hey," I whispered. Johnny took my hand and stroked it with his thumb.

"Are you okay, Olivia?" Thomas asked, his voice velvety soft.

"Yeah, I'm fine." My thoughts jumped to the confrontation with Lucifer's two wives. "But what was going on—"

Thomas put his fingers on my lips. "Sshhh, rest." He laid me flat, brushing the hair off my face. His hands landed on either side of my head and squeezed.

"Ow!" I screamed, sitting bolt upright. "That felt like a spike shoved through my brain, asshole!" I slapped my hand across my mouth, appalled at my offensive language.

Thomas scowled. "Excuse me?"

I glanced over at Johnny. "Maybe you want to attempt that again, Olivia," he said, "with a healthy dose of respect."

"Sorry, but that hurt!" I rubbed my temples in an attempt to alleviate the burning sensation.

"Maybe I pushed too forcefully," Thomas said. "You were upset. I was trying to infuse serenity."

"Really, Thomas? Lousy technique. Besides, there was something, I mean, yes, something I wanted to ask you…" Only now I couldn't remember the question. Not fair that brain farts happened up here, too. "Never mind."

I threw myself back onto the bed of fog to regroup. God, how I hated the dank, dreary Astral Plane, the land of perennial twilight. It always seemed like the sun was just about to rise or set, but nothing ever actually happened. The first time I'd arrived it took a while to figure out the terrain. Most of the newly dead appeared distorted and gray, as if merely extensions of the mist. After I'd been here a few times, I understood no one had control over what came next. We could only linger until The Powers That Be got around to assigning our next placement.

Throngs of ghosts wandered aimlessly, people trapped in their death attire. Blood and gore soiled their shirts, pants, and dresses. Contusions marred their faces and limbs, and some were missing entire appendages. Good thing we could float. Of course, as I'd learned during a previous time here, these injuries were just leftover memories and eventually the ghoulish aspects faded, and everyone appeared more like their old selves. The longer one stayed the more *normal* they looked, more solid. Usually.

People spoke in the faintest whispers. Mostly, the sounds of sorrow and unrest came. Whimpering, theatrical sighs, sobbing. Many had waited years to obtain a new life with no end in sight. Once, I'd tarried more than a century to be reborn. Although I do recall working in some type of garden during that time. However...I couldn't imagine where.

Exhaustion weighed me down, and I closed my eyes. The swirling fog wrapped me in the chilly swath of death. The melancholy didn't feel as bad this time, which made me wonder if I'd finally gotten accustomed to this whole death and rebirth cycle. Nah, I decided. It still sucked.

"What did you do, melt her friggin' shoes...?"

"I had to before..."

Johnny's and Thomas's words came uncertainly, as if they spoke underwater. I tried to focus on their whispers. "Did you say melted shoes? Is that why I couldn't save myself?" Neither answered me. I eyed Johnny suspiciously. He looked at Thomas. I shifted my attention to Thomas. Who then peered at Johnny.

"It's classified as need to know," Johnny claimed.

"Well, then you guys are terrible with secrets. Newsflash. I'm dead, not deaf." Thomas bit the inside of his mouth while Johnny swallowed hard. I went on, "What's the matter, guys? You're acting straight up bonkers."

"We're not having this conversation," Johnny said, putting his hand firmly on my forehead and shoving me back into the pool of fog. "Nap time."

I sat up. Uneasiness poked at me. For some reason

things felt different this time. Something was...*off*.

"I'm outta here," Thomas said. He leaned in close, and his hands zoomed toward my head. I jerked back defensively. "I'm not going to hurt you, Olivia. I'm sorry about before." Taking my head in his hands, he placed a soft kiss on my brow. "Good luck, sweetheart. You're off my list, so this is sort of goodbye." He winked at me. "She's all yours," he said to Johnny and then vanished into the eddying clouds.

Off his list? Confusion grabbed me, shook me. What did that mean? *Sweetheart?* He'd never called me that before. And a wink? Totally bizarre.

"What's with Thomas?" I asked Johnny. "What does being off his list mean?"

"Nothing for you to worry about."

Could Thomas be handing me off to somebody else? I must have pissed him off big time when I called him an asshole. "Sounds kind of, umm, worrisome. Are you sure?"

"Drop it," Johnny said.

"Fine. By the way, nice job, Mr. Knight In Shining Armor. What happened? Were you napping when that truck hit me?"

Johnny's expression lightened. "You're a regular riot."

Sitting cross-legged on the misty ground in a black T-shirt and well-worn jeans, he finger-combed his choppy sable-brown hair off his brow with both hands before placing his forearms on his knees. We could be two friends hanging out in the backyard if it weren't for the fact I was dead, he was a spirit guy, and the preponderance of fog of course, the eternal gloom.

"So, what's the plan?" I said.

"We wait for Otis."

Ah, my spirit guide. Otis. What a character. He reminded me of an old-fashioned train engineer because he always wore a pair of beat-up, navy-and-white pinstriped overalls complete with cap. He had only one foot. I never asked him for details. Seemed impolite.

Heaviness settled in my chest. The misery of this whole dying thing itself was awful, but as my mind cleared I reminded myself of the vagueness of this journey ahead. Sometimes it made absolutely no sense. Apparently, I hadn't achieved my objective yet. And truthfully I wasn't sure what that even meant.

"Hey, where's your head at?" Johnny said. I blinked. Thankfully, he'd interrupted my further descent into the valley of grief. Haltingly, he added, "Why so quiet?"

Oh my God, I just freakin' died! And at nineteen! Now I was being held against my will in purgatory with absolutely no say-so over my future. What did he expect?

Then again, since Johnny appeared to be in a chatty mood, maybe I should take advantage. I flashed my most innocent face. "Johnny, can I ask you something?"

"That's a loaded question coming from you, Olivia. Once you open a door, there's no going back."

"Well, I've never regretted picking *any* lock. Look, I once asked Thomas if you guys were angels, and he emphatically told me no. So, if you're not angels, what are you?"

"Next."

I sighed. I doubted I'd get anywhere, but I didn't want to give up yet. "Come on, give me something. Scraps. You know I'm not going to just forget about it.

I can't." Johnny examined me, thoroughly and hard. I wouldn't turn away from his intimidating glare. An interlude passed.

Now, *he* sighed. "I guess it's about time you knew." Johnny scrubbed his face with his hands, then turned away. "We call ourselves the Travelers and we guard the Light. That's all I'm saying."

I gasped. "Travelers? Like aliens or something?"

"No. Not aliens, and please, don't press me on this. I've already said more than I should. No more revelations until your journey is concluded."

My eyes scrunched, my mind in overdrive. "Concluded?" I said, my voice shrill.

"Okay, you get one more pearl from me, so listen. Eventually, the cycle of rebirth ends for everyone. In my opinion, you're almost there." He crossed his arms over his broad chest.

"Then this place isn't the final destination?" I said way too loudly, my words reverberating as myriad dead heads shifted toward me. A lady in a feathery church hat got too close, her face and body chopped up, like jigsaw pieces not quite lined up. The victim of a sadistic killer? I gave a firm nudge and sent her gliding in the other direction. "I've done my time? I get to graduate to something better? Is that what Thomas meant?"

"Maybe. That's if you don't screw up between now and then." His stern admonishment made me squirm.

"May I just ask one more thing?" I mumbled, afraid of pushing him.

"As long as you understand I might not be able to answer."

"How long will it take for me to get to...*then*?" I

hoped it wouldn't be another hundred years or more.

"Depends. And it's not a done deal until you arrive. So just hang tight, and do what you're told for once."

After a pause and with zero enthusiasm, I managed to say, "Will do."

"Promises, promises."

Chagrined, I dropped my gaze down to the bloody laceration on my shoeless foot, then noticed the raw burns on my legs, my arms. What did my face look like? It wouldn't be real blood, just memory, but would still prove gross.

I dragged my hands down my face in an effort to erase my frown. "So," I said, trying to sound unburdened. "How come you didn't keep me from becoming road-kill? Isn't that your job?"

Johnny winced. I was definitely giving him more aggravation than usual. "You have such a way with words, Olivia." Well, he had me there. Smart-ass Miller. I'd heard that before. Subtlety had never been one of the tools in my toolbox. I could never color within the lines either.

Now that Johnny had hinted I might soon jump off the life-cycle-treadmill, maybe this death was different in some way. It certainly *felt* different. "Was I scheduled to go today, or not?"

"I'm never going to live this down, am I?"

"That first crack was me inserting the knife. This one is me twisting it."

Johnny hesitated. "It's...complicated, Olivia. Thomas got the order to come and get you, ahead of schedule. He had to hustle."

"What? Why?"

"Can't answer. Above my clearance level. I just do

what I'm told. Something I suggest you take note of."

For some reason I had nothing to say, which for me, was about as rare as a total eclipse happening while all known planets in the cosmos align.

Johnny peered into the fog. "I wonder what's keeping Otis? I told him to meet me here at 2100 hours. I'm going to find him. Stay put, sunshine, and don't get into any trouble while I'm gone."

"Yes, sir." I saluted him.

"Like I said, a regular riot." Johnny phased into the thick mist.

I leaned my chin on my knees and wrapped my arms around my legs. This could take a while. I missed my devices. My phone. My tablet. My foolproof recipe for preventing boredom—

A pair of shabby black work boots entered my field of vision.

"Hey," a male voice said.

I had no intention of engaging anyone in conversation. You never knew what kind of people you'd meet here, and besides, most of us weren't in the best mood at the beginning anyway. I ignored him, hoping he'd leave me alone.

"Hey!" he said louder. "I'm talking to you."

I scrolled my eyes up his body. He wore those thick, insulated, tan coveralls, the kind that guys wear when they work outdoors at some kind of manual labor. The suit was nearly shredded and caked in a mixture of fresh and dried blood. A gash disfigured his right cheek and glanced across his eye. Soot covered his face.

Creepy. Stop creeping on me, Creep.

"How long you been here?" he asked.

I couldn't totally blow him off since he was close

enough to touch me. "Just arrived by twilight express," I said.

A huge puddle of fog drifted across his face, and he whisked it away with his hand. "Jesus, this stuff is suffocating!"

"Breathing isn't a requirement here," I reminded Creep.

"I know, smarty pants. It's just, well, it makes me feel like I'm drowning or something." Two spirit guys tenderly deposited an elderly woman on the ground nearby. She must've died peacefully, not a scratch. We both watched quietly until Creep broke the silence. "Well, what the hell happens now? Is this Hell? Are we jailed forever?"

A parade of the dead moseyed along, as if sleepwalking: completely nude males, old and young, who'd apparently died by fire—their skin charred and blistered—somehow they'd gravitated toward each other. "Not Hell, just the Astral Plane," I said. "First timer?"

His jaw dropped. "This happens more than once?"

"Yeah. You're here until they decide you're ready to be born again. Didn't your soul collector or guardian explain how this works? And how come you're alone? Someone usually stays with you."

"Don't know. Guess I wasn't all that pleasant now that I think about it. A glorious bastard, I reckon. So is somebody gonna tell me what to do next? Or do I just sit here until some flunky arrives?"

"That attitude, dude, isn't gonna get you anywhere. Literally." I did feel sorry for the guy, however. The inaugural experience is totally mind-bending. "You need to wait for your spirit guide to arrive. He or she will tell you where to go next. Either they put you to work or you get recycled right away. Not sure how those decisions are made."

Creep frowned. A downright sinister expression. Macabre. "Bet I can find a way to entertain myself in the meantime."

"Hey, buddy, leave the chick alone." A giant soul collector grabbed Creep by his nape and dropped him to his knees. Scrambling nimbly upright, Creep delivered a right hook, landing a direct hit on the guy's nose. Oh my God. A fight? Seriously?

Creep's blows didn't appear to do any damage, but they both fell to the ground, rolling around in the fog. I crawled away to avoid getting caught in this ridiculous mêlée.

Another soul collector, or maybe a guardian, swooped in, and they flattened Creep into the bed of mist, like two pissed off cops subduing a criminal. "You're close to getting tossed to the Dark Side," barked the soul collector, "and this place is Paradise by comparison."

"Here's my little ray of sunshine," came another male voice from behind. Otis stood next to Johnny.

"What's going on?" Johnny said, gesturing to Creep while bodyguards escorted him deeper into the nether regions of the Astral Plane. "Did that guy bother you?"

"No. Looked like police brutality to me." I struggled to stand. "Hey, Otis." My knees buckled, and I grabbed at Johnny's black shirt to keep from falling.

"Whoa! Easy!" Otis said as he and Johnny grasped my elbows.

"I'm okay," I sputtered, regaining my composure.

Johnny refused to let go. "Sure? I won't leave until you've convinced me."

"Stop stressing. No worries."

He scrutinized me. Once, twice, and then again. "Time to say my goodbyes then." He leaned in and kissed my forehead, holding me longer than necessary. Finally releasing me, he said, "Behave yourself, doll face." With that, he simply evaporated. Gone.

Doll face? What was with the cutesy names?

Otis smiled warmly and said in his usual cheery tone, "If you're okay to walk, I'll take you over to meet Margaret. I don't think you've ever been introduced."

"Lead the way," I said, trailing behind him and focusing on his single black sandal as it appeared and disappeared in the ground-fog. I wondered if this was a temporary assignment like the others, or if this was...*Then*? "What will I be doing?"

"You're to work at Chrism Center with the dead babies."

Chapter 5

The pitch blackness calmed Ravana, like death...mute and inevitable. The trickling groundwater slithering its way down the cavern walls welcomed her home, the dampness soothing. The staccato sounds of whimpering punctuated the silence, music to her ears. She turned toward the desolate soul, felt his youth but couldn't see him in the darkness. Extending a sharp fingernail toward the wall, she pointed at the candle that sat in the black metal wall sconce. The tip of her finger glowed. A tiny beam of red light hurtled toward the wall and struck the wick, her aim perfect as always, even in darkness. She did it twelve more times until all thirteen candles shimmered unsteadily, casting the room in a haze of crimson light.

Ravana craved magic, the way it built up inside her, its voltage zigzagging within as she tamed it and sculpted it like clay, unleashing it bit by bit or all at once. It didn't matter. Enchantments were a means to an end. Victory, sacrifice, pleasure. All tangled up in a web.

Taking a seat in the chair at the end of the long oak table, Ravana stretched her legs over the tabletop and crossed her ankles. The thought of putting up with Lilith's usual rants already rankled. Leaning back in the chair, she balanced her weight on the rear legs and tossed the mane of dark hair over her shoulders. Pulling at a loose thread on the knee of her black jeans, she flicked the errant string onto the ground. Ridiculous that humans would actually pay $700 for jeans that looked like they'd been trampled by a freight train. Still, she felt pretty damned hot in them. Ravana folded her arms over the front of her expensive purple velvet jacket and waited. The young boy sat in the chair across from her, his grimy face streaked with tears.

The clack of stiletto-heeled boots against stone heralded Lilith's arrival. Her spikey hair shone with the redness of the candlelight. Most people would think it a trick of the light, but her hair shimmered exactly the same in the bright of day.

Lilith ripped off her crimson leather gloves and threw them on the table. Her black leather jacket and tight jeans made it seem like she'd just jumped off a Harley, except for the boots perhaps. She said, "What are you doing with this wretched creature?"

"Amusement." Ravana gawked at the miserable youngster, but his gaze stayed glued to the floor.

"Why do you have him gagged and shackled in handcuffs? Why don't you just use a spell?"

"Sometimes I just like doing things the old-fashioned human way." A smug grin settled on Ravana's face.

Lilith ignored the presence of the whimpering child and took a seat across from Ravana, leaning against the high-backed gilded chair. A plump black spider skittered across the tabletop, and Ravana scooped it into her hand, held it captive for a few seconds, then popped it into her mouth.

"Blazes!" Lilith cried. "You know I hate when you do that! It freaks me out!"

Ravana swallowed. "I know, darling. Why do you think I do it?" She loved annoying Lilith. It was almost too easy.

Lilith shook her head and scooted her chair closer to the young boy. "He is a pretty specimen," she cooed, stroking his dirty blond hair off his forehead. "How did he wind up on the list of the damned at such a tender age?"

"He killed his best friend. I had to work him pretty hard, but eventually I managed to push him in the right direction. His guardian proved a challenge, I might add. Those pain-in-the-ass do-gooders really get on my nerves."

"Tell me about it." Lilith laced her fingers together. "You have no idea how hard I was working Ryan behind John's back. I was just getting warmed up. But anyway...I've been snooping around on the Astral Plane, and I have news—"

"How do you manage to prowl around up there?" Ravana interrupted. "I can't last more than a few minutes."

"You forget that Lucifer and I were once residents of the City of the Sun. Our auras are still compatible with the environment. Although, being so close to the sun is painful. I think I got sunburned. Does my face look red?" Lilith patted both cheeks with her fingertips and frowned.

Well, of course her face looked red. The whole place glowed in freakish red light. Ravana didn't answer at first, but then something struck her. "Where's your necklace? The one you always wear?"

Lilith's hand flew to her neck. She felt around. "Blazes! I don't know! I must have lost it!"

"Wasn't it a gift from Lucifer?" Ravana almost felt sorry for Lilith. It was her favorite possession.

"On our wedding night, yes." Lilith shoved her hands down her shirt and rooted around.

"Stop that," Ravana said, "and I've got things to do, Lily. I agreed to meet you here because you said it was important. So spill."

"Cranky, just like always." Lilith sighed. "Your little pet here isn't enough to brighten your mood?" Lilith patted the terrified boy's head, then turned toward Ravana. She thrummed her fingers on the hard wooden table, adding to Ravana's annoyance. "Hmm. Where was I?" Lilith had a knack for trickling out information. Ravana couldn't decide if she was just mentally slow or perhaps she did it on purpose to annoy her. Probably both. "They plan to keep Olivia buried in Chrism Center until the next term at Ecclesia Hall begins. There isn't much time once they recruit her into their army. If she discovers her powers before we get to her, it's game over, and I don't have to remind you what the ramifications will be."

Ravana cringed at Lilith's words. "I know," she muttered. "Do you have a plan?" Ravana's mind rolled around a myriad of sinister musings. She had no intention of relinquishing her station in the Underworld to anyone, especially not Olivia.

"Not yet, we can't really get near her until they put her to work among the mortals," Lilith said, pushing against the table and leaning back in her chair. The tension in Lilith's face gave Ravana hope her plan would work. If she played this with skill, Lilith would crack under the pressure and do her work for her.

Lilith grunted. "Maybe we should just kill her and

be done with it. If she's eliminated, then this stupid game will be over, and we could go back to business as usual."

Exactly the line of thought she needed Lilith to follow. They both knew they couldn't murder her, not yet, although the thought of squishing the little lightning bug under the heel of her favorite black boot made Ravana's heart leap.

But what about Lucifer's master plan to bring forth the prophesied Triangle of Darkness? A feat requiring three powerful auras, capable of sucking all light from the sun, plunging Earth into eternal darkness. The City of the Sun would be destroyed and the Scepters along with it, and Lucifer would have his revenge against Michael for banishing him eons ago.

Ravana feared Lilith's aura wouldn't be strong enough to generate the magical triangle. She needed to draw Olivia into the fold for two reasons: as a backup for Lilith in the event that Lilith couldn't perform as needed, and to keep Olivia out of the Scepters' arsenal.

However, Lucifer had other intentions for Olivia, and in that regard she and Lilith were like-minded. As soon as Olivia played her role, Ravana would find a way to eliminate her, and Lilith too. The Kingdom of Hell would be hers, and Earth her playground for all of eternity. A dark, dead, cold Earth. She smiled at the thrilling thought.

Unfortunately, the Covenant also prevented anyone from taking Olivia against her will and that included the Scepters. The task required a delicate hand, something Lilith could never manage.

"Don't be ridiculous, Lily, we can't outright slaughter her. Lucifer would be furious. And the

Scepters would easily go to war over this."

"Not if we made it look like an accident." Lilith quirked her eyebrows.

"Let's not rush into anything," Ravana said, trying to hold Lilith at bay. "Brilliance requires much thought and planning." An interlude of apprehensive quiet elapsed. "I have an idea, a way to get Olivia into some serious trouble with the Scepters." She walked around the table and faced the boy. Raking her talon-like fingernails through his dirty blond hair, she grabbed a hunk of it and jerked. "Peter, dear, how would you like a reprieve from an eternity in Hell and earn your way back into the Light?"

Chapter 6

Sauntering into Chrism Center felt like I'd been dropped into a vat of liquid sunshine. I gazed up at the oversized sun and shielded my eyes. The ever-present chill ran from me, an unwelcome intruder in this sunny place. Maybe this job wouldn't be so bad after all?

Margaret greeted me with a wide smile over too-perfect white teeth. Tall and thin, her skin coffee-hued but with a splash of cream, her luxurious auburn locks cascading down her back in long ringlets of spun silk. I couldn't decide exactly what color her eyes were, maybe violet.

She handed me clean clothes—a gray sheath-style dress and sandals, a welcome relief from the bloodstained shirt and shorts. One sneaker never made it to the Astral Plane, still wedged beneath the tire of the mangled Porsche, and Otis had discarded the other one so I wouldn't limp all the way here.

Margaret escorted me to the nursery, but honestly it looked more like a kennel. I inhaled sharply at the sight before me. Babies, encased in crib-like enclosures sealed with something resembling Plexiglas, filled the giant room. My first thought was they'd suffocate in there before I remembered breathing wasn't really an issue. They looked like translucent ghost babies, whereas my form appeared more solid. I wondered why. They seemed contented enough for dead babies, whatever that meant. Margaret opened the clear plastic top of one of the enclosures and told me to pick up the baby. On second thought, this *was* going to be awful.

I glared at Margaret in disbelief. "Yeah, I don't think so. There's no way I'm touching that thing." Margaret frowned, crossing her arms over her ample chest, pressing her mouth into a straight line. "Look," I continued, "I don't mean to be difficult, but I'm not one of those women who gets all goo-goo eyed around babies. They make me uncomfortable, and especially deceased ones." I never really enjoyed Tyler and Keith much as babies. They proved so needy and they cried a lot and were…messy.

Margaret's eyes narrowed. "This is your job, you don't have a say in it. Just do it."

"Please don't make me repeat myself," I countered with entirely too much attitude.

"We are in the business of saving souls here, young lady."

"Well, I'm not! I'm simply stuck between placements." Margaret glowered, and I feared I might have stepped on a proverbial mine field.

"Surly doesn't suit you, Olivia. Maybe you want to rethink this. I can always find another placement for you." Her voice unnerved me, haunting in some way. "After all, I wouldn't want to send you to—"

"Fine," I relented. It's not like I had much of a choice anyway. "I'll give it a shot. But I'm telling you right now I'll be terrible. Don't say I didn't warn you."

In my last job in the afterlife I'd been assigned to keep the first-timers on the Astral Plane from wandering away. That was like herding sheep, really stupid sheep. Half the time they wouldn't listen, buried under their own sad memories of a life lost. Mostly, I'd just come up behind them and push them back where they belonged. At least this place was warm and sunny.

I dipped into the plastic crate and scooped the baby up, settling it into my arms. Ick! Ick! Ick! Like holding a jellyfish, it totally skeeved me out. The baby squirmed, and I struggled to hold him. His dark eyes locked onto me as a wave of sadness twisted my gut.

"Better," Margaret said, warming slightly. "Now, here's what you need to worry about."

Oh joy, could this situation get any worse?

"First, you must keep your mind separate from his, or the sadness of his limited memory will invade your spirit. These souls can't process what's happened to them, and so they wallow in their abandonment. We try to negate that by giving them lots of love and attention until they're ready for rebirth. So resist the invasion of his despondent aura."

I shut my eyes and pushed back the negative energy swarming me. I focused on something pleasant: a beach, a sunset, a pristine snowfall. The pain of sadness lessened, and my eyelids fluttered open.

"Second, be prepared for the occasional loss. Sometimes they are too far gone to keep cohesive." Margaret's expression stiffened with a certain somberness, what I interpreted as solemn respect for the infant's plight. "When they are lost, they simply disaggregate into tiny droplets of energy, and you will be responsible for collecting them. It's a daunting task and one none of us relishes. If it happens, please call me right away, and I will show you what must be done."

Margaret instructed me to return the baby to his

enclosure and then gave me a specific ward assignment, telling me to work my way through the line of cribs, giving each baby as much time as I could stand. And so, I set about my tasks begrudgingly and banished the thought of losing a baby.

Departing the Astral Plane was a relief. The constant sunshine contrasted starkly with the perennial twilight of the land of the dead, where no sense of day or night existed or the passing of time, just the creepy impression of being immersed in some form of suspended animation. A time paradox of sorts.

I didn't think about Earth much any more. Most of the sadness had evaporated, and I felt more like my old self. Besides, life on Earth was a lot of work by comparison. My energy level here stayed pretty high, which I could maintain without ever having to eat or sleep.

Then, what might have been one month or a year or five decades later, I found myself struggling with a particularly ornery baby. He evaded my grasp and dissolved into a rain shower of sparkling light. A piercing scream heralded the exact moment. I gasped, then shouted, "Margaret! Come quick! Hurry!" My eyes stayed locked on my feet and I didn't dare move. Tiny puddles resembling mercury—liquid metal—skittered across the floor like tiny silver balls ricocheting inside a pinball machine.

Margaret sprinted into the room and stopped short.

"Oh my God! Margaret, I'm so sorry! I don't know what happened!"

"It's not your fault," she said with an odd tranquility. "We need to gather up the soul shards." She retrieved a tiny white container from a nearby cabinet and settled onto her knees. "Come," she said, "help me sweep them up."

I tried to assimilate the idea that this child no longer existed. What had caused it to become unstable? I asked Margaret to explain.

"Can't really say. Some souls are stronger than others. It's still a mystery. It just happens. The first time is hard for all of us." Margaret screwed on the lid and left the container on a shelf near the door.

I probed Margaret about what would happen to it. She immediately got snippy, telling me I didn't have the proper clearance level to know. What was this, the friggin' C.I.A.?

No matter how much I strained to banish it, I couldn't dispel the awful image of a soul disintegrating in my hands. Thoughts of death consumed me. So different from mortals dying, something I fully understood, well, sort of, anyway. But this, the apparent demise of an immortal soul…Why?

I saw one of the new girls, Alice, standing off to the side, having witnessed the horrid event. She wasn't really new to the afterlife but to Chrism Center. The sound of the front door crashing into the wall behind it startled me. I looked up, inhaling sharply. He strode into the room with an air of authority. The muscles in his upper body strained the shoulders and sleeves of his gray jumpsuit. He stood tall, well over six feet, warrior blood definitely pulsing through his hot body. The dazzling array of imaginary sunshine coming off him sent a heat-wave through me. His right hand clutched a knotted black cord with little red gemstones bookending each knot, which he quickly hid behind his back.

Alice whispered close to my ear, "That's Gabriel!"

I whispered, "Who?"

"Gabriel, he's one of the Scepters," she said.

Ah, the head honchos in the hierarchy. The mighty Scepter's intense dark gaze fell on me, and my throat closed up. I wondered if he'd come in response to the lost soul, and my whole body tensed.

"Hello, Olivia." His bass voice echoed across the room. "Peace be with you." He paused, then turned to my coworker. "And you, too."

Holy crap! He knew my name?

Gabriel pivoted and headed down the hallway, presumably in search of Margaret. I gaped in silence.

"Geez," Alice said, "that was weird. He knows you?"

"Don't ask me how."

"He didn't say my name, and I've been dead like thirty times."

I blinked in disbelief and swallowed hard. Why would I be someone Gabriel knew?

Gabriel's voice grew loud, and I skulked off into the shadows with Alice. It sounded like Gabriel and Margaret were about to have an argument, and I prayed it had nothing to do with me.

"You're keeping a close eye on her, right?"

"Yes, of course!" Margaret answered. "It's not like they can get to her here."

"I don't know," Gabriel said, annoyed. "Look what one of the guardians brought me." He lowered his voice, but tension iced his tone. "It looks like Lilith's necklace."

Margaret sucked in air. "W-where did he find it?"

"On the path between the Astral Plane and here."

"Honestly, Gabriel, it's not likely Lilith could get to the Astral Plane without Lucifer knowing it and you know he's abided by the Covenant for 300,000 years. He'd never let her come here."

"True, call it intuition, but somehow we think Lilith is acting on her own."

I crouched in a corner with my arms wrapped around my knees, and Alice squished up beside me. She whispered, "I wonder who they're talking about?"

"I've no idea." Then, too loudly, I added, "Who's Lilith?"

"Shush!" Alice plastered her hand across my mouth. The conversation between Gabriel and Margaret halted, and I feared we'd gotten caught eavesdropping.

Gabriel finally said, "I only wanted to confirm she's safe, so I could assure Michael."

"How soon can you get her to move on?"

"Not sure, Michael is still being pretty stubborn about letting her out on her own."

"I suggest you hurry. The sooner she's out of here the better."

Gabriel must have escaped out the back door because we didn't see him leave. Emerging from our hiding place, Alice said, "I think maybe they were talking about you."

I stared at her in astonishment. "Me? Why would Lucifer or this Lilith give a hoot about me?"

"I don't know. You're probably right. Most likely it's one of the babies. I heard Lilith likes to steal babies."

"That makes more sense," I said, relieved at her offer of a more reasonable explanation for Gabriel's visit.

****

Sneaking out, I broke into a jog to keep up with the ghostly courier who'd collected the tiny white soul-coffin. We reached a fork in the pathway, and he veered left instead of going right toward the Astral Plane. I found myself heading into unknown territory. Considering we were supposed to be on the Light Side, as opposed to the Dark Side, it felt scary and creepy…like walking into a cemetery, although no tombstones littered the fog-covered ground.

An enormous white wrought-iron fence emerged through the veil of gloomy mist. Images of screaming babies etched into a giant archway loomed over the gated entrance. The courier took a large silver key from the jumpsuit's pocket and unlocked the gate, opening it with an inaudible push.

An overwhelming dread blanketed me. I shouldn't be here. Why did I always do stuff like this? Impulsive. Again. I thought of my mother and all the times she'd castigated me for acting without thinking. Even dead, I seemed to have this problem. *Turn around, do it, right this minute, and make tracks back to where you belong.* But something nudged me forward. And so I disregarded that inner voice of warning.

An enormous fountain came into view. The rim enclosing the bubbling pool of what flowed like water had more of those distorted baby faces carved along its sides. Silvery blue streams erupted in a giant geyser. Through the veil of drizzle, I made out a swirling eddy near the center. There! The courier glided up to the fountain and disappeared inside. I waited, crouched low to the ground, buried in the fog. A small jet of indigo fire flared upward from deep inside the fountain. A baby cried out, followed by the eerie stillness of death.

I frowned. The courier emerged perfectly dry, slipped the white container into the pocket of his suit, and slid past me. Either he hadn't seen me or didn't care. I desperately wanted to see inside the mysterious fountain but couldn't afford to get myself locked in this spooky place. So I trailed him back to the exit, careful to stay out of sight. But now I realized I hadn't thought this through very well. If Margaret found out...

I stood there in a stupor when the handle clanked and the lock clicked. My heart sank. *Trapped*. Now what?

My form wasn't that solid, perhaps I might be able to squeeze through the metallic bars in the fence, but as I reached to grab the bars, sparks erupted. I recoiled. Did they have some kind of invisible force field set up? I felt like a cornered beast.

"Friggin' great," I said.

I paced around the perimeter of the mysterious fountain, contemplating whether I should investigate this strange place. Did I dare go in? It appeared dimmer and quieter than before. But...I had no idea what I'd be stepping into.

Slipping out of my sandals, I waded into the ankle-deep rippling water. Sadness and despair swamped me, like when I picked up a new baby at Chrism Center. Awash in bubbling water, I struggled to maintain my footing on the slippery floor. I entered a dry space and wiped the water from my face. Opening my eyes, I gasped. Oh my God! Barely a few feet from where I stood, a giant blue funnel of water violently swirled. I could have fallen right into it!

Thousands of crying baby faces circled the cosmic

drain, their tiny piercing eyes glaring at me. *Okay, get a grip, Liv, these are only babies, they're already dead and you needn't be scared, right?* A wave of horrid images washed over me. Did this fountain recycle these souls? Did it send them to the Other Side? Would they be lost forever? A freakish thought struck. Could this be Limbo? Ugh, I'd heard stories about such a place for the lost souls of babies but never imagined I might actually see it for myself.

My feet started to lose traction on the slick marble. The floor took a downward slant and I slid toward the whirling vortex. I lunged backward trying to regain my footing, but to no avail. Panic engulfed me as I visualized becoming soup in the blender of life. At the last second, two hands grabbed under my armpits snagging me from the brink of extinction. I landed face down on the foggy damp ground. Marble baby faces, snarling like rabid creatures, ogled me.

"What was the last thing I told you?" he said behind me.

Dread seized me as I recognized the familiar voice. Johnny. Slowly getting to my feet, I noticed I was perfectly dry. What was that stuff that mimicked water? It felt like water. I slid the palms of my hands over each other as if wiping dirt off them.

"Do I win a prize if I answer correctly?" I said.

"I told you to behave yourself."

I didn't answer right away. "Sorry, but I'm having a really bad day. I killed a baby." I dropped my hands and shifted my eyes downward.

"First of all, you're lucky I got here in time, and secondly, you didn't kill that baby." Johnny peered down at me with his soulful brown gaze.

"You heard?" I cried.

"Yeah, I heard. It's not your fault."

I let out a huge sigh of relief. "So Margaret wasn't lying?"

"You can take her at her word." He hesitated and then added, "However, if you'd slid down the funnel into the Fountain of Lost Souls you'd have disintegrated into thousands of pieces and been absorbed into many new souls. Not all of them human either."

Now that was an odd notion. What would I have become...a toad, a cat, an opossum? This gave a whole new meaning to life on Earth. What about a thorny rose?

"Then, I guess I owe you thanks," I replied.

"You're welcome." But Johnny continued to glare at me. I wasn't off the hook.

Finally, I said, "What?"

"When Margaret finds out where you went, you're going to be in serious trouble."

"I can handle Margaret," I said, gathering my sandals and sitting down on the rim of the fountain to slip them on.

Johnny waited until I finished. "Let's go, sunshine." He put his hand out, and I took it, letting him pull me to my feet. One arm circled my shoulders while the other gathered the back of my knees. I clasped my hands tightly around his neck, brown eyes to brown. A smile spread across his beautiful face. "You're a piece of work, you know that?"

He smelled just like Thomas, and I couldn't decide which of them was cuter. A tie, maybe? Definitely. I grinned. "Yeah, a regular riot, but you love me anyway."

The air crackled, the light blinded me, and suddenly we were back on the grounds of Chrism Center. How did he and Thomas always manage to appear and disappear in a twinkling?

Walking though the front doors of Chrism Center, I ran right into Margaret, her foot thumping.

"Where have you been?" she shrieked.

"I-I went for a walk."

"No more of *that*," Margaret yelled.

Three seconds became a lifetime. "I'm sorry, Margaret. Okay?" I knew I had to grovel, but demeaning myself wasn't really in my repertoire. "Look, I had to find out where those soul shards went."

"I told you that was none of your business." Margaret's eyes constricted.

"Margaret, I won't lie to you. The truth is I had to know. I don't expect you to understand. But I'm just not good at taking somebody's word for anything. I prefer to find out stuff for myself."

The creases in her forehead softened. "What I'm about to say is for your own good," she said, rubbing her temples. "Until I tell you different, you're confined to these premises. Is that clear?"

Seriously? Grounded? Permanently? Before things got messier, in my most contrite voice I said, "Yes, ma'am."

And to think, I'd just sworn I wouldn't lie.

Chapter 7

I'd absolutely no desire to be stuck in this baby-recycling center for all eternity. There must be some reason I'd lived all these lives, a greater purpose that would help me understand the cycle of life and death.

Time passed in its strange other-side way, mostly uneventfully. Tiresome days, although time wasn't really measured that way here, menial jobs of tending lost souls and angry babies, even that garden at some point. Waiting for a placement or new life constituted boredom ad nauseum. Then one day while wrestling a robust babe with a vicious grip on my hair, Margaret came over to talk to me. "Olivia, overall you've done an excellent job since you've been here."

"Thank you," I said, gushing with pride at Margaret's expression of unsolicited praise. All this time I'd considered myself a major pain in her butt.

"It's time for you to move on. I've received word you've been called into service at Ecclesia Hall Academy where you will be trained as a soldier for the City of the Sun."

My imaginary heart stopped. I'd thought Chrism Center had become my own personal hell, at least until I got jettisoned back to Earth again. But then Johnny had hinted at something different this time. Maybe I'd finally arrived at *then*!

"Soldier?" I pretty much shrieked. "What does that

mean? Where is this City of the Sun?"

Margaret gave a wry smile. "It's both here and there, on a constantly shifting corner of the Astral Plane. Difficult to describe. But you're to report immediately. Let's get the paperwork started, shall we?"

Paperwork?

Margaret handed me a five-page document and a white mechanical pencil. I stared in astonishment. "Seriously, Margaret? Don't they know everything about me already?" I drifted back to thoughts of the C.I.A. Wasn't there some form of otherworldly background check they could access? I had the impression that there was a record for all of us somewhere.

"You give us too much credit, Olivia. We aren't quite as all-powerful as you seem to think. Now get to work on it and make sure you proofread. Let me know when you're done."

I settled onto the floor to begin my task. The first question asked how many lives I'd lived, my age at each death and to list any accomplishments during each lifetime. Okay, I knew I'd lived twelve lives but couldn't remember some of the pertinent information for each. I deliberated why. Was my memory eroding with the passage of time? Or maybe fog had finally replaced my gray matter? Some things remained crystal clear: I could recall this death and the one before. I'd only made it to forty-five that time, felled by anaphylactic shock. The one before that? Although a memory of working in someone's garden drifted through my consciousness, I had no idea where that could have been and so I glossed over it. I had to write,

"Can't remember" over and over. When Margaret assured me I'd filled out everything sufficiently, I relaxed, figuring she knew what she was talking about.

Margaret gave me a uniform to wear, like the one Gabriel sported and that courier guy, too. It resembled a flight suit. The lightweight shiny gray material flaunted the academy crest proudly over your heart. A wavy circle of silver thread surrounded a large ornately scripted "E." A pair of golden wings attached itself to the letter's lower area like tiny feet. Godspeed.

I shared an uncomfortably long hug with Margaret, like she was reluctant to set me free, and then headed out on the path to find this Ecclesia Hall. I gave each baby a kiss goodbye, surprisingly sad at leaving.

Arriving at the fork on the golden footpath where Margaret instructed me to turn right, I frowned. I'd walked by the spot plenty and never noticed anything. Continuing along the well-trodden path, I stopped abruptly. My jaw dropped. Not more than fifty feet in front of me stood an enormous structure made entirely of gleaming green marble. I felt like I'd arrived at the Emerald City, and my gaze shifted to my feet. No ruby slippers.

The fog thinned, replaced by brilliant sunshine and puffy white clouds floating against a perfect blue sky. Only a small amount of fog lingered near the ground, small wispy white eddies at my ankles. Nervousness swarmed me as I contemplated entering the unknown.

Ecclesia Hall loomed twenty stories high, crowned with a tall turret dotted with circular stained glass windows. In fact all the windows on the facade were made of multi-hued glass. I cautiously approached the formidable building and stood in front of the over-sized doors where large gold letters announced I'd arrived at my destination. Two intimidating men dressed in the gray uniform bordered the door. Guardians, I assumed, and they looked like they wouldn't take crap from anybody.

I surveyed the crowd of new recruits, all uniformly clad. Everyone—an equal number of males and females—appeared to be about my age and seemed so serious. No one spoke, which just added to my nervousness. I waited first in line until the guardians instructed me to enter, a metal tripod with a crystal globe obstructing my passage.

I stepped forward.

"*It's her*," I heard one guardian whisper to the other. I wondered what they knew about me. Then I realized his lips didn't move. How could I have heard him? Could I be experiencing some form of telepathy? Was that what Johnny and Thomas were doing when I heard them talking about melting my shoes? Hmm.

"Good day, Olivia," the one to my right said in a rather solemn voice.

"Uh...you too," I croaked, anxiety escalating inside me.

"Welcome to Ecclesia Hall," the other guardian announced. "After you enter, submit your forms to the Recorder sitting behind the front desk. Congratulations on being chosen for Special Services."

"Thank you. I-I'm honored."

The guardian ordered me to place my palm on the crystal sphere. An eerie silver light erupted, and the orb jumped off its perch. "Oh my God!" I cried, trying to grab it before it smashed to smithereens.

The alert guardian made the save a split-second

before it would have crashed onto the stone step. His eyebrows arched. I felt my expression twist into terror. I hadn't even touched it!

The intimidating guardian continued to eye me suspiciously. Not a great way to make a first impression! "No matter," he droned politely.

"Yes, no harm done," assured his cohort. The doors magically sprang open, and I crossed the threshold, my name mysteriously echoing through the oversized foyer. But as I passed through the door a shudder wracked my body. I heard them. *Trouble. Most definitely.*

The huge vestibule held twin staircases curving upward and guarded by dark oak bannisters with ornately carved ivory spindles. Floor-to-ceiling windows lined the gleaming marble walls paned with stained glass images of warriors fighting evil monsters from eons before. Huge scarlet blooms lined the periphery of the lobby, spilling out of golden vases encased in wrought-iron stands. Hundreds of snow-white candles rested in shiny silver wall sconces. The fragrance of flowers mixed with the scent of candle wax reminded me of sitting in church.

In front of me: a gray and white marble reception desk. Behind it sat a rather aged gentleman wearing a pair of old-fashioned gold spectacles. Classical music wafted in from the far recesses of the building and I smiled, recognizing Mozart's overture to *The Marriage of Figaro*. My brothers used to call this "bagel music." We awoke to the sounds of Mozart, Bach, or Beethoven on Sunday mornings and ate bagels seated around the dining room table.

"Welcome to Ecclesia Hall, Olivia," the elderly

gent said as I handed him the forms.

"Thank you," I squeaked. Where had my voice gone?

The old man perused the forms. His bushy white eyebrows sat like tufts of dandelion feathers above his mischievous azure eyes. Excitement somersaulted inside me. I struggled to contain it. Dreaming about doing something important was one thing, but…now I worried that maybe I'd overshot my aspirations.

Between the two grand staircases the queue of new recruits passed the front desk through a hallway and into a gigantic open-air auditorium. The smell of smoldering candles made me think of a birthday cake and I remembered my last one: pink frosting atop white cake adorned with ripe red strawberries. It saddened me to think I'd never have another birthday after fate snatched me at the tender age of nineteen. Banishing this morbid thought, I dutifully followed the procession into the polished oaken pews, shuffling feet announcing our arrival. Mosaics of colored light from the stained glass windows splashed across the parade of potential soldiers as we silently took our seats. The spectacular windows reflected fierce animated warriors engaged in combat, like a hologram. I slid across the cold slick bench, anxiety clenching my gut. A soldier? Me? I wasn't quite sure I was soldier material.

The stage at the front held five enormous carved gray marble thrones with crimson seat-cushions. Hundreds of candles in golden sconces lined the stone walls and giant crystal vases stuffed with silver, white, and gold flowers rimmed the room's perimeter. I involuntarily shivered even though the air proved quite warm. The wooden doors behind us shut with a thunderous bang. Everyone jumped. Two men, literally giants, marched to the front and then pivoted, standing at attention while staring straight ahead.

The air electrified. I didn't think the sky could get any brighter, but it appeared like someone had focused colossal klieg lights on the platform. Audible gasps arose as four mega-muscled men emerged from plumes of white smoke. I almost thought I was at one of those Wrestle Mania events I'd seen on TV!

Each stood well over six feet, shod in knee-high leather boots with gleaming silver buckles down the sides. And they were...*ripped*. Togas wrapped around their muscular torsos and barely covered their nether regions. I immediately recognized Gabriel.

A gust of wind whooshed past during their arrival, swirling my hair into a mini tornado of brown ribbons. Strangely, none of the candles went out. Each took a seat on one of the massive marble chairs, fixing their intense gazes on the assembly of squirming apprentices.

A tall willowy figure stepped out from behind the middle unoccupied seat. Flaxen hair cascaded down her back, and her brilliant ivory gown sparkled with every step. Atop her head rested a garland of silver flowers shimmering like moonbeams. As she came to the lip of the stage, her perfect pink lips parted.

"Welcome to all, and may peace be with you," she said in a lilting voice.

The personnel in attendance robotically answered in unison, "And with you."

"I'm Director Bath Qol. Welcome to Ecclesia Hall." She paused and beamed a bright smile. She sure didn't look like a soldier but more like a fairytale princess, and I wondered at her role.

"This will be your base of operations as well as your home during training. I welcome each of you as apprentices to our elite Special Force." It sounded like I'd been recruited into the heavenly version of the Navy SEALs. Now that was downright scary.

"We've been following each of you for ages to determine if your aura continues to evolve along the proper pathway." Uneasiness poked at me. Exactly how long had they been watching?

"For those not born here, we are the Travelers and have taken it upon ourselves to protect and nourish the collective soul of Earth. This requires us to remain forever vigilant in building positive energy in the cosmos. In the event the negative forces tip the balance in the wrong direction, then the world as we know it shall cease. Thus, we are the caretakers of this world, and it's a responsibility we do not take lightly.

"You may notice you're all the same age, nineteen exactly. This is no coincidence. We've used this as our marker for the age of reason since time began. Age is more subjective in the case of mortals and too complicated to explain because mortals have served a varying degree of prior lives. Suffice it to say you have been in a state of suspended time here in the afterlife as you awaited placement."

Huh? How long had I been in this suspended state in Earth time? Months? Decades? Would I be frozen in the body of a nineteen-year-old forever? I wasn't sure if that would be good or bad. Bad, I decided.

The director paused for a minute, her long fingers intertwined in front of her tiny waist and trim hips. "Half of you are former mortals and the other half were born Travelers. You'll work in groups of four: two mortals and two Travelers. Mortals will undergo our transmutation process tomorrow, and if they pass, will officially become part of our Traveler family."

We weren't all mortals? I looked around trying to distinguish who might not be a former Earthling, but I couldn't see any differences. And *transmutation?* It sounded a little Frankensteinian, and I refused to allow my imagination to play with the idea. Bath Qol's beautiful voice pulled me from mental disarray as she continued the orientation.

"At this point I'll take a moment to introduce our honored guests. The Scepters are the most powerfully evolved of our kind. They sit at the head of our Court and are the highest ranked guardians and warriors, our generals should we need to go to war. Again."

I surveyed the four men seated onstage. Quite simply, they were incredibly handsome, like an image I had of Greek gods. What were their lives like? Where did they live? Did they travel back and forth to Earth to save souls?

Bath Qol continued, "After I present each honored guest you will file forward and press your right palm against one as means of introduction. Then proceed through the back hallway and take a seat at a table in the rear chamber. Your name is listed at the entranceway along with your seat assignment." She glided back toward her chair, hair and gown flowing behind her in a dizzying array of sparkles. Her musical voice called out "Gabriel," and he stood, his dark gaze settling over the crowd like a wave of shimmering heat.

She introduced Raphael, the one to Gabriel's right, then Uriel, who sat to her far left. As a palpable momentum kept building, she introduced the tallest of the four as "Michael, our Lord High Commander." A quiver shot through me. The enormity and power of his presence like nothing I'd ever felt.

The director came forward once more. "Approach," she commanded. The two guardians at the front suddenly came alive and urged the first row of new recruits forward. They sorted us into lines. In all, I figured we numbered about two hundred. I sat halfway back on the right-hand side. Each prospective apprentice stopped before one of the Scepters, pressed a palm, then suffered through an awkward moment and waited for release. It seemed easy enough, although the thought of getting this close to one of them filled me with jitters.

I approached the mighty Lord High Commander. Lucky me, couldn't I have drawn one of the others? And I feared he was about to read my mind. He'd know I'd broken plenty of rules, had gone through twelve lives to get here, and I probably wasn't warrior material. I could never measure up to these guys.

My turn. I visualized getting hauled out any second. I stared at his massive hand as he held his palm out to me. An oppressive heat stifled me. Or perhaps this unbearable temperature came from somewhere within. I prayed not to faint. Our hands connected, and energy surged through me, tiny embers shooting from our clasped hands.

Holy shit! What the hell?

I froze, willing the lump in my throat to disappear. The Lord High Commander furrowed his brow, his intense brown eyes searing me. He forced his thick fingers through mine and swallowed my entire hand in his. Electricity sizzled between us. Our gazes dueled, a dance of wills.

After what seemed like an eternity he freed my hand. The guardian standing alongside raised an eyebrow. I ignored the urge to run and hide—where would I go? Was it too late to change my mind? Babysitting suddenly seemed like a better option than being a...*soldier.* Instead, I skulked away to follow my predecessor into the rear chamber, my hand throbbing.

Chapter 8

The line of apprentices moved through the archway to enter a cavernous chamber featuring circular wooden tables and attached half-moon benches, the towering walls painted a bright blue to complement the cobalt and white tiled floor. Massive, beautifully crafted tapestries adorned the walls—a bearded ram next to a great horned bull, a spidery red crab…that cunning lion. Truly something to behold. I twirled slowly, viewing them all: Aries, Taurus, Gemini, the zodiac's twelve signs. Hmm.

Once inside, everyone seemed to relax, and conversations sprouted up, albeit slowly. While waiting to find my seat assignment, someone tapped my shoulder. A young man with reddish-brown hair and dark irises stared back. He stood about a head taller than me, and his expression stretched to the point of being gigantic, over-the-top.

"What was *that*?" he said, his voice having a smooth, rich flow. I detected a twinge of an accent. British? Or maybe Australian, although he sounded more formal than the rugged speech of an Aussie.

I swallowed, hard. "What was what?"

He spoke in a conspiratorial whisper. "That thing the Big Guy did to your hand?"

I bet nobody referred to the Lord High Commander as Big Guy if he was within earshot. Although it did have a ring to it. I said, "You saw, huh?"

"Nearly flashed a million miles away. I was standing right behind you."

I leaned in close and whispered, "Truth? I've no idea, but it scared the crap out of me, like I'd stuck a fork in an electric socket or something." I glanced around hoping no one overheard this absurd conversation.

"Electric socket?" he inquired. I bit my lip. How could he not know what—"Probably an Earth thing," he added, a bit calmer. "I've been trying to cram as much info as I can about your planet recently. By the way, my name's Andrew, but everyone calls me Drew."

"Olivia, but same as you, call me Livy or just Liv." I put my hand out yet it hung in the empty space between us. Drew didn't move.

"Are you going to shoot a lightning bolt through me?"

"Life, and I guess even death, are risky ventures," I said with a grin forming. Drew hesitated a second, then reached out. Our hands clasped in an awkward handshake, and luckily I didn't electrocute him. We beamed in shared relief.

"Mortal?" Drew said.

"Afraid so."

"Traveler. Great to meet you, Livvv-y." His voice lingered on my name, making it sound exotic and strange.

"Pleasure, Drew." A beat later, I asked, "Is that a British accent? Or maybe Australian?"

Drew sank his hands into the back pockets of his flight suit. "Well," he confessed, "I've been studying some of your famous male actors and perhaps I picked up their speech patterns."

Who had he been studying, the Hemsworth brothers? A giggle tried to sneak out but I swallowed it fast. "Well, whatever it is, it sounds tight."

Drew smiled. "Do you know anybody here?"

"Not a soul."

We located our names on the master list and happened to be seated at the same table. Coincidence?

"I guess we're about to become either best buds," Drew said, "or, as you humans say, 'thorns in each others' sides.'"

"So you have been Googling us humans!" Oh, no. What a stupid, stupid thing to say. I'm the dumbest girl alive. Or dead. And then, for some inexplicable reason, I bounced on my toes.

A petite young woman approached our table and offered her hand. What a knockout. Emerald green eyes bracketed by long, dark lashes, peered over her Barbie-nose and pert grin. A tumble of strawberry-blonde curls outlined her face. Compared to her, I was too tall, too skinny, too...drab. Ugh. I watched for Drew's reaction. If this honey showed up at my last school, the guys would be covering their loins with notebooks. But Drew appeared totally unfazed.

"Hi," she said a tad too brightly. "So, I guess you guys are part of my team. I'm Kadie. Traveler."

Before I could respond, another voice said, "Hey, guys, I'm Seth. Former mortal." Seth stood about five feet ten inches with a swimmer's body, long and lean with gangly arms and legs. He sported carefully mussed chestnut-hued bangs that nearly covered his brown eyes. We could be twins. Our hands made contact and, thankfully, no sparks flew.

We took our places at the table, and an unwelcome lull persisted. I kept thinking about the eerie encounter with the Big Guy. What happened back there in the Great Hall? Would it go unnoticed, or at least be forgotten? Something unsettling stirred within, seeds of gloom.

Suddenly Drew turned into an unlicensed motor-mouth, relating my disturbing moment with the Big Guy. Kadie and Seth flashed matching scowls, their eyes scrutinizing me as if I were some wayward character from a fairytale—the well-intentioned imp who always messed things up. I resisted the urge to say I owed them no explanation and simply shrugged.

We sat through the rest of the orientation while the director introduced the staff and assigned rooms. Nervous energy flitted about as each group was dismissed, students scattering here and there. Guess we were all new school-kids with first day jitters. Paired as roommates, Kadie and I approached the winding staircase to the second floor to locate our quarters, but I never made it past the first step. A guardian escorted me to the director's office. First, I'd nearly smashed the crystal globe on the front steps, then I got zapped by the Lord High Commander. Now I was about to get grilled by the director. Death—the gift that just kept on giving.

I entered an imposing space with a round stained glass window depicting a magnificent warrior woman, scantily clad and aiming an arrow at a fire-breathing demon. I immediately noted the resemblance to the director. Beneath it a bench seat was covered in a quilted white cushion. An impressive ivory desk stood near the back wall where Bath Qol sat primly in her chair. She pointed to one of two chairs, and I took a seat across from her, somehow feeling too small and too exposed. Like a bug about to be stepped on.

"Olivia, my responsibilities here require I provide a nurturing environment while simultaneously training my apprentices to be accomplished warriors who'll defend themselves and protect the souls in our care. I've had this duty for many centuries and witnessed untold events I could not have foreseen. Today, however, I experienced something completely unprecedented."

Here we go. The zillion-dollar question. What caused the electric charge with the Big Guy?

The director continued, "I sense you understand what I'm referring to. Has anything like this ever happened to you before?"

"Am I getting kicked out?" The thought of returning to Chrism Center irked me.

"Please, focus. What exactly occurred when your palm connected with the Lord High Commander?"

"Well," I began, "I j-just placed my palm against his, and this peculiar sensation occurred. Little flames shot out, and he kind of frowned. Maybe someone was pranking me and the Big...I mean, Lord High Commander."

"Whatever the case may be, Olivia, I will get to the bottom of this. I'd hoped you could provide some insight."

"No, ma'am, I'm afraid I'm just as much in the dark as you are." Yet somehow I had an almost premonitory feeling it was...awful. Like an omen.

"Very well, but you have attracted my attention, so I want you to promise if anything else extraordinary happens you will alert me."

Already in our dorm room, Kadie sat in one of two upholstered wing chairs covered in a butter-colored fabric. She laid the book she'd been flipping through—*Crisis Intervention: The Fifth Dimension*—on the cream-tinted table between the chairs, nearly knocking over the green-fringed lampshade in the process.

"How'd it go with BQ?" she asked, propping her feet on the matching ottoman. I gave a rundown of the director's cross-examination, and she didn't seem overly concerned.

"She seemed more curious than angry," I offered, surveying the perfectly square room. Tiny yellow flowers stenciled on vanilla walls bathed everything in a reassuring warm glow. I walked to the open circular window overlooking a lush garden of white lilies and lavender daffodils. Gray marble fountains shaped in a menagerie of wild animals spewed shimmering water into the air. Flagstone pathways led into the surrounding woodland of willowy trees laden with fragrant low-hanging fruit. Sweet nectar perfumed the air. Almost like a postcard from Eden. When the oversized monarch butterfly nearly collided with my nose, I jerked backward.

Turning, resting against the windowsill, I eyed the twin beds covered in pastel golden quilts. "I haven't slept in…I'm not even certain. Months or years, probably."

"Sleep?" She picked up the book again, started flipping through its pages, then rose and tucked the book on the shelf of a corner bookcase. "We Travelers don't sleep. We—how should I put this? We *meditate*."

Well, la-di-da. Was she a guru too? Hobnobbed with Gandhi on her days off? Geez. I plopped down on the bed nearest the window and snuggled into a pillow. Comfy.

Kadie pointed to a massive antique wardrobe, crafted from cedar and featuring heavy brass handles. "I'm supposed to show you around, get you settled in. So ask me anything you want."

I had a million questions but decided I'd ration them, hoping not to overwhelm my new friend.

Kadie took my place on the windowsill and nodded toward the far wall. "That closet's stocked with nightclothes, spare flight suits, sheath-style dresses and tons of shoes. It replenishes itself."

"You're kidding?"

"Nope," she said. "And there's the powder room on the left."

Hmm. I hadn't attended to much in the way of grooming lately. My curiosity piqued, I jumped up and went to investigate. I entered the bathroom and caught my reflection in one of the matching oval mirrors above the sinks. I startled, not having seen myself in forever. No evidence of the fatal accident, thankfully. My maple brown hair, twisted into the braid I'd been accustomed to wearing—no muss, no fuss—appeared frizzy and dull. But my complexion was clear, a bit pale, eyes bright however. I did look like my old self, just a little worn out, weary.

"Nice digs," I said, returning from the bathroom.

"It'll do."

Hmm. Maybe this was a step down for Kadie. Perhaps her family home was the Traveler's version of Buckingham Palace, down to the snobby airs. Crumpet?

Later, we moseyed down the hallway and met some of our fellow female recruits, who lived in rooms identical to ours, except for the colors. The girl cattycorner from my room, Rachel, spoke in manic, super-fast syllables, gushing over the fact that her boyfriend, Jesse, had also been recruited. Although I found it odd that the whole time she talked she regarded others but wouldn't even glance at me. Meanwhile Meghan, all four feet ten of her, a hundred pounds soaking wet, blabbed about the rivalry between her and her brother and how pissed he was when she got into Ecclesia Hall and he didn't. This training program must be prestigious. Ivy League for the recently departed? Except the Travelers weren't technically dead. This whole existence still confused me.

Just as we were leaving, Rachel said to Kadie, "This your mortal?" Finally, I existed. Ha! Rachel pointed her thumb in my direction yet still didn't look at me. "Hear she's already causing a stink."

"Don't worry, I'll keep an eye on her." Kadie slipped her arm through mine.

"I can take care of myself." I said, wrenching my arm free. Then I felt embarrassed, Kadie probably meant well, and I'd overreacted.

Rachel invaded my personal space, her giant head of black curly hair making her seem taller than she was, her unnaturally light blue eyes made me think of a rabid husky. She regarded me carefully and said, "I get bad vibes from you, sis."

"First, I'm not your sis. And second, we mortals don't scare so easily."

"Come on," urged Kadie, tugging my forearm again.

"Go get your beauty sleep," Rachel said. "You humans really, really need it."

Giggles erupted from a few other girls, and I had some choice words for them too. Just as my mouth opened, two hall monitors appeared at the door, announcing curfew. The friction dissipated as all the recruits behaved like nothing out of the ordinary was happening. Another day, another time. Kadie and I headed back to our room.

"What a bitch," I said as Kadie shut our door. "The nerve."

"Just forget it, she's only one person. We'll steer clear."

"Or maybe she should steer clear of me."

With that, we readied for bed and I climbed inside my sheets to await morning. I couldn't recall when I'd last witnessed a sunset or sunrise. Here, the Travelers simulated night and day, as well as Earth's time zones. Nothing to do now but stare at the ceiling.

Of course, Mr. Sandman didn't pay a visit and so I decided to count as high as I could, losing count somewhere after eleven hundred and fifty-something. My lips were still moving when I heard chimes clanging. The beginnings of orange-gray light dawned in the sky. Across the room, Kadie mumbled something and I heard rumblings in the rooms adjacent to ours.

Up and at 'em, Olivia. One step in front of the other. Time to face the unknown.

Chapter 9

Food? The meeting room from yesterday apparently now served as a dining hall.

I couldn't figure out what we were doing here. I hadn't eaten anything in ages. As a mortal I'd been fond of things like ice cream, pizza, and that glorious culinary invention—French fries. But I'd never seen any evidence of afterlife cuisine. Maybe they ate that freeze-dried stuff designed for astronauts?

The director introduced a five-foot-tall, rather rotund gentleman as "Horatio, our master chef."

Horatio twisted the ends of his black mustache, then folded his hands and parked them on his belly. "We sustain ourselves with what I like to call galactic rocket fuel. Even here, we operate under the weird and dizzying laws of quantum physics, so it's formulated as a liquid to allow for high density with low volume." He strode over to one of about twenty stainless steel machines resembling convenience store soda dispensers. He slapped his hand against the mechanism's front panel. "The liquid portion is available from these spigots. Simply press down the lever and ease the concoction into the glass." A gold-colored beverage streamed into the large tumbler. It appeared...*turbulent*...swirling and bubbling, releasing wispy violet vapors as if a mysterious force controlled each molecule. Horatio placed the glass on a small table.

"The oxidizing agent, or propellant—in tablet form, is kept separate." He reached into a white jar like those on each of our tables and unwrapped a neon pink wafer trapped inside silvery cellophane. "The propellant pumps fuel into your internal combustion chamber. You simply drop in the pellet and wait for the rainbow."

He plopped the tab into the liquid and tapped his foot, lingering. The churning increased and a vibrant multi-hued foam erupted, like some psychedelic Wizard of Oz beer. *"Cheers!"* Horatio chugged it down in four long gulps. "Delicious," he declared, wiping his mouth with the back of his hand. "So invigorating, refreshing." Slamming the glass on the tabletop, he added, "You can store a great amount of fuel in your current form. And if you continually energize, you'll last many weeks on Earth without refueling." He pointed to trays displayed at the serving tables. "Then there are cookies. Not just any cookies, but more of, shall we say, mood enhancing edibles." He winked, the glint in his striking amber eyes hinting at something playful, mischievous. "No nutritional value, just *comfort* food. Caution, it's hard to eat just one."

Horatio directed us to serve ourselves.

I sat before the ominous liquid.

Seth said, "Maybe it's like Red Bull or that 5-Hour Energy shit?"

Unconvinced, I continued to stare at the mysterious potion.

"Just do it," Kadie ordered.

"Don't be a chicken," Drew said.

"Hey, ease up, weren't you guys a little freaked out

the first time?"

Drew smirked. "Well, the thing is we're not allowed to drink this stuff until we're old enough to flash. But once, when I was five—" His eyes darted back and forth.

"Finish your story," I said, momentarily distracted from imbibing the enigmatic brew. His gaze grew distant as a string of seconds elapsed. I waved my hand in front of his eyes. "Yoo-hoo?"

My eyesight pixelated, like a bad satellite image or an attempt to censor graphic TV moments. When my vision cleared, I glimpsed a living room where a little cinnamon-haired boy sipped from a large silver beaker. He immediately vanished and almost hit the window of a bakeshop. Getting to his feet, disheveled, he peered at the confections, then disappeared again! He rematerialized in a lake, landing on his head before teleporting to the shore.

"Holy crap," I said, half chuckling, half out of breath. I refocused on Drew's adorable face. "What did you just do?"

"Psychic holograms. It's easy, you'll master it soon enough."

"You mean broadcast like YouTube inside somebody's head?"

Drew narrowed his eyes. "YouTube?"

"Never mind." I'd reached my ridiculousness quotient for the day.

"Well, anyway, they didn't find me for three hours. I flashed myself all over the neighborhood."

He pushed into my mind again. "I can see it, like it's happening right now." Infantile Drew on a playground, atop a giant hill where he beat his chest as

King of the Mountain, and back again to the bakery where he helped himself to a jelly donut. His parents shook their fingers at him. They put him on a leash, leaving him in his soaking-wet clothes until the effects wore off. I had to admit the image of him tied to the dining room chair proved downright hysterical. I suppressed another chuckle. "I'm not gonna fly around the room like a drunken bumblebee, am I?"

"I'd think you have more control than a little kid." He looked down his nose at me. "At least I hope so. Come on, now or never."

A bit of Turkish delight never hurt anyone, right? Famous last words. Breathe, one thousand, breathe. "Never or now." I dropped the pellet in, let an interlude pass, and chugged the potion down. It tasted sweet, syrupy, yet bitter and searing like coffee, no...arctic cold...I expected brain freeze...no...maybe fizzy?...nope...it slid down my throat like a cotton candy milkshake, maybe. My taste buds exploded. Flavor overload. My tongue wandering in a wonderland of lemony tang followed by sweet raspberry gelato. A warm, squishy marshmallow floating in hot cocoa. Butterscotch. Toffee. Candied walnuts. All I wanted was more.

Heat surged through me. Oh, oh, not ready, not—I feared I'd morph into some gigantic extraterrestrial, like a mutated super-hero...The Hulk? Spidey? I inspected my arms, my legs, expecting my body to radically change, or a giant S to be branded on my chest. Nope.

I nibbled on a cookie. They reminded me of those holiday waffle treats my grandmother made. But...Oh my God. The rush! My fingers and toes tingled, hot drum beats danced under my facial skin, spreading. The urge to fly across the cosmos seized me. Then I got a case of the giggles. "Best goddamned cookie *ev*-er!"

Seth held up the tasty morsel, hesitated a trice before popping the whole thing into his mouth. His eyes lit up. "Holy shit." He did a little jig in his seat. "What's in these things?"

In unison, Kadie and Drew leaned in, whispering, "Magic!"

The insane effects calmed after a few minutes, and I felt in control, although exceptionally...*peppy*. The warning chimes rang, and our foursome made our way to room fifteen for the morning briefing. We drifted to the back and chose seats in high-backed chairs surrounding a round table. In all, I counted twenty-four apprentices, each group at its own table. A tall, black man glided through the doorway dressed in the standard flight suit and sporting shoulder-length ebony hair. A single strand fell across his face and he pulled it back and tucked it behind his ear. He moved about the room so swiftly he seemed to be everywhere at once.

"Well, well, well," he began, "welcome, welcome, welcome!" Did he intend to talk in threes, threes, threes for the entire briefing? His name was Aidan, Commander Aidan, to be exact, but we could just call him Aidan. His gray eyes twinkled with mischief. He introduced his assistants: six impressive figures who stood at the back of the room, two of them women.

"Good morning, and peace be with you," he offered.

"And with you," we responded in unison.

"Before we begin let me remind you that at the end of today's briefing former mortals will have their auras transfigured. Report to the Ministration Building promptly at noon. It's the large white structure with the four smokestacks. The entire transmutation process doesn't take long and is relatively painless. The remainder of you may use the afternoon to explore the campus."

I winced. Exactly how painless was "relatively painless"?

"Afterward, we suggest you rest until tomorrow, to allow your adjusted aura to stabilize. Occasionally there's slippage and the procedure must be repeated. Within twelve hours you'll be good to go."

A clear glass orb about six inches in diameter sat atop Aidan's lecture desk. It appeared identical to the one at Ecclesia Hall's front door where our names were announced upon arrival, the one I'd nearly shattered into smithereens. The memory made me cringe. He pressed a button on his lectern, and simultaneously a similar orb popped up from the center of our tabletops. A crystal ball? Everyone jumped back a little. Could it see into the future?

Aidan explained the orb would be used to project our mental images onto the screen—like a video projector for your thoughts. "Travelers can push images to each other, but this will take some practice for former mortals." Well, I'd already done this with Drew. Maybe I'd be a quick study.

A map appeared on the screen behind him. "On your way to your first assignment you must pass through the Astral Plane, so I expect the former mortals to acquaint their partners with the terrain. Your first trip to Earth requires that you target a predetermined destination. Your primary task is simply observation, but you must also practice controlling your visibility.

You will learn how to rearrange your atoms to suit your needs. To be clear, at our core we are essentially energy, a unique balance of light and electricity with the ability to harness quantum particulate forces of the universe..."

What? I suddenly became fearful that a lack of knowledge in both physics and astronomy rendered me a blithering idiot. Having taken AP Physics in high school, and both organic and inorganic chem at Columbia, I thought myself reasonably schooled in how matter and energy interacted.

"...Which allows us to assume solid form—human form—while still retaining the ability to explore space and the higher dimensions of parallel universes."

Yikes! Definitely over my head with this stuff.

"We would be unable to function and specifically unable to procreate if we hadn't incorporated human particulate matter into our forms. Also, being so close to the sun, it would be difficult to keep our energy cohesive."

I turned toward Seth to see if he shared my confusion. He just stared at the commander with his mouth open. Yeah, I decided...he's in the same place.

"Before we get into the details of this first assignment I'd like to brief you on some of the basics regarding your missions. Our mechanical navigation system will allow you to locate our established *wormholes,* which are links for space travel and are held open by negative mass cosmic strings."

I gulped and my eyebrows shot up. *Wormholes?* Finally, I decided to just think of all this new stuff the same way I thought of computers or television. I had limited understanding of how they worked but no problem using them.

The assistants distributed what resembled sophisticated wristwatches while Aidan continued. "But in order to travel through a wormhole you need to learn how to flash. This requires you to disaggregate and then re-aggregate your form. You can flash anywhere, but in order to travel galaxy-long distances you need to flash through an established wormhole.

"Now, those of you born here already know how to flash on a small scale and will be responsible for getting your partner to Earth by tandem-flashing. Of course, you'll be traveling at lightspeed."

Holy crap, if I remembered correctly that was like 670 million miles per hour. Geez!

"All right then, my assistants will hand out the coordinates for your first destination. You will execute your assignment tomorrow and be prepared to report the following day."

My hand shot into the air. "Yes, Olivia?"

"No training? No practice? You're just throwing us out there and hoping we don't crash and burn?"

Aidan smirked, momentarily covering his mouth with his hand. "Olivia." I got the distinct impression he was trying to be patient with me. "This is the easy stuff. There will be plenty of training when we get to more demanding aspects of your vocation. Trust me."

Well, I wanted to trust him but…traveling through the cosmos at the speed of light? Praying that we'd land at the correct location because of a fancy wristwatch? I wasn't convinced.

He put his hand up which probably prevented me from saying something stupid, the entire class already focused on me. "Your Traveler teammates are more than capable of getting you to the appropriate destination. Just as you are proficient at navigating them through Earth's cultural nuances."

We ended in a stalemate. He hadn't persuaded me.

Our assignment was slated for a small town in New York. The whole flashing-through-a-wormhole thing had me seriously terrified, and I guessed I'd know soon enough if a crash landing was in my immediate future.

"We have a well-stocked wardrobe area where you may select the appropriate costuming. Those of you who've been human will have the advantage since you've walked among mortals. Follow me." He pivoted on his heels.

Arriving at Wardrobe Central, I realized it wasn't a room but more of a warehouse. The ceiling loomed about a hundred feet high with racks of clothes scaled all the way up the walls. Aidan informed us, "You may browse through the racks, or use the directory screens over on the left that index every item. If you know specifically what you want simply type in the name, push *Enter*, and the rack will move down with your selection.

"You can also type in something like "hospital" and several suggestions will pop up. You can pick the season of the year and the proper size. When you're done simply deposit the used clothing in the laundry chute." He pointed to a square white opening in the wall near the entranceway. Wow, free laundry service. Too good to be true, as I recalled the tedium of such chores.

"Browse around for something matching the locale for your assignment. Our particular base of operations covers only North America so you'll find yourselves in areas with similar costuming, language, and culture. Before departing, have one of my assistants check your attire."

Kadie and I returned to our rooms and put away our mortal clothing for tomorrow's mission, then strolled toward the dining hall. Drew and Seth met us at a table. I gazed at Drew's handsome profile and a rush of warmth spread through me. Gosh, he was getting under my skin, and I imagined what it might feel like to kiss those beautiful lips of his, and suddenly…my whole body glowed.

We'd swigged our fuel and gobbled a few cookies, the effects not as extreme as the first time, when Kadie reminded us that Seth and I still had an appointment at the transmutation laboratory. Reluctantly, Seth and I sought the exit, leaving Kadie and Drew behind. I wasn't in a big hurry to head over to the ominous building with the smokestacks. Smoke meant *fire*.

"It kinda looks like a power plant," I said as the lengthy line of former mortals approached the doors to the gloomy building.

Seth said, "Yeah, it doesn't look very welcoming."

"I hope we come out better than Frankenstein's monster," I joked.

Seth glared at me. "Oh, great, that's really helpful. I bet you told scary ghost stories to your kids, too." Embarrassed by my quip, I lowered my eyes and shut up. Why was I such a smartass? I needed to work on that.

"Well, now or never," I said.

Seth grimaced. "Never or now."

A jolly, round woman greeted us at the door and led the parade of nervous recruits down a long, sterile, white-tiled hallway. I immediately thought of a hospital. Six unmarked, windowless white doors taunted me. What might be going on behind them? I listened for moans, groans, or screams. It felt like walking to my execution, but then I remembered...*I'm already dead.*

"Okay," Seth whispered, "I'm freaking out." I nodded agreement, then linked my arm through Seth's, uniting us in our escalating anxiety.

Ushered into a spacious lecture hall, we beelined for the back rows. A pointy-nosed angular woman with short gray hair and a clipboard came to the front. "All right, I'm sure you're all anxious to get this over with, so let's start." Countless sideways glances darted around the room.

"Each of you has been identified as having a strong aura similar to our auras, and it will only require a minor modification to synchronize. Afterward, you'll essentially have all the same characteristics of those born here. It's vital you begin refueling after you're discharged to support your adjusted aura. By the time you complete your training you'll be fully grown adults. There's one exception however, you won't be able to reproduce until some time after that."

"Free birth control? That's cool," I muttered. I didn't know where that came from. I felt Seth's stare. "Oh my God, you didn't hear that, did you?"

"What you should be concerned about is if *they* heard you," Seth murmured.

"Oh, great." I slid lower in my seat, trying to be inconspicuous.

"Maybe they have super hearing or something. We've no idea what these guys can, or can't, do. You need to be more careful. I'd like to not get in trouble on the first day."

"Sorry, sometimes I'm just a jerk. But really, I haven't thought about sex in a long time, have you?"

Seth slumped in his seat too, bringing our heads to the same level. "The birds and the bees? Can't say that I have."

"How many times have you died?" I asked softly.

"Fourteen. You?"

"Twelve."

"And you made it old enough to have sex?" Seth said.

"Of course. Lots of times."

He leaned in closer and held up his thumb and forefinger, marking off about an inch. "I was this close to scoring on this really hot chick in my sociology class before I got yanked off the planet."

I reserved comment.

Seth added, "From what I can tell so far it seems like Travelers have the same, you know, parts as we do."

I thought about that for a moment. "Kadie appears to have all the necessary equipment on the outside. What about Drew?"

"Let's just say he…uh…measures up."

My eyes widened. The image of Drew naked sent a quiver through me. He was my partner. I shouldn't be picturing him naked. I shook my head, hoping to dislodge the image. "I can't believe you actually said that," I uttered a tad too loudly. A case of the giggles seized me and Seth broke into a grin.

"I can't believe we're having this conversation. I just met you," Seth said in a low voice, chuckling.

"This conversation is totally ridiculous."

"Something funny back there?" the woman with the clipboard barked.

Seth and I struggled to regain our composure. My new best friend spoke up. "No, nothing…sorry."

"And you, Olivia, you're amused?" the teacher queried.

"Um, I always laugh when I'm nervous. Apologies."

Clipboard Lady's face relaxed. "There's nothing to be nervous about. Let's get on with it." The lecture continued as Seth and I avoided the stares of the other recruits. Making asses of ourselves on the first day. This just kept getting better.

"Are there any questions on what I've said so far?" Clipboard Lady asked. No takers. "Everyone will be scanned tomorrow morning before leaving the dining hall to make sure all is well. Only rarely have we had to repeat this process, but it has occurred."

Names were called. Seth and I fidgeted and squirmed, waiting not so patiently for our turn. When it came, we walked together behind a technician alongside two other pairs of apprentices. We entered an unmarked white door where six gurneys sat in a neat row against the back wall. A transmutation specialist waited near each, while another supervisor guy with a clipboard stood in the room's center. I hopped up on the starched white sheet covering the hospital cot. A kind gent named Elijah assured me this would be over before I knew it.

I kept reminding myself that I wasn't really alive so I didn't have anything to be afraid of, right?

Chapter 10

Elijah explained that he'd run his hands over my prone form, drawing my aura to the surface, and then simply smooth it out. It sounded easy enough, but...
"Piece of cake," I said with false bravado. Elijah beamed. I wondered: Did he know what cake was?

Elijah settled me comfortably on the gurney, but then froze. He held my wrist in his hand. "How did you get this mark?" He rubbed his thumb over the raised red crescent.

"I don't know. It's a birthmark. Why?"

"Nothing, it's just rather interesting. It's a perfect arc. Most birthmarks are more...irregular. It looks like a tattoo." He continued to run his thumb across my skin, gently, soothingly, as if I had some deformity.

"Trust me, Elijah, I've never gotten a tattoo."

"Hmm..." he muttered thoughtfully before releasing my hand. "Let's get down to business, shall we? A few things I must explain before we start. You've always had your aura, just like all mortals, which is basically pure energy. On the Astral Plane you were in a state of suspended animation. You didn't have to eat, breathe, or do anything you used to. Most of your form is like muscle memory. But you can't stay that way forever. Make sense so far?"

"Sort of...So, how are you guys different from us?" Elijah had started something I didn't think he'd bargained for. I had unlimited questions.

"We're actually more alike than you might think. However, we have what I call an internal furnace. Anything you consume now will basically burn up while at the same time fuel your aura."

So that answered the no toilet in our bathroom conundrum.

"But," Elijah continued, "our food won't nourish your aura as much as the energy from good deeds will. Once the transformation is complete your aura will be self-sustaining, requiring only a small amount of fuel and air, like combustion. However, if you're totally deprived of these things, eventually your aura will be extinguished. Think of it like the pilot light on a gas stove."

"A what?"

"Never mind," Elijah said, shaking his head.

"Okay," I said, "but if you don't have any organs how do you experience things? Can you feel pain, heat, or cold? How can you love someone if you don't have a heart?"

Elijah appeared bemused. "Olivia, most of these things happen in your mind, *not* your bodily organs. And, by your mind, I don't mean your brain. The energy of your consciousness can exist without human organs. Actually, it's now even more evolved than ever. I'd describe it this way, humans have both a physical heart and what I'd call an emotional heart. This is where your devotion, your emotions, and love exist. We all, in our own way, have a heart."

Okay, I thought, that made perfect sense. Kind of.

"But there's more to this than you might imagine," he added.

Uh-oh.

"When we're on Earth, the atmosphere and the force of gravity solidify our form and we appear human, but mostly it's our perception, we think of ourselves as human, so we look that way. While you were a citizen of the Astral Plane, you may not have felt like you had a body, but you appeared that way to us."

Good, I decided. I could handle that.

"Just one more thing I want to prepare you for. As soon as the transformation is complete you may have a tremendous urge to breathe. Think of it as firing up your furnace. It takes a burst of initiation energy to get it started, but afterward you'll be fine. You can calm the feeling by simulating breathing. Got it?"

"I think so."

"Great, then let's get started."

I tried to remain reasonably calm figuring this would be over shortly. Elijah smiled reassuringly as he placed his hands over my head, slowly moving them toward my feet. A colorful array of light snaked around his open palms. The magnificent rainbow swirled into a tiny funnel of dancing light beams. Elijah's outstretched hands suddenly vanished inside the spinning vortex. I looked on with amazement. Who knew?

A violent explosion erupted in my head. Electrical current ripped through me followed by rushing hot air spiraling inside my own wind tunnel. The shock hit Elijah like lightning and hurled him through the air. He smashed into the far wall, then slid to the floor and landed with a thud. The other technicians rushed to his side to revive him. Seth sat up on his gurney along with the other recruits. Their contorted faces mirrored my shock. Oh my God! What was wrong with me? Twice now I'd displayed unexplainable phenomena.

Elijah sagged against the wall, dazed. At least I didn't kill him! Sufficiently frazzled, he struggled to his feet and regained his composure, then inched toward my side.

"Oh my God, Elijah, I'm so sorry! Are you all right?"

He studied my face, his voice deep and foreboding. "Olivia, nothing like this has ever happened before. I'm guessing your aura is exceptionally strong and I'm going to need some help to rearrange it. We'll try it with two of us this time." He hesitated before adding, "Focus. Think of your aura as a cohesive controllable entity."

"I'm not sure how to do that."

"I'll guide you."

"Okay," I whispered, or was it more of a whimper?

Elijah crooked his finger to call over a second technician who didn't appear all that anxious to participate. The two of them stood alongside the gurney as I lay there dreading a repeat performance. "All right, Olivia, close your eyes. Visualize your aura in its rainbow state and imagine it contained in a bathtub. Immerse yourself and then put your head under the water. Pull your colorful aura tightly around you. Can you visualize what I'm saying?"

"Trying." I closed my eyes as ordered.

"All right, now don't think of us at all, just contemplate that image. Keep concentrating until I tell you to stop."

I kept my eyes tightly shut as the vision formed in my mind. The warmth of the rippling water calmed me. Multihued energy surrounded my head as I drifted under the water's surface.

ZAP! I sizzled like a cut power cord, throwing sparks everywhere. Hot wind whistled in my ears, the intense air pressure suffocating. My eyes flew open in time to see both Elijah and his assistant crash into the far wall and hit the floor with two thunderous clunks.

"I'm jinxed!" I yelled, sitting up. No one came to their aid this time. Everyone appeared shocked, not the electrical kind, well, except for Elijah and his buddy. The two weary technicians returned to my side, their hair morphed into Albert Einstein style. Elijah raised his hands in the air as if to dispel the panic pervading the room.

"We'll get it, Olivia, hang in there," he said, appearing a little irritated, but I could hear the resolve in his voice. He intended to get this done even if it killed somebody, and I sorely hoped it wouldn't. This time, four ministering technicians stood around my bedside, none acted too thrilled to be involved. Elijah instructed me to use the same image but to picture a lake this time. Apparently my aura couldn't be contained in a bathtub.

I let myself float effortlessly in the lake's crystal-clear water. My head slipped below the glassy surface and the multicolored light once again made to escape. I *sucked* it back in. Hair swirled around me, long chocolate tangles in a brilliant rainbow. I drifted downward into the deep water holding my breath until it felt like my lungs might burst. I focused on keeping my energy cohesive, the cool water battling the heat rising from somewhere deep inside me. I was a dead weight lying at the bottom of the lake, my arms and legs wriggling around me like wayward tentacles. A terrible thought erupted: electricity and water are a bad combo! The urge to spring to the surface overtook me. I needed to breathe. Now!

A distant voice called to me, "Olivia, Olivia, can you hear me? Open your eyes. You can release yourself from the water."

Another voice. "I thought we'd have to put her in an ocean to get this done."

My eyelids fluttered, opened. I didn't recognize the surroundings at first. "Am I dead again?" I blurted, hearing the panic in my voice. "Did I drown?"

"This is Elijah. You're here with me. Everything's fine, it's over."

Then it hit. A giant boulder landed on my chest. Gasping for air, I spiraled into a darkness I feared I couldn't flee.

"Breathe," the technician commanded. "It will help." I struggled to inhale, gasping for the breath I hadn't needed in a long time, but I found it difficult to escape the whirlpool of shadows threatening to swallow me whole. Sluggishly emerging from the murky tunnel, the room's luminosity banished the terrifying darkness. Elijah helped me sit up. Dizziness swarmed me. Seth and the others huddled near the exit door, a series of frowns marring their faces.

"Better?" Elijah said, more kindly than he should after I'd surely practically killed him. Twice.

"I think so." At least I hoped.

He patted me on the back a few times. "Rest for a minute, and when you're steady enough you can go with the others." The poor guy seemed exhausted. He ran his fingers through his wiry hair in an attempt to return it to its former state. Before leaving my bedside he smiled, thankful I guessed, that I hadn't killed him....then gave my hand a little squeeze. Perhaps as a safety check before he released me into the wild.

"You're excused," the flustered supervising technician announced to the band of newly minted Travelers. "But please remember the instructions to refuel and rest for the remainder of the day." A collective sigh of relief resonated from all the ministering technicians.

Seth put his arm around my shoulders. "You okay?"

"I think so, maybe a little woozy," I mumbled through a wave of nausea.

Seth let out a loud breath. "So weird. I haven't needed to breathe in a long time."

"I'll say!" The dizziness dissipated as I slid off the gurney and into Seth's waiting arms.

Leaving the Ministration Building, Seth supported my shoulders, keeping me steady. "I know I'm starting to look like a freak show," I complained. But Seth remained silent as we ambled on. "First that incident with the Lord High Commander and now this. I don't understand why this stuff keeps happening." I feared Seth didn't want to be seen with me.

Finally, he said, "Look, don't feel bad. You didn't do anything wrong, and maybe there's a reason for all this. Obviously you've got some powerful energy running around in that body of yours. I'm sure it will be put to good use at some future point. Try not to overreact."

We sought out Kadie and Drew, locating them seated at a large, round table on the far side of the dining hall. "Hey! How'd it go?" Kadie said, moseying toward us with Drew beside her.

"A little out of the ordinary," Seth said.

"Oh? Well, come on, we found this cool place," she said, leading us toward the exit.

The enormous room contained comfy couches and overstuffed chairs in a variety of arrangements. Square tables covered in red matting held chess sets, decks of cards, and even poker chips. Wooden chairs with burgundy cushions surrounded each card table. Thousands of books filled floor-to-ceiling bookcases that lined the dark wood-paneled walls. No windows, and the only hint of outside came from the French doors near the back of the room that opened into a garden. The recessed lighting made it feel as if I was in an exclusive club for the rich and famous. Hmm, maybe being a Traveler meant I *was* a member of an exclusive club.

We settled into an unoccupied seating area. The guys took the couch and perched their feet atop the coffee table, arms crossed over their chests in matching poses. Kadie and I sat on the loveseat opposite them. "So," Drew said, "everyone is talking about what happened with you. Spill."

That didn't take long. I sighed, then buried my face in my hands and mumbled, "Seth, you tell them. I don't have the energy."

"I beg to differ," he said. "Apparently you have plenty of energy, and therein lies the problem." He wasted no time in relating the entire fiasco to my new friends. Seth finally finished with, "You should have been there. Watching those old guys scrambling around and landing on their asses totally cracked me up."

Drew couldn't contain himself a second longer. He

slapped his knee, his laughter erupting. Kadie searched my face, seemingly hesitant to join in the hilarity. I surmised she was trying not to hurt my feelings, but eventually she joined in too, as the unrestrained merriment became contagious. I smiled. My transmutation probably would have gotten a zillion hits on YouTube.

"This room is cool," I said. "What else did you guys discover while we were tied up in the torture chamber?"

"Come on," Drew urged, "we'll take you on a tour." Outside, a garden dotted with park-style benches and patio tables and even a few hammocks welcomed us. A giant field bordered the garden where some kids kicked a ball around and others played on a basketball court. Insane. It must be for educating our otherworldly brethren about earthly ways. Each player shot for the basket. No one missed.

Lush green trees shaded a cobblestone pathway snaking through the decorative shrubbery. Exotic flowers in a multitude of vibrant colors sprang from the fog-covered ground and tiny familiar creatures ambled about, sort of like a shimmering version of Earth. A quartet of over-sized sparkly monarch butterflies flew here and there, circling my head a few times, and then drifted off. I gazed over my shoulder as they vanished into the treetops.

I reflected on what a crazy twenty-four hours it'd been and could only imagine what the rest of my stay would be like. Then again, maybe I shouldn't think about it too much because I might totally go berserk.

Chapter 11

Ravana entered the Madison Avenue coffee shop with Lilith in tow. Her smart black business suit made her look like a high-class exec, and actually, she *was* here on business. She and Lilith needed to talk, a conversation Lucifer couldn't be privy to, and Earth provided the safest place to avoid his attention. He rarely left his home turf these days, content to let others do his bidding. That suited Ravana just fine. It irritated her that he had such a high opinion of himself and relied on a bunch of demon-slaves to cater to his every need, but on the other hand it gave her freedom to be on her own. The thought of waiting on him hand and foot made her cringe. Domesticity didn't suit her.

Ravana sensed Lilith's foul mood. Nothing new there. They took a table near the front window. Lilith slipped her favorite red leather jacket onto the back of her chair, then tousled her shaggy crimson locks with her fingertips. Ravana examined her. "You always look like you just rolled out of bed, Lily."

"I don't sleep. Neither do you. And what I do in bed has nothing to do with sleeping or my hair."

"It's just an expression, Lily." Ravana took the white cloth napkin and arranged it neatly on her lap.

Lilith propped her elbows on the table and folded her hands under her chin. "It's an insult, Vana, something you're particularly adept at. In my *humble*

The Wives of Lucifer

opinion, of course."

"When have you ever been humble?" Ravana taunted her. Lilith shook her head in annoyance. Ravana rebuked herself for baiting Lilith in the first minute of seeing her. She needed to keep control, or she'd never get done what she needed to.

"So why did you pick such a fancy place? You won't find anything to munch on. Their kitchen is probably too clean."

"What are you rambling about?"

"Don't roaches rank with spiders on your list of favorite snacks?"

Ravana glowered. "Be careful, Lily or I just might shove a few down your throat."

"Go ahead and try!" Lilith threatened. "We haven't had a good fight in at least, what, a week?"

Neither continued the derisive banter. Shifting gears, Lilith said. "You realize there are two do-gooders sitting behind you?"

"Who?" Ravana said.

"Two illustrious detectives from the NYPD?"

"No matter. Things will still go according to plan. Maybe we'll get lucky, and they'll shoot somebody by mistake."

"Well, we can't take them if they're not on the list."

"True."

The waitress interrupted. "What can I get you ladies? Do you need a menu?"

"No," Lilith said. "Just tea for me. Black."

"And you, miss?" the perky blonde waitress said.

"Coffee. Black," Ravana's curt voice rumbled from her diaphragm. The waitress disappeared into the kitchen. "She's so damned cheery."

"Speaking of cheery," Lilith said, "I hear Little Miss Sunshine nearly blew up the Transmutation Laboratory at Ecclesia Hall. I'd find that amusing if it didn't vex me so. If she learns what she can do with that aura of hers before we get to her…well, I can't even ponder it…"

"How do you find out this stuff? Were you on the Astral Plane again?"

Lilith smirked. "Not this time, but I have a contact. Someone at the highest levels." She waved her hand in the air.

"Really? Do tell."

Lilith laughed too loudly for a Madison Avenue coffee shop, and Ravana surveyed the patrons, embarrassed. She should know better than to take Lilith anywhere nice.

"You're joking, right? I'd have to be an idiot to tell you my secrets!" The waitress arrived with coffee and tea, placing the tea in front of Ravana while Lilith got the coffee.

"You incompetent idiot!" Lilith barked. "We order two drinks, and you can't even keep that straight?" The young woman blanched.

Ravana leaned across and exchanged the cups. "Honestly, Lily, can we not go anywhere without you making a scene?" The waitress skulked away.

"Where were we?" Lilith asked, adding too much sugar to her tea.

"Want some tea with that sugar?" Ravana chided. She bit her bottom lip, upset at her compulsion to taunt Lilith. No matter how hard she tried, something sardonic always seemed to slip across her bright red lips.

"Are we here to talk or are you going to waste time being obnoxious?" Lilith chastised. "I have other things to do. And if you force my hand I might just take care of Little Lightning Girl myself."

"Fine," Ravana snapped. "You were telling me who your contact is in the City of the Sun."

"Really, Vana? I'm not falling for that crap."

Ravana reminded herself again that she needed Lilith. Although both were exceptionally powerful, they didn't exactly have the *same* gifts, and she required Lilith's special abilities to implement her plan. Shaking off her frustration, she moved on. "So, did they finally get her aura transmutated?"

"Unfortunately they did, although it took four of them to do it."

Ravana's mouth fell open. "Four?"

"Yup."

"That's a bad sign…for us."

"I nearly forgot! That's not even the worst of it!" Lilith said, pausing to sip her tea.

Anger oozed through Ravana. The thought of anything that could make her plan even more difficult was one thing, but Lilith's joy at teasing out information just iced everything with frustration. Through gritted teeth she said, "Don't torture me, Lilith, what else?"

"Torture…what a lovely word." Lilith smiled. "I do enjoy a good torture session. And this isn't even close to what I'd really like to do to you."

Lilith's smile turned wicked and Ravana wanted to lean across the table and smack her. "Go ahead and give it your best shot, Lily. You'll be under my heel."

Before Ravana's anger shifted into the red zone she reined it in. She gulped coffee, hoping the bitter liquid would distract her rising fury.

"Oh, all right," Lilith said, ignoring Ravana's retort. She leaned in close. "Apparently, our little lightning bug shot some serious sparks at the Lord High Commander during the meet and greet. I had to laugh. I would have loved to see that for myself."

"What do you mean? Her aura hadn't even transmutated yet. How could she have that kind of impact? His aura is the most powerful in the universe. Unless…holy shit, you don't think…?"

"Oh yes, I most certainly do. She has the same aura as Michael and you-know-who…" Ravana shuddered to think. She hadn't anticipated anything like this, and it put a whole new spin on confronting her archenemy. Lilith grinned smugly. "My, my, you look a tad terrified, Vana. I don't think I've ever seen you like this."

Ravana gave a tinny laugh and flicked her hand as if swatting a fly. "Terrified? That's ridiculous. It's merely a detail I hadn't considered."

"I wouldn't dismiss it so easily. Now it's absolutely crucial we get her under our control."

Ravana nearly convulsed, her insides fumed, but she wouldn't let Lilith see that. "We'll simply have to work harder to accomplish our task. The stakes are just a little higher."

"Agreed. We can do this," Lilith said. "We *have* to." She added more sugar to her tea and stirred it with the shiny silver spoon. "Nice silverware. Maybe I'll bring some home."

"And what are you going to do with it? It's not like

you host fancy dinner parties," Ravana said.

"I just like shiny things." Lilith licked the sweet tea off the spoon and slipped it in the pocket of her red jacket. "So how's your plan with Peter coming? Do you think it will work?"

"I'm sure it will. Olivia's such a bleeding heart she won't be able to resist him. The trouble is we have to wait until she starts her assignments on Earth before putting him in place."

Lilith leaned back in her chair. "Where are you holding him?"

"Right now I've got him under guard in the west end dungeon, but I'm going to need your help to move this chess piece so I can finish the setup."

"Fine, whatever you need." Lilith had turned too agreeable, and Ravana grew suspicious. She couldn't trust Lilith worth a damn.

"I'll let you know when the time is right," Ravana said.

Lilith nodded. "What I'm really worried about is interference from John and Thomas. They had her pretty well under control the day she died." Lilith sighed and drank the last of her tea. "That Thomas has always been a nasty son of a bitch, and I'd just as soon avoid him."

Ravana didn't want to have to contend with the two of them either, but she didn't think she'd have to. John had a new charge to mind, which left little time to babysit Olivia, and they kept Thomas pretty busy with his death duties. Ravana asked, "So what else has your contact told you? Anything we can act on now?"

"Olivia should be able to traverse wormholes by the end of this week, so I'm guessing she should be here soon. She'll have her team with her, so we probably can't do much other than rattle her cage a bit. Start making her doubt herself."

"How are we going to manage that? We need to get her alone. It's going to be nearly impossible if she's always with her little posse."

"They don't concern me. They're newbies. The ones we really have to worry about are Thomas and John. They're experienced, powerful, and they have connections."

Ravana considered their options. They had to be careful not to spook Olivia. The best plan would be to convince her she belonged with them. Cajole, coax, invite…If it came to a show of force, things might blow up in their faces. Literally. And she had Peter as her backup plan. "Let's just scope things out when she makes her first trip to Earth, then we'll plan something more intimidating."

Lilith drummed her fingers on the table, the starched white tablecloth muting the sound. "Waiting. It drives me crazy."

"Great. You're crazy enough…" Ravana said.

Lilith grimaced. "Oh, so now we're back to insults. Can't you focus for ten minutes without resorting to your snide comments? Don't forget, you need me. It's going to take the both of us."

The waitress returned with two fresh cups. "On the house. Sorry I mixed up your order. I'm not having a very good day."

"Like we care." Lilith snorted. The waitress removed the used cups and scurried away again. Ravana blinked at the waitress who promptly tripped and cups and saucers went flying.

"You didn't?" Lilith exclaimed.

"I did. Just a little spell…and besides…" Ravana smirked. "Her day is about to get worse."

"How lovely." Lilith chortled and then dumped sugar into her steaming cup of tea. "And, 'on the house'? Really? It's not like we were going to pay anyway."

The pert waitress stood alongside the two detectives, having just returned with their change when two masked gunmen entered, taking everyone hostage. They collected money and valuables and nearly escaped. One of them grabbed the waitress around the neck and walked backward toward the exit.

"Nobody moves and no one gets hurt!" said his accomplice.

Ravana put out her foot and he tripped. The waitress attempted to run, but the robber aimed his weapon and shot, hitting her in the back. The detectives returned fire. Bullets flew, the waitress shrieked, everyone screamed, cowering under tables.

"Duty calls," Ravana said, rising from her chair.

"Two more for our side," Lilith chirped.

Ravana grabbed the souls of the robbers by their collars and dragged them toward the door. She wiggled her eyebrows at Lilith. "A pity we can't take the waitress."

The two women and their dead prisoners vanished in a flash of crimson light.

Chapter 12

On the way to the dining hall the next morning, the former mortals had to get cleared by one of the ministering techs from yesterday. To do that they ran their hands quickly across everyone's foreheads to make sure their auras remained intact. The whole process appeared rather routine and uneventful until I showed up.

"Uh...Good morning, Olivia...perhaps we can move a little closer to the wall to check you out?" the nervous technician said. So, did he think if he got blown off his feet the impact might be minimized by standing against the wall?

He motioned to his buddy to come over and stand behind him. Was the second one supposed to act as a cushion for the guy in front? Not fair. They braced themselves for impact. If they could've perspired, I envisioned beads of sweat dripping down their brows. The director appeared out of nowhere. "Is everything okay, Olivia? I heard your transmutation wasn't exactly routine yesterday." Great. I'd wound up on the director's radar once again.

"Has anything with me been routine so far?" I answered rather impertinently.

"Proceed," the director said to the technician, ignoring my insolence.

He instructed me to face him, adding, "Let's get

this over with." His palms moved toward my forehead. A crowd gathered, everyone apparently eager to witness my sparkling personality firsthand even as I fervently prayed I wouldn't send anyone flying into next Tuesday.

The techs' squinting faces belied their anxiety. They appeared to be peering into a bright light when in reality they stood in the dimly lit hallway. I chuckled. I doubted closing their eyes would offer much protection against my overzealous aura.

The scanning technician held his trembling hands in front of my forehead. The crowd's anticipation manifested itself as its own form of adrenaline. Pressure began to build in my chest. The urge to breathe strangled me. Remembering Elijah's words, I imitated the motions…in and out…in and out. Calmness replaced the feeling of panic as the scan progressed. I sensed every person in the room holding his breath, the tension palpable, and then…thankfully…nothing.

"Oh my God! I'm okay?" I exclaimed.

"You're good to go, Olivia," the tech said, overly enthusiastically.

"Yay," I said, facing the crowd. Everyone scurried away. Some appeared a little embarrassed, while others seemed disappointed and, to my relief, Bath Qol had vanished.

"No light show today!" I announced loudly through the megaphone of my hands. "Sorry!"

We ate a quick breakfast and spent all day in monotonous briefings. After dinner we wandered through the milling throngs of the living dead on the dreary Astral Plane, in search of the exit point for our first interstellar voyage. It didn't seem quite as depressing as I remembered. Most of the fog hung near the ground, and the sky appeared brighter. I marveled at the change. Was it my perception or reality?

Kadie and Drew said they thought it a terrible place and were sorry Seth and I'd spent so much time there.

A familiar face appeared out of the fog. Dressed in his pinstriped overalls, Otis, my spirit guide, emerged through the glistening mist, his jolly face its own brand of sunshine.

"Hey, Otis!" I called out. His eyes lit up even more when he saw me.

"Olivia!" he said excitedly, marching in my direction. "I heard the good news, congratulations! Welcome to the fold! You look wonderful."

"Then my appearance matches my mood." I introduced him to my new friends, and we chatted each other up for a few minutes. Telling him we had a tight schedule and had to run, we shared a quick hug and bid each other farewell.

Just as we exited, another familiar face caught my attention. Thomas, my soul collector, sat cross-legged in the fog beside a sad-looking man of about thirty. A somber scene, and the emotions of my death briefly resurfaced. I didn't think I'd ever see him again.

My team realized I'd lagged behind and backtracked to stand next to me. Kadie murmured softly, "Someone else you know?"

I whispered, "My soul collector."

"Pretty hot for a soul collector," Kadie said.

"I know and he always treated me with such kindness, you know, like he really cared."

"He probably did. Soul collectors have a lot of emotion, love even, for those in their care, sometimes too much."

"He said something strange before he left me last time. He told me I was 'off his list' and he wouldn't see me again. Do you think he knew what lay ahead for me?"

"Probably, although he might not have had all the details, and nothing is definite until it happens anyway. Something could've changed your pathway between when he left you and the time you were chosen. You know, free will and all."

As I recalled my unauthorized trip to the Fountain of Lost Souls a shiver snuck up on me. That could have been a career-ender if Johnny hadn't swooped in for the rescue.

"Come on," Kadie urged quietly. "He's working, and we have to go." She took my hand to lead me away as I continued to peer over my shoulder at Thomas. And so we left that sad place in search of our exit point.

I brushed the sadness from my soul and my spirit lightened, focusing on the good things I had now, these wonderful new companions and the opportunity to do something great in the world.

Before long, we encountered the sign we sought. In giant block letters it announced:

YOU ARE NOW LEAVING THE ASTRAL PLANE
TO ENTER THE ATMOSPHERE OF EARTH.
PEACE BE WITH YOU.

The fog appeared much thicker here, and we couldn't see more than a few feet in front of us. Seth warned to keep a sharp eye in case the entrance to the main wormhole surprised us and the ground suddenly disappeared. Again I had that strange thought. What were we standing on? Interplanetary clouds?

We stopped to set the coordinates on our fancy watches, double-checking them.

"Okay, let's do this," Kadie said.

I kinda thought maybe we should have practiced this. A little training couldn't hurt. But apparently the Travelers were sort of a "do or die" organization. And, at this juncture, I wasn't sure what alive or dead even meant.

Drew took my hand. I looked up at him wondering why. "I want to be careful," he said. "Seth might be right. If this wormhole sneaks up on us, I don't want to lose you."

We tentatively approached the exit, when shortly we ran into a sign above a fifty-foot wide slide:

EXIT THIS WAY

Aidan had informed us we'd effectively be using some type of a turbo booster to get into the wormhole. I wasn't quite sure how to approach this.

"Come on," encouraged Drew as he took a seat on the oversized slide. He reached out his hand, and I took it, settling myself next to him. "Sit behind me," he suggested, "wrap your legs around me, and hold tight to my waist." Kind of like riding with a guy on a motorcycle, I thought. Yeah, a wild ride on a Harley!

"Okay..." I said, trying to sound enthusiastic. My breasts pressed into Drew's back and a blaze of heat raced through me. I feared sparks might erupt, but thankfully they didn't.

Kadie and Seth moved into identical positions only with Kadie in front, and we sat in brief silence.

Drew settled his arms over mine, securing me against him. "Ready?"

My enthusiasm vanished. "Not really," I answered.

Jumping back on my virtual Harley, I tried to convince myself I wasn't about to become...what? Heavenly road-kill? One of the Fallen? Yikes! I had to stop over-thinking this before I chickened out.

"Don't be afraid. I've got you," Drew said, pulling me out of my reverie. The same words Thomas always used to ease my anxiety just before we ventured into the great beyond. "Now or never!"

"Never or now," I muttered.

Drew gave a push, and we were off. The speed exhilarated me, the cool air whistled past my ears—that's if I still had ears—but then, searing heat swarmed me. How long would this take? Would I be able to withstand the sensation of being on fire until we hit Earth?

I tried to keep my eyes open, but couldn't see anything but sparkles, as if flying through a fireworks display. I smelled smoke and tasted metal, something I'd experienced only when I'd died and en route to the Astral Plane. My atoms felt in disarray, in ionic chaos, molten, like metal evaporating. Could I be disassociating? Like the baby at Chrism Center...rendering my soul into droplets of mercury?

A clap of thunder and our speed began to diminish. We landed on our feet with perfect precision, yet then tumbled to the ground. Kadie and Seth arrived right behind us. The four of us lay there, panting, overjoyed by utter triumph.

"Oh my God, we made it!" I cried. My ears popped. I gazed into the sky above and couldn't believe I'd just come from...up there! Totally insane. Seth and I shared in the astonishment of our return trip to Earth.

"Wow, that was a lot easier than I thought!" Drew

said.

Kadie laughed, a nervous titter. "Yeah, surprisingly it was. I can't say I was all that confident at the onset."

Seth gave her a wary look. "Now you tell me?"

Kadie stuck her tongue out. Seth shook his head. Standing, I straightened my appearance and extended a hand to Drew, pulling him to his feet and picking grass out of his windblown hair. His blazing dark eyes shimmered heat through me. Damn. I wanted to kiss him. Badly. And I began to think he wanted me, too.

Chapter 13

We entered a street of neatly kept homes with lawns covered in a mosaic of orange, red, and yellow leaves. The air smelled fragrant with the perfume of a fall harvest. The sinking sun spewed blood-red light across the skyline. Our calm mood abruptly vanished as three frightful creatures came into view. The one in front sported pointy red horns sprouting from his forehead and gore smeared across his face. Two ghosts followed him. None of them stood taller than four feet.

"You've got to be kidding me!" Seth said, as the three devilish munchkins passed us by.

"Geez," I exclaimed, "you'd think they might have mentioned this before they sent us out!"

Kadie and Drew both took a step backward and gasped. Kadie said, "I didn't know humans could look like that! Are they dangerous?"

Seth and I didn't respond to Kadie's question. "I can't believe it," Seth said to me. "It's friggin' Halloween!"

"What's Halloween?" Kadie mumbled.

I sighed, knowing this wasn't going to go well. We made our best attempt at explaining Halloween. But bribing frightfully costumed children with candy in order to prevent them from vandalizing your house sounded ridiculous once we'd said it out loud.

It took a few minutes for our buddies to refocus on

the mission. The town appeared busy as people went about their last minute chores, navigating the small parade of creepily attired children visiting stores and businesses in pursuit of treats. Kadie and Drew explained that except for the outlandish costumes, the physical environment wasn't all that different from their colonies, but they did feel a little strange as they moved around, sort of heavy. What a relief, the thought of explaining the entire physical structure of Earth would have been daunting.

"Do you think the mortals can see us?" Kadie wondered aloud.

"I'm not sure," Seth said. "It doesn't appear so yet."

A small dog trotted over and sniffed at my feet. Could it see me? Aidan had explained animals didn't follow the same rules as humans. They could often sense the presence of a Traveler when humans couldn't, but the scruffy little mutt lost interest and trotted off to find something, or somebody, more interesting.

Next, two women approached and I focused on being visible. The one on the left had coal-black eyes and long dark hair fashioned in a sleek ponytail. She wore a short jean jacket with the collar turned up, over a white T-shirt and tight black jeans. Her companion flaunted short, shaggy hair dyed a bright crimson color and too many piercings in her face to count at a single glance. She wore sunglasses, even though sunset foreshadowed.

Both of them stared *at me* as they walked past. "Those women saw me, I'm real!"

"What women?" Drew asked.

"The two that just walked by, one with crazy red

hair and face piercings and the other a long black ponytail..." I turned to point them out. No one was there. "Nobody saw them?"

"Nope," their collective answer came. I frowned.

A pack of five boys riding bicycles came upon us next. I said, "I'm going to run out in front of them and see what happens."

"Okay," Drew said with a tinge of hesitation. I darted into the street. The boys ran right through me. It felt like someone had just attached me to a vacuum cleaner and sucked all the air out of me.

"Got any other brainy ideas?" Seth said. "First you see people who aren't there and now this. We're going to flunk this assignment if we don't figure things out quick."

A too-big part of me doubted my ability to perform the required task. So far, things hadn't exactly been going according to plan. Perhaps I wasn't cut out for this work. "Maybe it's something we have to do willfully," I finally proposed.

"Kind of like mind over matter, you mean?" Seth said.

"Yeah."

"All right, let's try to be seen, to be human," Seth suggested. "Everybody concentrate."

"That's not so easy when you've never been human," Kadie said.

Good point, I thought, as we returned to the sidewalk and walked four abreast toward Center Street.

"Visualize interacting with the mortals," Seth instructed, our self-appointed quarterback, apparently.

A young man and woman approached from across the street. I found him incredibly handsome and immediately thought of my old boyfriend. Had he moved on? Was he kissing somebody new these days? The notion depressed me, and I shoved it aside.

As the couple neared, Seth pretended to trip. The man reached out to keep him from falling. "Hey, are you okay?" the cute guy said, gawking at Seth.

"Thanks, buddy. I wasn't paying attention to where I was going," Seth said.

"No prob," the stranger said as he and his companion continued on their way. Seth gave me the thumbs-up, which he then had to explain to Kadie and Drew.

We ambled through town. The sidewalk was bumpy and irregular, and I had to judiciously plot each step.

"Let's head back to Eccli Hall," Drew urged.

Yes, let's. I exhaled relief. But then confusion knitted my eyebrows together. "What did you say? Eccli Hall?"

"Yeah, that's what everybody calls it," Drew said. Kadie nodded.

"Okay, then." I shrugged in Seth's direction, and his shoulders flexed upward, too.

The sun had set, the velvety blue-black sky revealing a celestial map. The town's hustle and bustle had stilled, save for a few leftover kids begging for treats. As folks headed to their houses for supper, I envisioned my family sitting at the dinner table, my chair empty. I should've made it home for dinner more often.

A decrepit old man slumped on a bench near the field's entrance where we'd arrived. He mumbled to himself in sleep, chin on his chest. A sense of purpose consumed me. I situated myself next to him. Was I visible?

"What are you doing?" Drew asked.

"Not sure," I said. "Let me just sit for a minute."

Two boys came into view. They seemed to be about thirteen or fourteen. Stopping before the sleeping man, their voices rang out, raucous and obnoxious. "Hey, old fart, taking a nap?" the taller boy said, snarling. He wore low-slung, baggy, black jeans with a long silver chain hanging from his belt. His torn gray sweatshirt fit too tightly on his scrawny body. Greasy black hair fell into his muddy-brown eyes. The other boy, similarly clad, puffed on a cigarette. He brought his face close and exhaled the foul smoke into the elderly man's face.

"Hey, mister, you want some?" The taller boy sneered. The groggy man lifted his head. The boy pulled a small liquor bottle from his back pocket and dramatically waved it about, then tipped the bottle and poured some of the brown liquid into the man's lap. The man attempted to rise from his seat in an effort to bolt, but the boys forced him back onto the bench. A cigarette lighter appeared. Without thinking, I swatted the lighter from the boy's hand and it flew into the air, skittered across the pavement, and slid down a grated storm drain.

The boys exchanged expressions of shock, whirling around in search of someone, or some*thing*. Seth confronted them, doing his best tough-guy act. "You better leave before I call the police and tell them you tried to set this man on fire." Seth pulled a cell phone from his front pocket. *What was he doing with a phone?*

Fear spread across their faces and the boys absconded into the field, vanishing into the descending darkness. Drew asked, "Should we chase them?"

"And what if we catch them?" I said. "Beat the crap out of them?"

Katie said, "We did enough, guys. Let's head back."

We arrived home uneventfully, and Seth and I took the lead on the path back to Eccli Hall.

"Pretty weird being back on good ole planet Earth, huh?" Seth said.

"Yeah. Strange, for sure."

Although initially invisible, willing my atoms into a cohesive entity had truly made me human. My breath, my pulse, my flesh, all felt normal. Conversely, on the Astral Plan I seemed more like a hologram, able to glide, using less energy and force to ambulate. Plus, telepathy facilitated communication when you were comfortable with someone.

"Do you spy on your former family much?" Seth asked.

"I used to, the other times I died, but this time, not so much. It helps to keep busy, not like on the Astral Plane where you have nothing to do all day."

The pain constricting Seth's features saddened me. "I can't help watching my mother. She hasn't adjusted well."

Although I'd heard the death circumstances of quite a few recruits, I hadn't talked about this with Seth. He'd drowned in his backyard pool while practicing a back flip and wound up breaking his neck. His mom was in the kitchen but didn't find him until too late.

"I never should have been doing something so

stupid. I feel awful about leaving my mother behind with all this guilt. It haunts her. She's never going to forgive herself."

Seth's story disheartened me. "I know it's hard, Seth, but we need to remind ourselves that what we experience on Earth is temporary, merely a chapter in a long, long book."

"You're right. But it still gets to me."

Solemnly trudging homeward, we shared a silent interlude of grief.

"By the way," I said, "what's with the phone?"

"I don't know, when I picked out my clothes I saw it on the shelf. Couldn't resist. I miss my iPhone more than I care to admit."

Shaking my head, I wondered. Did it get service up here? Doubtful. Besides, who would we contact? Getting a call from a dead person would be ill advised. "You're nuts," I offered.

Seth's laughter rumbled. "Listen, since you already think I'm nuts, there's something I want to ask."

"Okay, shoot."

"This is going to sound crazy, but when we were on Earth, I kept thinking about sex. Like, every chick I saw I was attracted to. I thought about it a lot as a mortal, but this was addiction territory, even for me. Do you think there's something wrong?" I couldn't believe he'd said that. I had the same feeling, thinking about my old flame. And so that's what I told him. After a pause, Seth sighed. "Really? I thought it was just me."

"It's the Libidinous Spirits," a voice from behind us interjected.

We stopped and turned toward Kadie.

"Excuse me?" I said.

"The Libidinous Spirits, Spirits of Lust, or 'The Lusties,' as they like to call themselves," Kadie stated matter-of-factly.

"What the what?" The pitch in Seth's voice increased.

"She's right," Drew said, giving me a mischievous wink. His eyes were molten chocolate under those long lashes. I could get lost in those eyes.

Kadie continued, "Lusties mostly hang out on Earth trying to tempt humans to behave badly. But their favorite pastime is to prank newbies like you."

Both corners of Drew's grin seemed to almost reach his ears. But now I wondered if my desire for him was due to ethereal pranksters. Annoyed, I said, "What can be done about it?"

"*Nada*," Drew offered. "Just ignore them, and they'll get bored and move on to someone else."

He knew Spanish?

"Okaaay…" I grabbed Seth by his upper arm as we neared the front door, whispering, "I can't believe they're acting like it's no big deal."

"Maybe we've got just as much to learn from our new pals as they do from us," Seth said quietly.

"I guess so." I smiled, couldn't help but notice his chin stubble. "Growing a beard?"

He reached for his chin. "What?"

"I think you need a shave."

"You know, I thought so, but I couldn't really believe it."

"Does Drew shave?" I hadn't noticed stubble on Drew, but he had much lighter hair than Seth.

"There are shaving supplies in the bathroom medicine cabinet."

"I guess you have your answer then."

"Yeah, and that sucks. One advantage of being dead was you didn't have to worry about all that personal grooming shit."

Hmm. Now that I thought about it, my underarms and legs needed some grooming.

Back at the dorm, Kadie and I returned to our room. She said, "A few more hours before the next briefing. Not hungry, so I'm going to chill."

"Sounds like a plan." We plopped down on our beds. I closed my eyes and rested the back of my head in my hands. The movie of our newly completed mission played in my mind. I couldn't wait for the next field trip and hoped my buddies felt the same.

"I do," said Kadie.

I sat bolt upright. "What did you say?"

"I said 'I do.' I feel the same way. I can't wait for the next assignment," she said, her nose already in a book.

"Since when can you read my mind?"

"You're pushing your thoughts to me," Kadie said.

"What does that mean?" I gaped at Kadie like she had two heads.

"It means we can read each other's thoughts. Remember when Drew did it to you in the dining hall that day?" Oh yeah, when he showed me how he'd sneaked some fuel from his dad and flashed around his neighborhood. "Don't act so freaked out. If you don't want anyone inside your head, then just keep your thoughts to yourself."

"How do I do that?"

"Trial and error, basically. You'll figure it out."

I pondered this new ability and tried to decide if it

was a good thing or a bad. I could definitely see pros and cons. "Hmm…"

We both sank into a hush as I considered what other oddities might occur along this journey to being fully vested warriors. I mused over tomorrow's briefing focus, the City of the Sun's Seven Kingdoms. Where the Scepters resided. A thrill shot through me. Would we get to see them up close and personal?

A girl could certainly hope.

Chapter 14

Standing before the closet in my underwear, I grabbed a clean jumpsuit from the top shelf.

"Get me one too, will you?" Kadie asked. I tossed it on her bed.

I needed information, vital info, and she was the only one I could turn to. "Kadie, question?" But then I wondered, could she read my mind? Did she already know what I was thinking?

"Fire away." She sat on the edge of her bed and slipped her well-toned legs into the clean jumpsuit.

"Are there any rules about dating here?"

Kadie looked at me. "You've got the hots for Drew, huh?"

"Kadie!" I tried to appear shocked, my face probably in some oddball contortion. "Are you reading my mind?"

"I didn't have to use telepathy to figure that one out."

"It's that obvious, huh?"

"Umm, *yeah*."

"Soooooo?"

Kadie rolled her eyes. "Livy, honestly, for such a smart and experienced soul, you're acting like a dork. It works the same here as it does anywhere."

"That's not an answer. Deets?"

"Well, I wouldn't exactly call it dating. There's

nowhere to go. If you're falling for Drew, just flow with it. There aren't any rules that forbid love."

"Okay." I needed to think. I really wanted to know if we were allowed to have unadulterated toe-curling all-night sex, but somehow I couldn't bring myself to blurt that.

"He's a cutie pie!" Kadie said. "And a good guy, to boot." I didn't offer a response. My mind traveled to places I hadn't been to in the longest.

Later, in the dining hall I picked at my wafers, wishing it was pizza, while we waited for the guys. I sipped at the blue liquid in my cup, concluding it definitely tasted like a watery version of maple syrup. But my mind was wrapped around thoughts of being wrapped around Drew.

Taking our seats in room fifteen, our long-limbed instructor arrived a few minutes after. "Sounds as though everyone is in rather good spirits this morning!" he said. Did he realize he'd just made a joke? "Let's have your reports."

Aidan randomly picked on Jesse to go first. Jesse sat across the room from me, but his girlfriend, Rachel, was only two seats away. They hadn't been assigned to the same team which I heard royally pissed off Rachel. Although, *everything* seemed to piss her off. Aidan told Jesse to place his palm on the orb at the table's center, explaining all he had to do was project the thought and the memory would materialize.

Like a movie, the foursome's trip appeared on the screen. In high def, living color, too.

Each group got a turn to report and the requisite awkward moments incited the occasional smirk or giggle. Apparently we'd all forgotten we were being recorded as we went about our business. The Halloween aspect made for some amusing reactions, but Aidan simply ignored the glitch and actually appeared somewhat entertained by the whole thing.

When our turn came, Aidan chose Kadie. Her comment about Thomas being "hot" garnered a huge laugh. Kadie didn't find it quite as funny as the rest of us, however. I watched for the appearance of the two women who'd given me the evil eye. But nothing. Of course, if Kadie hadn't seen them…Would they be visible if my hand controlled the orb?

Aidan frowned when I seated myself next to the old man. He continued to grimace through the entire report and then asked me why I'd gotten involved in what he called "an unauthorized intervention."

I told him an overwhelming urgency insisted I sit next to the man. "So," I said, "I waited, and my friends lingered with me. And then, the boys came along and tried to hurt him. Obviously we needed to protect him and you saw the rest."

Aidan listened closely while everyone waited to hear his verdict. He had his chin resting in his hand, which in turn rested on his other arm perched across his chest. "Hmm…this was supposed to be a simple assignment with no real interaction, and I had no intention of allowing you to perform an intervention. Certainly not on your first trip. I'm concerned you weren't properly prepared. There are certain rules for interventions and also specific dangers I haven't addressed. However some other force may have been at work here, so I don't think I can hold you fully responsible for your actions."

What other *force*? I didn't like where this was

going.

"Although I'm quite pleased by your performance, you must understand interventions will be assigned with strict protocols in order to keep you safe. Never are you to intervene without prior permission. Agreed?"

"Yes, sir. Won't happen again."

"Good."

Rachel leaned over and whispered, "Like I keep saying. Trouble, you."

Switching gears, Aidan said, "Today, I'll give you a quick overview of the realm of the Seven Kingdoms."

The assistants distributed guide sheets to us as Aidan began his lecture. "The City of the Sun is vast and not only includes the Seven Kingdoms, but also the colonies where Travelers are born and raised, and Chrism Center where we nurture the souls of babies until they are ready for recycling. Many other structures and institutions are located in outlying areas, but are too numerous for today's discussion.

"Entrance into the Seven Kingdoms is only permitted if you know the names of the guardians at the main gate. You'll see them listed on the back of your guide sheet. Memorize them in the event you ever have business there, and then destroy the paper.

"Gabriel's crest identifies the main gate since he's chief of the Announcement Bureau. Don't veer too far left of the archway as that leads directly to the Fountain of Lost Souls. It's a dangerous place and is off limits."

Uneasiness crept over me as I recalled my unauthorized field trip to that infamous fountain. I considered sharing this experience with my teammates. Then thought better of it.

The sheet gave us a map of each kingdom, the

Scepter who ruled it, and a depiction of his crest. Huh? I thought only four Scepters existed, but seven kingdoms meant at least seven Scepters.

The label for a prison caught my eye. Who was incarcerated? Mortals or Travelers? I wanted to ask Aidan but found myself too shy. So unlike me. I always had my hand up in conventional schools, sometimes to the point of being annoying.

"Each kingdom, and the Scepter who rules it and resides there, maintains a specific area of responsibility. For example, the Sixth Kingdom, governed by Raphael, houses our scientific laboratories, the Department of Healing, and the Fountain of Life where souls are reborn to Earth. Most of this is explained in the printed information I've given, so I won't go into further detail. However, I'd like to take a few minutes to emphasize the status of the Seventh Kingdom, as it's the most significant in terms of our mission.

"The Court of Justice is located within it, as are the Offices of Death and War as well as the main vault housing our energy source, known to us as the Flame of Life.

"Michael is the highest ranking guardian and warrior in the City of the Sun. He serves as the magistrate of the Court and Commander in Chief of all our legions and is responsible not only for Ecclesia Hall but all our recruitment centers." Aidan paused. "Any questions?"

Quelling my hesitation, I swallowed hard. My hand went up.

"Yes, Olivia?"

"Uh, there are prisons marked on the map. Who are the inmates?"

Aidan leaned back against his desk and crossed his arms across his chest as if settling in to tell a story. He sighed and his eyes fixed on the gray-tiled flooring. "Well, Olivia, they are combatants left over from the war between Michael and Lucifer." He paused and the silence grew uncomfortable. "When the humans first evolved on Earth, we charged ourselves with helping souls navigate through their birth and death cycles until such time as their energy becomes pure. Lucifer and Michael disagreed on our purpose, and when we realized Lucifer and his followers had become so covetous, boastful, and excessively proud, even lustful of young mortals, we had to remove them from service. Lucifer attempted to overthrow the City of the Sun, but he lost the battle and fell to Earth along with his most devoted followers. Others were captured and remain our prisoners. Needless to say, Lucifer is still enraged over his exile and fights every day to steal souls from us, thus preventing them from achieving grace…and peace…through the cycle of reincarnation. And so these prisoners have been sentenced to what we call the 'measureless judgment.' Which…is an eternity of waiting and waiting for…well…absolutely nothing."

I shivered, asking, "This war had nothing to do with any angels, correct?"

"No," Aidan said without hesitation. "No angels. No wings, no halos, no harps. That's pretty much a mortal misconception. It's only been us, forever and always." I pondered his words.

Aidan continued, "Those were trying times. We seldom talk about them anymore, and we never want that kind of battle outcome to be repeated. We shall remain vigilant in this regard, and it will be something you'll monitor for us in the future as part of your sacred responsibilities."

Oh, joy. I didn't relish the thought of acting in the capacity of otherworldly police. Then again, what an honor.

"Anything else, Olivia?" prompted Aidan.

"No, sir. Thank you."

"You're very welcome." Aidan continued his lecture, naming a bunch of Scepters I'd never heard of and whose names I couldn't even quite pronounce. My mind started to drift, but thankfully Aidan ended his lecture before I totally zoned out.

Chapter 15

The weekend flew by, and Monday found us off to Atlanta on our first real assignment, delivering a message to a dead woman's husband. We wormed our way in by pretending to be visitors from the food bank and assisted the inebriated father in getting the house—and what remained of his family—in some semblance of order.

I went out the back door in search of a trashcan to deposit garbage. Upon arrival, I hadn't noticed the house bordered a cemetery. Without warning, the evening temps drastically dropped and my breath streamed out as white mist. A black crow swooped down over my head and I ducked. A crow flying at night? The errant screech of an owl echoed. I pivoted on my heels. The large bird swept over my head, and I crouched low.

Quickly dumping the trash into the plastic can, my chest panged, telling me to run for shelter. Fear amplified into terror. Blinding red light paralyzed me, my arms pinned to my sides as my feet zoomed away from the ground. My back slammed into a stone wall, and my head thudded hard against cold cement. The strangling grip around my upper arm would definitely leave a bruise. A metal door creaked open, and the unseen force shoved me inside a frigid dark place where I fell to my knees. A black marble coffin filled the tiny chamber. The dank mausoleum smelled of mildew. Decay.

I managed to stand and backed away, finding myself trapped in a corner. Two women moved in close, too near, the same ones I'd beheld walking down Center Street during my first mission. The ones only I had seen.

"Well, if it isn't the adorable Little Lightning Girl." The woman with jet-black hair snorted.

"She is lovely, Vana," her cohort said. "It seems like every time she reoccurs she gets blessed with the beauty of Bathsheba."

Who were these women, and what did they want from me?

"Time works against us, Lily," Vana said to her companion, although her gaze never left me. "And how I hate disguising myself as a crow to avoid detection by the Scepters. It's beneath me."

"Shapeshifting was never your forte," Lily said. "Admit it, Vana, I'm better than you at pretty much everything."

"Don't start, Lily! We have equal status in Hell."

"You're lucky I put up with you at all!"

I watched as the two women volleyed threats between them as if I wasn't there. For some reason I couldn't move, like some invisible force had a magical hold.

"Please, Lily. Just stop. We're in this together."

"Not by choice! This was my kingdom first. Lucifer gave me his kisses long before you."

Vana negotiated a step toward Lily, her long index finger only an inch from Lily's chest. Her voice grew deep, resonant. "Don't overestimate your powers, or your station in the Kingdom of Hell, Lily. And don't underestimate me either. That could prove lethal."

Lily growled through clenched teeth, her fists tight at her sides.

Vana's arm withdrew. "Enough! We waste time, just tell her already."

"I will not," Lily countered.

The two women argued while I'd been trying to figure out a means of escape.

"Fine," Vana said. Her dark, feral eyes might melt a glacier. She inched forward. Sharp stripes of moonlight percolating through the side window's bars streaked her onyx-colored hair. I pushed my back into the cement wall praying for escape. But my invisibility trick didn't seem to be working. "I regret the subversive tactics, Olivia, but it's impossible to get you alone."

"Who the hell are you?" I said, my voice cracking.

"Now that's complicated," Lily said. "But we're your family, you bear our family crest." Suddenly their anger evaporated. They both pulled up the sleeves on their black capes to reveal matching marks, crescent-shaped red scars with the horns pointed toward their hearts. If they had hearts. Somehow, I doubted it. Not even emotional hearts.

"Show her, Lily," Vana said as Lily reached for my arm. But Lily didn't have to, for I knew. I peered down at the ominous mark emblazoned on my skin.

"Ah, see," Lily said with a satisfied nod.

"I don't understand, what does this mark mean?" I braced myself, fearful of her answer.

"It means you belong to us. Your destiny is to rule the Underworld alongside us."

Dumbfounded, I couldn't answer. I fretted, who

were these ominous creatures? I'd no idea how to make an escape, as they seemed to possess powers that gave them tactical advantage. I had to…call for help. But how? Panicked, I sent out a mental S.O.S and prayed Kadie would hear me.

A finger snapped, and I felt as if I were under water.

****

Ravana grabbed Olivia by the throat and pinned her against the slimy wall. Olivia hung like a rag doll.

Lily shifted toward Vana. "This isn't going to work. We're never going to convince her."

"Then we'll resort to something drastic," Vana said. "It's obvious that she's not about to come willingly. Since *I* am the Immortal Queen of Witchcraft perhaps I'll resort to a curse. I daresay I'd rather enjoy casting a spell on the little Traveler."

Lily guffawed. "What merriment, but you know we can't get away with a curse. A suggestion instead? Something inescapable, hypnotic. No memories either. We can't have her remembering. Just plant the idea she's playing for the wrong army. Hurry, she's been off the grid too long. The Scepters will catch on to what we're up to if she's out of sight much longer."

****

Dazed, I fell on the floor in a heap. I pleaded to Kadie. Then Seth, and Drew. *Help me!*

"Nice try," Lily said. "But we've blocked that. They can't hear you."

Crap.

Vana's cold hand grabbed my throat and lifted me, shoving me farther up the cement wall. My hair pulled against the coarse concrete. I winced. "Beware, Olivia, this discussion is far from over."

The night erupted in scarlet flashes, and then everything went black. A foggy haze engulfed me, and I couldn't remember where I was or what I'd been doing. Worse than when Thomas made that attempt at trying to calm me. Nausea flooded my insides, and my head throbbed. The trashcan sat overturned with the contents strewn around my feet. I knelt to clean up the mess, yet dizziness overwhelmed me, and I sat down on the snow-cold grass to keep from toppling.

"Livy?" His voice startled me, and I emitted a small squeak.

"Geez, Drew, you scared the crap out of me!"

He hoisted me up, his arm trapping my shoulders in a comforting embrace. "I couldn't find you. What have you been doing out here?"

Something happened. I struggled to recall the chain of events: an errant crow flew by, the screech of an owl, and I lay on the ground with the trashcan dumped at my feet. Then I had a sick feeling. "Stop making a fuss, I'm fine," I said, although I wasn't.

Drew held me by my shoulders. "I don't believe you. You look awful."

I put my arms around his waist, and he hugged me. His warmth banished the chill from my body.

"Oh Drew," I mumbled into his chest. "You make me feel safe."

"Safe isn't a word I'd use when it comes to you. I think you're pretty capable of keeping yourself safe. But I do like having my arms around you."

I smiled into his shirt. *Me too.* I gazed into his beautiful face, nervousness tingling inside me.

"I've got it bad for you, Liv," he confessed.

My insides took a tumble. My aura raced, expanding. "Me too."

Drew leaned in, and the heat of his mouth on mine cascaded quivers of desire through me. A soft, gentle kiss to which I responded eagerly. He tasted sweet, so very sweet.

The house's screen door flew open. "Caught ya!" Seth said. I recoiled from Drew's arms. "We're in here trying to save the day while you two suck face? Seriously?" He slammed the back door.

Drew broke into a wide grin. "To be continued," he said. We finished cleaning up the trash, and he tugged me by the hand toward the house.

We returned to find Kadie and Seth in the living room talking to the distraught father. "I can't believe I've fallen apart like this," the man said to Kadie. Drew and I sat on the living room couch beside Seth. "My wife would be furious if she saw this. I guess she does see, that's what you're telling me, isn't it?"

Kadie said, "She sees you. We're sure you can get your life back together, Dan. So does Erin."

"Is she," the man choked out, "is my wife okay?"

"She is," Kadie said in comforting tones, "and she'll be much better once she knows you and the children are all right. Then she'll be able to move on."

Message delivered, we entered the dank night air to make our departure when uneasiness struck me. Someone was here, hiding in shadows. Something bad was about to happen. I searched the darkness for danger. Something moved. A shadow…no…two shadows. The dark silhouettes disappeared among the tree trunks. Was something really there or were my eyes playing tricks?

"Come on," I urged, "let's get out of here. This place gives me the heebie-jeebies."

I clutched Drew's hand. Traveling through the cosmos at astronomical speed, I almost believed I could let go of him, but I wouldn't. Holding onto Drew made me feel safe, warm.

Back in our room, Kadie asked if I had tried to flash yet. Embarrassed, I admitted I was afraid. "Why?" Kadie inquired with concern.

"Not sure. What if I'm some kind of mutant and can't do it? Things haven't exactly gone according to plan so far."

Kadie rubbed her chin. "Come on, give it a try. I'll help."

I bit at my nails. "Okay. As long as you're here. Tell me, please, what to do."

"First, take your fingers out of your mouth. You look like a two-year-old. And try to relax." Kadie placed her hands firmly on my shoulders. "Now, close your eyes and try to feel it. To start, keep your aura tight inside you. Keep track of all your atoms, then push them out. But be careful. Don't overthink. Wouldn't want you to blow up."

"That could happen?" I cried. I pictured myself disintegrating into tiny mercury-like shards skittering across our room's floor, like that angry baby in Chrism Center.

"Probably not, but in your case you never know." Kadie smiled, even as shock infused my face. She offered, "I'm kidding!"

"Not funny," I said. Because it wasn't.

"My bad." Kadie's hands tensed. "Now close your eyes and let yourself evaporate, but do it slowly. Then suck it back in."

Kadie's confidence encouraged me, so I cleared my mind and tried to recall the sensation of flying through the cosmos with Drew. I opened my eyes, disappointed. Nothing. "I knew I wouldn't be able to—"

Kadie clapped her hands. "You did it!"

"I *did*?"

"Yup, perfectly. Now try and go somewhere."

"Wow, I can't believe it! Okay, where to?"

"How about out to the garden and back. Wave to me when you're down there."

I stood in front of the open window. "Now or never," I mumbled under my breath.

"Never or now," Kadie said.

I closed my eyes and coaxed my atoms to drift away. Shocking. I could actually see where I was going. I hit the soft grass and sucked my atoms back in when a terrible epiphany struck. What if I put myself back together deformed: upside-down, inside-out? Kadie and Drew's simple yet wise words returned. *Don't overthink this.*

Kadie leaned out the window sporting an impossibly huge grin. She motioned enthusiastically. "Excellent. Come on back."

And I did. Wow. Deceptively easy.

A few hours passed and as I undressed for bed, Kadie startled me with: "What's that mark on your arm?"

"What mark?" I asked, gazing down at the birthmark. It had already garnered too much attention, and apprehension invaded me again.

"The one on your upper arm, your left one."

I frowned at Kadie's unexpected response and examined the mottled skin near my shoulder. I had no memory of what caused the bruise. "Honestly, I've never seen this before."

Chapter 16

Ravana entered the west end dungeon dressed for the Metropolitan Opera Ball. Valentino himself had clothed her, in the flesh. The elegant black evening gown hugged her lush curves and the plunging sweetheart neckline showcased her double-D breasts. Her smooth skin glistened in the iridescent candlelight. "Bring him to me," the Princess of Darkness ordered.

"Yes, Your Majesty." The hellish prison guard bowed slightly, then skulked away into the dimness. Ravana pointed her finger toward the stone wall. A silvery spark skittered across the jagged rock, spreading into a web of shimmering threads. A huge full-length mirror with a silver frame appeared. Ravana gazed at the image in the glass. She stroked her lengthy dark tresses, tucking one sleek strand behind her ear. The diamond drop earrings reached almost to her collarbone. The matching barrette pinning back the left side of her hair sparkled, shooting tiny rainbows across the slimy rock wall of her glorious dungeon. A satisfied smile crossed her face as she slid her hands down her hips, caressing the fine plush ebony velvet ending at her ankles.

A figure emerged behind her. Lilith. "My, my, don't we look stunning."

"We?" Ravana said. "You look like you're off to a hog-tying contest."

Lilith's lips set in a terse line. "Really, Vana? I was trying to pay you a compliment." Her penchant for leather aside, Lilith wore seriously distressed jeans and a tight black T-shirt, and countless silver bracelets on each arm. Her scarlet locks were gelled into spikey points and her favorite earrings with the dangling crescent moons sparkled in the incandescent crimson light. A red and white bandana circled her neck, tied into a double knot at her throat.

Ravana chastised herself for once again baiting Lilith, who'd come to do her bidding. Ravana cleared her throat. "You're too sensitive, Lily," she said, shrugging off Lilith's comment with a wave of her perfectly manicured hand. Lilith stuck her tongue out.

"Really, Lily? I know you have a fondness for babies, but must you act like one?"

Lilith actually laughed. "Is this one of your special mirrors?"

"You ask questions you already know the answer to."

"I do envy you this skill," Lilith said.

Ravana ran her fingers through her hair again. "It is a convenient method of transport. It keeps my hair from getting too windblown."

"So, where are you going all gussied up?"

"I have a secret liaison with a senator after the ball. But by the time I'm done with him it won't be so secret. And when his wife finds out, it's going to be the end of his career, and I'll have removed another one of those damned do-gooders from government service."

"Music to my ears."

"Let's get down to business."

Lilith's gaze fell to the back of the dungeon as if

anticipating someone. "So, you're ready to place Peter?"

"Yes, the guards are bringing him now. The subconscious threats aren't getting us anywhere. It's time to up the ante. You'll bring him to the Astral Plane and let him stew there for a while. Put him somewhere in the back, so no one notices him. I'll let you know when to place him with Marilyn Shannon. You know where she lives?"

"Yes, I located her."

"Good. I'll take it from there."

"Your Highness," the guard interrupted. "Pardon my intrusion, but I have brought the boy as you commanded." Again he bowed. Ravana peered down at Peter, his clothes dirty and ragged, his face smeared with grime.

"Free him from his shackles," the Princess of Darkness ordered. The guard released the prisoner from bondage and retreated, bending at the waist, then disappeared into the dungeon's recesses.

"Peter," Ravana said. "Your time has come, little man. My friend, Lilith, is going to escort you back to the Astral Plane…"

Lilith huffed a laugh, distracting Ravana from issuing her directive.

"What?" Ravana snapped.

Lilith smirked. "You just called me your friend. I'm touched."

Ravana closed her eyes and counted to ten, then opened them. "A slip of the tongue."

"Well, blazes. I thought you were going soft on me."

Ravana shook her head. The urge to smack Lilith

fizzed up inside her, and she struggled against it. She pivoted to Peter again. "Listen carefully. You are to wait on the Astral Plane until Lilith returns for you. The next time I see you we'll rehearse your story. You are not to tell anyone about our little agreement. Clear?" Peter nodded his head. "Use words, heathen."

"Yes, ma'am," he whispered.

"Good boy. Remember, Peter, if you fail at this task I will bring you back here, where you will remain for all of eternity. Understood?"

"Yes, ma'am." Peter whimpered.

"All right, then. Off you go." She took her index finger and pushed him toward Lilith as if touching something that would soil her dress, which it most likely would. "He's all yours."

Lilith tugged Peter along by his hand and said, "Let's go, little guy." Before she exited the dungeon she said, "Have fun tonight."

"Oh, trust me. I will." Ravana gave her signature wicked smile. Studying her slim profile in the mirror, she cocked her head to one side and practiced her alluring pout. The guy didn't stand a chance. And then she walked through the mirror, taking it with her in blinding red flashes.

Chapter 17

With messenger rotation completed, acting as healers was next. Before setting us free, Aidan explained the special powers of what he called *the kiss of light*, a healing gesture to be utilized in cases of unscheduled deaths. On very rare occasions it's administered when a soul dies under malevolent circumstances. He warned us to use it only in cases of extreme emergency. In essence, we'd be giving away fragments of our aura, diminishing us. It was forbidden for use by anyone other than our elite force. Guardians, for example, were never permitted to employ it to save their charges. He also instructed us not to merge our auras with any other life force—ever. For instance, if we possessed something like an animal and it died, we'd be bonded to the creature's aura for all of eternity. A ghastly thought.

On our way to a small town in Maine, Drew and I sought out a young girl of four. We found the house straight away, skulking unseen into the child's bedroom. She'd been sent home to die. Entering her room, we found her asleep in her small bed, attached to oxygen and an IV tube. A monitor quietly beeped near her bedside. She appeared so tiny, frail, nestled snugly in her bed covers. Nearby, her mother, Robin, slept on a small cot.

Drew went over to the little one's bed while I sat

with the mother. I gently moved the hair from her face and kissed her on the forehead. "Don't worry, Robin. Today your prayers will be answered."

Drew removed the oxygen mask from the child's face and disconnected the IV needle from her tiny arm. He shut off the machine and a deathly silence shrouded the room, lit only by a Barbie nightlight. Climbing into her bed, Drew cradled the child in his lap, nestling her up against his chest. I suddenly found myself overwhelmed with emotion as I watched Drew hold the child with such tenderness. He was a natural at this. Yet I wondered. Why were some souls spared and others not? No one ever tells us why we're sent to intervene and of course we always go without inquiry.

"She's pretty low," Drew said. "Think you need to come over here."

I nimbly climbed onto the bed opposite him. We wrapped our legs around each other's waists, cradling the child between us. Our hands intertwined as our healing auras melded into a glowing cocoon. I drew the sickness into me, slowly, uncomfortably. A chill shivered through me, like the time I'd donated platelets for an ill friend. Drew mirrored my distress, his pallor gray. Thankfully, the feeling passed quickly.

The child's eyelids fluttered and her green eyes opened big as saucers. She beamed at me, then shifted her gaze to Drew, revealing her baby teeth.

"Hi," she said.

"Hello there," Drew said. "How are you feeling?"

"Hungry."

"That's good," he said.

We broke our healing embrace as Drew picked the child up in his arms, rising from the bed. Drew tossed her in the air a few times. She giggled loudly. Robin stirred so Drew placed the child back in her bed. But she wouldn't be contained and immediately stood, jumping up and down.

"Mommy, Mommy," she called. Robin rose from the cot, tripping in her haste to reach the child. I kept her from falling, but she didn't notice. Within seconds her husband ran into the room anticipating the horror he'd expected for many nightmarish months. To his shock, his daughter frolicked on her bed, mysteriously detached from the tubes and machines.

"What in heaven's name?" he said with alarm.

"I—I don't know. I dozed off and awoke to this!"

"How did she get unhooked? And the machine is shut off."

"Seems impossible..." Robin said and then, "Olivia!" She scooped the child into her arms.

I did a double take, wondering how she knew my name. She shouldn't be able to see me! Drew rescued me. "The child's name is Olivia, she's not calling you."

Only Drew had read the assignment sheet and he'd apparently left that little detail out, or maybe I hadn't been listening. I blew out a slow stream of breath. "That freaked me out for a second."

"Mommy, I'm hungry, can I have waffles?"

Robin, her husband's arms secured around both her and their child, said, "Sure you can, honey, sure." She kissed her husband. "It's a miracle."

"Can they have waffles too?" little Olivia asked, pointing in our direction.

Uh-oh. That was our cue to make a getaway. Aidan explained that the younger the child, the easier it was for them to see us, even if we tried to be invisible.

"Who, baby?" Robin scanned the tiny bedroom.

"The angels, right over there," little Olivia said, pointing again. She leapt onto the floor and stood squarely in front of us.

"We have to go now," Drew said to the child.

"Do you smell that?" Robin said to her husband.

"What?"

"I distinctly smell maple syrup. Can't you smell it?"

"Actually, yeah, I do. Strange."

This wasn't the first time we'd heard that either, and I couldn't really explain it. Maybe it was our own spiritual pheromones.

"Don't go!" Olivia said loudly to us. "You just got here."

"We'll meet again someday, Olivia," I promised.

"Who's she talking to?" the dad said, tilting his head to the side and pursing his lips.

Robin gazed out through the window, to the stars. "Thank you, thank you, thank you."

Once outside, Drew and I slapped a high-five. Job well done.

"I love this gig!" Drew said, immediately before our lips touched.

Joy and satisfaction consumed me. Such a privilege, the opportunity to save a child. Tomorrow the doctors would declare little Olivia cured and everyone would call it a miracle. If only...if only they knew just how true that was.

"Let's take a walk before we head home," Drew suggested.

I snuggled against his side as we strolled toward the nearby town. Tucking my arm under his, he pulled me close and our steps synchronized. We entered a busy street. Music punctuated the air as local bar patrons crowded around the entrance puffing cigarettes. A clearly inebriated young woman stumbled out the door followed by a man.

Drew yanked me back, avoiding a near collision with the couple.

The guy grabbed the girl by the upper arm as she stepped between parked cars and into the street. The man scooped her up in his arms and settled her onto the sidewalk. A city bus nearly clipped her. "Jesus, fucking Christ, Krystle! You almost got killed!"

The girl screamed, "I'm sick of this fucking shit! Every girl flirts with you!" She lingered, staring at him, then fell into his arms. He hugged her tightly.

That voice. I recognized it...Oh my God...*Ryan.*

Drew noticed me stiffen. "What's wrong?"

"I...I..." What should I say? Should I admit I'd somehow stumbled into my old boyfriend? The last guy I'd had sex with? "It's nothing," I muttered. "For a second I thought I knew that guy."

Obviously, Ryan had moved on. I should feel bad, but I didn't. Ryan paled in comparison to Drew. By like a million times over. I deserved better. And yet he'd saved that girl's life.

****

After several weeks of healings, we rolled into crisis intervention mode, and excitement transfixed the classroom. Aidan explained how we'd be sent in when an unscheduled death occurred. In this capacity we gained ultimate authority and empowerment to intervene, whereas a guardian was never allowed to save their charge's mortal body. That seemed unfair to me, but then I remembered Johnny saying that the purpose of a guardian is to watch out for one's immortal soul, not the human body.

The following evening found Drew and me off on a mission to prevent a kidnapping. We'd spent nearly an hour in the garden last night, smothered in each other's breathless kisses. I touched my chafed chin, a residual effect from all the kissing against stubble. Worth it. So worth it.

Drew sat beside the kidnapper, who had the baby perched on her lap behind the steering wheel. I hovered in the truck bed of the beat-up white pickup. A chill instantly troubled me. I noticed someone sitting across from me. He seemed about twelve, but I didn't recognize him.

"Who are you?" We spoke at the same moment.

"You first," I said. The strange boy had a raggedy appearance and a dirty face. Apprehension prickled my skin.

He grunted. "I don't have to tell you nothing. Your kind screws me over."

"And what kind is that?"

"You know, guys like you, the guys with the Light inside." I fully expected him to spit at me. He sneered, shouting, "I'm trying to work here, and guys like you are always getting in the way."

"You mean you're working this kidnapping?" I couldn't hide the shock in my voice nor on my face. Could this be a creature from the Other Side? Words of warning surfaced as I tried to recall what I'd learned from Aidan. How serious a threat could he be? His body translucent around the edges, I guessed he might be a fledgling demon. In other words: not exceedingly powerful. Even though once they attached themselves to a family, bad luck ensued.

"There are two of us," I said. "You're no match for me, much less me and my partner."

"I'm just getting started," the boy said with vengeance. "And I've had my eyes on this Shannon lady for a long time. My turf."

"I can tell you with complete confidence that we're going nowhere until we've performed the necessary intervention," I said loudly, then pointed my index finger toward the sky. "We go upward, not down, where you probably belong."

He started to cry. "I need this, I got to get it right. My last chance or they'll take me to Hell and torture me forever."

Don't feel sorry for him. Might be a ruse. "How did you wind up in this situation?"

"I did something terrible just before I died." His eyes fell downward.

"What? Tell me."

He kept his gaze averted. "I got into a fight, and the kid fell and hit his head. He didn't get up. Then somebody hit me. I didn't get up."

"You killed someone?"

"It was an accident!" He let out a raucous breath. "God! Why won't anybody believe me?"

"What happened to you at death?" I asked.

"My soul collector was not happy. She left me in a dark place in the Astral Plane. I tried to talk to anyone who would listen, but everyone kept walking by me like I was invisible."

"How did you wind up on the Astral Plane if you did something so terrible? Don't you belong, you know, on the Other Side?"

"You think I know? At first I thought she took pity on me, then she left me to figure the way out. She was so angry, but must've thought I deserved one more chance, even a slim one. She wouldn't help and I didn't understand."

"What about your guardian? I can't believe you were abandoned like that."

"He told me I was on my own until I figured out which Side I wanted. As far as he knew I was already damned."

Awful. Who were these guys? "Let me get this straight. You were abandoned on the Astral Plane and told to fend for yourself?"

"Pretty much. Then, one day, this lady came up to me and said if I did something for her she could get me off the Astral Plane and into a better placement. I'd been alone for so long. It was bitter cold back there."

His knee joggled up and down. He wrung his hands together in a tight moving circle. I wasn't sure if I should believe anything. His words came more rapidly. "She brought me here and as soon as I started following this woman, bad things happened. I think I'm some kind of jinx."

Demons could make their way to the Astral Plane and try and steal souls or even spy. They couldn't sustain themselves for long and easily plummeted back to Earth. Sometimes they could last longer in the Astral Plane's colder distant regions. Maybe this was just such an occasion.

Damn! I'd lost focus on why I was here in the first place. I peered through the window separating the cab from the truck's bed to assess Drew's progress. I put a finger to my mouth to quiet the unexpected hitchhiker. Must discern the situation in the front seat.

The truck swerved left. With nothing to grab onto, my knees slid across the metal floor and my shoulder crashed into the opposite side of the bed. The tires screeched, and the vehicle abruptly stopped. I flashed onto the pavement alongside Drew. He shot me a nasty look. "What the hell were you doing?"

"I had kind of a situation going on."

Marilyn Shannon exited the truck, the baby clutched to her chest. She appeared to be searching for something in the distance. The headlights cast her in a blinding glare. Drew peered at my new acquaintance and said, "Who's that?"

"That's my *situation*."

The baby began to cry, and the woman returned to the driver's seat. She settled the wailing child on the precarious perch of her lap—again. Drew said, "It appears as if your 'situation' just threw himself in front of the truck! The woman slammed on the brakes to keep from hitting him!"

"Sorry. I don't understand why he did that." Not that I actually had any control over him anyway.

Disdain crinkled Drew's expression. "We'll talk about this later. Right now I've got to try and reason with this woman." He materialized in the seat next to the kidnapper.

She shrieked. "Where did you…? Who are you?"

"I'm here to help," Drew said.

"Are you an angel or something?" Marilyn Shannon muttered.

"Sort of," Drew said. The woman's chin fell, but she didn't respond. "Why did you steal this child?"

After her initial shock at seeing the supernatural, the woman burst into tears. "My husband left me six months ago and I...I couldn't bear to live without him. If he thought I'd had his baby, he might come back. We could be a family again."

Her tears turned hysterical. Drew reached out and rubbed her shoulder. "This isn't the solution, Marilyn. You must consider the other family and their unspeakable anguish."

Drew kept at it, his persuasion skills flawless.

"You're right," Marilyn Shannon finally agreed. "I'll surrender." She gently kissed the baby's head before handing him to Drew.

I jumped back into the truck bed alongside my lost little soul. Neither of us said anything. I briefly wondered why Drew didn't get behind the wheel himself. Then it hit me. I bet he didn't know how to drive. Another problem I hadn't considered.

Arriving at the precinct, I watched Drew usher the woman from the truck. She tenderly cradled the baby in her arms. He escorted her inside, his arm around her shoulder in a comforting embrace.

And just like that, Marilyn Shannon was off our to-do list.

I spied my little demon-buddy crouched in the bushes near the side of the road. He wailed as I approached. "Stop it," I said. He covered his face with grubby hands and quieted. Tiny hiccups erupted in the night. "Why did you jump in front of the truck?"

"To help you get her attention so she'd listen to you."

"A bit risky, you think? What if she'd crashed the truck?"

"I reckoned she was probably safe with you two along for the ride."

"Not necessarily, not if it was her time to go."

"If it was her time to go, then I wouldn't have screwed up, would I?"

I contemplated his words. "Good point. But what made you go against your instructions?"

"You were the first one who ever asked what happened to me and you really listened. I want to do what's right, so I took a chance." His glistening gaze beseeched me. "Help me."

"I don't know. Maybe. I have to think about it."

Drew returned. "A lot of help you were," he quietly rebuked me before glancing at my new buddy. "Now, who is this wretched little guy and why's he crying?" Drew listened intently while I explained what I'd learned. He added, "So, looks like we've encountered our first demon-in-training?"

"Something like that. But he definitely stepped into the Light by stopping that truck for us. Besides, it appears he was duped into some kind of evil servitude against his will."

Drew frowned. "I'm not convinced. And we definitely could have stopped the truck ourselves. We're supposed to use our powers of persuasion before doing something drastic, remember? The rule is to remain invisible and inconspicuous."

"You're missing the point," I said. "He wants another chance, and I can't see why he shouldn't get one."

"Above our pay grade," Drew said.

"Then we bend the rules. I'm not about to let a soul who's headed for eternal damnation slip away if he wants forgiveness."

"Listen, Liv, I've been around you long enough to know you don't always think things through."

"You don't have to be a part of this. Go back to the spot where we landed, and I'll meet you there when I'm done."

"You're not going to do what I think you are—"

"Don't ask questions, and then you won't be implicated."

Drew's gloomy countenance made my stomach clench. I didn't want an argument. But I stood firm in my belief this soul could be salvaged. "It's always about free will with you, Livy. Sometimes I don't get it." He slid his hands across his face, covering a massive sigh, his eyes too serious for my liking. "I'll wait for you back at the takeoff spot. I won't leave without you. You've never made the trip on your own before."

"I'll be quick. Promise." And he trod off into the darkened woods.

My new friend sat on the curb as giant teardrops made tracks down his dirty face. His watery brown eyes unleashed a melancholy deluge inside me.

He muttered, "I'm sorry I caused trouble between you and your boyfriend."

"He's not my boyfriend," I blurted. I had to reconsider that. Maybe he was. "He's more like my partner-in-crime." A small hint of a smile flickered across the boy's visage. I bent down and put my hands under his armpits and pulled him upright. "Look, this is new territory for me. I may be able to help you find a way back. I've never done it before, and I'm not entirely sure it will work. I'm willing to try if you're truly committed to rejecting evil."

"Please, please. I promise I won't disappoint you. I know I can do good things, I know I can be better."

At that very second a wave of trepidation took me. We were no longer alone.

Johnny. Right next to me, saying, "Are you sure you want to do this?"

"Yes, one hundred percent, absolutely," I said with false bravado, thrusting my chin up for added emphasis.

"You're on unholy ground, sunshine," he said.

"Good beats evil every time," I said, trying to impress. "But first, why did he wind up on the Astral Plane if he was already damned? That seems like a mistake."

Johnny paused, his head subtly shaking. "I can't answer that. My best advice is to steer clear of the damned."

In a twinkling, Johnny vanished.

"Who was that?" Peter asked. "You gonna get in trouble?"

"Not for you to worry about, kid."

Headlights from an approaching car crested over the upgrade in the road ahead, and I grabbed my charge, slipping into the shadows of nearby trees to let the vehicle pass. Yet it didn't.

It stopped.

Chapter 18

The woman in the passenger seat rolled down the window. "Need a ride?"

"No, thanks. We're fine," I told her.

"But you're all the way out here in the middle of nowhere."

Intrigued, I wondered how she could see me, or my new friend, who was dead. The woman wore a tight black woolen cap and her turned-up collar hid the lower half of her face. She acted like a Good Samaritan, but her voice sounded sinister. I gazed past her and caught a glimpse of the driver. Her companion appeared tall, even while sitting down, and her dark eyes and matching hair seemed oddly familiar.

"We can be of assistance," the driver shouted, leaning toward the passenger window. "We can take you with us if you want to come, just say the word."

"No, really, thanks, we can manage." They stared at me. A sharp pain knifed my head. Like the time Thomas attempted to *calm me down.*

"Who ya talking to?" the grimy-faced boy said, enlarging his brown puppy-dog eyes.

My head pounded. I rubbed my temples in soothing circles. "Uh…I wasn't talking to anyone."

"Great. Now, you're talking to yourself. Looks like I hooked up with a crazy lady."

I shook my head in an attempt to shake off the

headache. "My name's Livy, what's yours?"

"Peter."

"Come closer, Peter." He took several steps toward me.

"Don't be shy," I urged. I placed my hands on both sides of his head. My mouth moved toward his face. Our lips touched. I summoned a long breath from deep inside me and blew into his mouth, then gently kissed his lips and pulled back. Slowly, the dirt and grime on his face vanished, and his tattered clothing renewed itself. His pallor warmed, and his eyes morphed from black to clear, brilliant green. His hair turned a rich brown color, and his posture became erect, making him taller. He seemed nearly whole, still a bit transparent, but definitely a huge improvement. He smiled at me, brilliant and dazzling.

"You did it, Livy!" he said, glimpsing his transformation. He turned his hands over and over again, inspecting them before softly adding, "Thank you."

Hot damn! Magical. Yet now I had no idea what to do with him. Make it up as I went along, I guessed. "You'll have to stay for a while. Redeem yourself through good deeds. Can you handle that?"

"I understand. I'll wait until you believe I'm ready. Then come for me."

"Those who tried to possess you may return. Don't be fooled."

"I'll be careful," he said earnestly.

"Then go, and fight the good fight for all the souls who need help."

"I won't let you down, Livy."

Peter walked in the opposite direction, and I

noticed his feet came off the ground just the tiniest bit. He waved goodbye.

And I said a little prayer.

****

Reaching the rendezvous point, I saw Drew leaning against a car in the parking lot, his hands deep inside his jean's front pockets. "The deed is done," I said.

Drew shook his head. "You're an idiot, Livy, but I love you anyway."

We arrived back at Eccli Hall in a flash of white light, and I ran upstairs to change clothes, having agreed to meet Drew out in the garden. Thoughts of what I'd done sat uneasy in my mind. Did I break a rule? Not technically, right? Although Aidan did mention something about not intervening without permission. However, this wasn't really an intervention. And I firmly believed my job was to save any soul I could. Damned or not.

I stripped out of my jeans and T-shirt and threw them in the laundry chute. I unbraided my hair and was in the process of giving it a thorough brushing when the director appeared at the door. That familiar sense of dread immediately set in.

"Olivia, you've been summoned to the Seventh Kingdom. You're to go straight away." She walked past me and over to the open window, gazing out at the clear evening sky.

I swallowed, painfully. This couldn't be good. A giant lump formed in my throat, and I struggled to respond. "The Seventh Kingdom? You mean where the Scepters live?" I blurted, not to mention feeling uncomfortable addressing the director clad only in my underwear.

"Specifically, the Lord High Commander. It's where he works and lives. He commands your presence."

"Why?"

"I think you already know," the director said, inhaling fragrant night air.

I stared at the back of her head, glad she couldn't see the dread on my face. "Do you think I've done something wrong?"

Bath Qol turned, hair and purple velvet gown swirling around her. "It doesn't matter what I think, it matters what you think. You must speak from your soul, Olivia. That's all I can tell you."

I studied her beatific face for signs of anger or disappointment but found her difficult to read. "How do I find it?" I muttered. I'd no idea where I put the map Aidan had given us. Facing my open closet I considered what garb would be appropriate for a meeting with...*a king.* I grabbed the white sheath-dress and threw it over my head.

"I don't suggest flashing your way there because you don't know where you're going. Take a right when you exit the front door and stay on the path. Seek the large iron gate with the mark of Gabriel. You'll know it when you see it. It's about a five-minute walk."

I focused on the closet door and gritted my teeth. Apparently I'd ruffled the mighty Scepter's feathers. Dread knotted my gut, my imagination traveling to a bad place. What punishment would the Lord High Commander inflict on me for my transgression?

****

The Kingdoms' imposing archway loomed large, and I studied it, the huge, black iron rendering of

Gabriel's crest announcing I'd arrived at my destination. My aura raced. Two somber guardians stood tall on either side of the massive gate. Crap! I needed to know their names to be allowed in.

The one to the right addressed me.

"You're expected," he said. Okay, so thankfully, they were overlooking the usual protocol.

"The Lord High Commander is waiting for you in his garden, Olivia. The pathway to the right leads directly to the Seventh Kingdom. The guards at the front door await you." He pushed his hand against the gate allowing me passage.

"Peace be with you," I mumbled, walking through the entranceway.

"And with you," he said. "May fortune shine upon you."

Another gate greeted me, this one had the Lord High Commander's crest mounted over an archway and the corresponding guardians opened the gate without a word. My feet refused to move as nervousness swirled inside me like wriggling caterpillars. A flutter near the side of my head made me jump. My hand flew to my ear. A large sparkly butterfly flew past my nose and I flinched again. Instantly, there were more…more…more…until a giant herd swarmed me. I screeched and thrashed. The two guardians came to my aid, swatting the insects away. I opened my eyes and searched the landscape. The butterflies had vanished, and the two burly guardians scrutinized me in bewilderment, then turned and frowned at each other.

The silence endured for too many uncomfortable moments.

Finally, one guardian said, "That was a bit of an

oddity."

"Ya think?" I said. Trying to regain some semblance of poise, I smoothed my hands down my sides in an attempt to put myself back together.

"Let's go," the other guardian said. "Mustn't keep the boss waiting."

I followed mutely as they led me up the ten-foot wide steps. "Go straight through the first two chambers and at the far back take a left at the Altar of the Sword. The garden will be directly in front of you."

Their eyes burned into me as they simultaneously pushed the solid gold doors open to let me pass. If the hinges had screeched, I would've sworn I'd arrived at Dracula's castle. A tiny "thank you" squeaked through the lump in my throat as I entered, suppressing the overwhelming urge to flee. All earthly signs of terror coursed through my body. Adrenaline? Sure felt like it.

A small flame flickered at the back of the far chamber near a colossal glowing sword embedded in a thick slab of white marble. The letter M was emblazoned on the handle. The sword effigy cast a warmth over me, and I guessed the enormous weapon belonged to the commanding Chief of the War Office. I wanted to touch it. I reached out, hesitating...my hand suspended in the air. Would it scald me?

I jerked my hand back and chewed on my fingernail, mesmerized by the massive lance. Too big for anyone to hold, never mind wielding it against an enemy. I shook my head in amazement.

Inch by inch, I goaded my legs to keep moving...

The garden doors stood ajar, and I entered cautiously. Its magnificent trees of silver and gold, with rosy fruit hanging from the branches, made me gawk.

Intricate vines laced through the canopies of shimmering trees and stalks of tall, red flowers lined the cobblestone walkway. The tall torches' flickering flames cast a buttery hue over the swirling fog at my feet. I felt incredibly small and insignificant amid this majesty. And there, under the shadow of a large willowy tree, stood the stately and magnificent Prince of the Seventh Kingdom.

Oh. My. God. Someone get me out of here.

I'd never seen him dressed in the familiar flight suit before. Actually, I'd never seen him at all after the opening assembly when he arrived in that seriously hot warrior ensemble. He had his back to me, his biceps and broad shoulders straining the limit of the lightweight gray fabric. Dark, shiny hair curled over his upturned collar, his head tilted slightly to the right, allowing me to glimpse his profile.

Now or never. I approached him slowly. Oh boy, I *sooo* did not want to be doing this. A hush soothed the night, yet the memory of my beating heart thundered inside me. Standing about five feet from him, I was sure he sensed my presence.

"You wasted no time, Olivia," he said, without turning around, the deep timber of his voice vibrating as if from everywhere.

"No, sir." I gulped, attempting to swallow my terror. "Bath Qol told me this was urgent."

"I want to discuss the incident." He hadn't moved a muscle. Me either.

"What incident, sir?" I couldn't believe I'd said that. Like we both didn't know why I was here. He turned to face me and lifted one disapproving eyebrow as he held my stare.

"Olivia, I try to watch over you. You're important to me and warrant my attention…"

Important? What did that mean?

"…I didn't see the incident of which I speak, as I was engaged elsewhere, but I've received reports of this unusual undertaking. I wish for you to explain to me what transpired."

I stood there like a child caught misbehaving. But I wasn't a child. Stand up for what you believe, speak your truth. And so I began to explain the sequence of events that led me to intervene in the life of a damned soul. Instantly, he interrupted.

"This will take too long. Please push me your thoughts."

Did I know him well enough to do that? Besides, once I let him in, maybe he'd have access to much more. Would this mean he could hear my thoughts anytime he chose? But I couldn't say no! Panic crawled through me like a slow-moving snake.

The mighty Scepter said, "I sense that you're vexed."

Oh no! Could he already be inside my head? "Uh, it's just, I didn't think it worked with someone I'm not emotionally close to."

"True, but if you're close in proximity it will be successful." He gazed at me intensely. I struggled to stand still as if ants were nibbling my toes. "Don't worry, this doesn't mean I'll be accessing your thoughts in the future. You have my word. Besides, you can always refuse me if ever I try such a thing."

Well, if he wasn't reading my thoughts he was doing a damn good job of guessing what I was thinking. I had no other choice than to believe him. "I'll do my best," I said weakly and mentally replayed the dubious deed.

"I see," the Lord High Commander said. "You've chosen to save a soul intended for damnation. And you utilized the Kiss of Light." His laser-like gaze pierced me. "I find that rather bold for one so young."

"I thought our purpose was to save any, and all, souls."

"The souls who are damned are forsaken."

I frowned at the mighty Scepter. "I don't understand."

"The choices and decisions they've made led them to eternal damnation."

"But I thought all of us had free will."

"We do. However, once a soul has chosen the other pathway, there's no coming back."

"But if we always have a choice of good over evil then I don't see why that shouldn't apply to everyone, dead or alive. Shouldn't we always have another chance to do right?"

My rush of courage suddenly vanished. Yet instead of a reprimand, he said, "Walk with me." I followed him deeper into the garden. "Would you like a piece of fruit?" He plucked a large red apple from an overhead branch. He turned toward me, his expression softening. "I assure you, it's quite pleasurable." He extended his massive hand in my direction. The apple shimmered invitingly in the bright moonlight.

I took the alien-looking fruit, avoiding contact with his skin. The memory of what happened last time when we'd touched flashed vividly like dazzling fireworks. I still couldn't explain what happened that day. But as he withdrew his hand, his fingers brushed gently against my thumb. *Sparks*. I swallowed hard.

The apple felt cool and slick against the skin of my palm. I brought it to my mouth, the fragrant scent filling my nostrils. Or was the sweetness in the air *his* scent? I couldn't help but ask, "This isn't a test of some sort, is it?"

The Lord High Commander's lips quirked upward. "Forbidden fruit? You already have the knowledge of good and evil, do you not?"

Hmm…He had me there. "I suppose so."

His smile broadened. "I assure you, Olivia, it's just fruit, solely for pleasure."

I bit into the crisp, cool flesh. A delicate sweetness tantalized my tongue, a flavor and aroma reminiscent of earthly apples. "Quite delightful," I said, momentarily distracted from our argument.

"I'm grateful you think so." He clasped his hands behind his back again and faced me. "Now, to continue, I admit I'm taken aback one so young, and inexperienced, would undertake such an audacious move."

"All due respect, sir, I think you know I'm not particularly good at following rules. I have a need for truth, and I don't care for rules that make no sense."

"Yet no rules mean no order," he countered.

"What sort of *order* allows a young boy to be damned? And for better or worse, I am independent. I make decisions based upon the situation and my instincts. I hope those of us who've been asked to perform the task of saving souls were selected because we have good judgment. How is that wrong?"

The Lord High Commander put his head down and rubbed his chin thoughtfully. "At this time, you're too young to express opinions on such things. We are not interested in saving the damned. They made their choice." His dark eyes returned to my face, his hands to his back. "As much as this pains me, for your own good I have no choice but to ground you until further notice." I couldn't decide if he was angry or…sad?

Confusion made me frown. I almost thought I'd gotten my point across. My lips pressed into a hard line. Anger seared my insides. "What? Why? This isn't fair!"

"Perhaps you should watch your tone," he said. Which nearly sent me over the brink. "These rules aren't arbitrary, Olivia. They are for your protection."

A loud sound whooshed from behind, accompanied by a huge wind gust. My hair swirled around me, a small chestnut-colored tornado. I rotated to face them, sucking in an invisible breath, an audible gasp. My fingernails dug into the apple's flesh.

They wore the accustomed flight suit and were incredibly massive up close. I just might faint. Apparently I'd ruffled a lot of feathers.

Gabriel spoke first, addressing the King of the Scepters. "We just heard, my lord."

"I've grounded Olivia," the Lord High Commander said gruffly. "She's out of service until, or *if*, I decide otherwise." He looked down his nose at me. My fear magnified to wrath.

Raphael's voice deepened. "I think you should reconsider."

"Why would I do that?" the Lord High Commander said, and I began to squirm. An argument between the Scepters seemed imminent.

"Because she'll never develop her skills if you

don't," Raphael said. "It's imperative she learn from her mistakes and move on. You can't protect her forever."

"Too dangerous," the Lord High Commander said, his jaw flexing. "I won't risk it." He puffed up his chest, and I cringed, perplexed by this difference of opinion. I thought of Michael as the all-powerful leader no one dared question.

Uriel spoke next. "Lord, perhaps we should impress upon Olivia that she must follow the rules to the letter in order to ensure her safety. That should be sufficient."

The King of the Scepters paced, his shoulders squared, his fists clenched. The stillness among the remaining Scepters made me fidgety. Everyone held his or her breath. It felt like a bomb was about to explode.

The Lord High Commander finally spoke. "On a probationary basis, she can continue serving. Yet if anything happens to her I will hold you collectively responsible."

Gabriel surveyed me carefully. "All right, Olivia, go now, but promise you will follow the rules more carefully."

I opened my mouth in the hopes of defending my actions but thought better of it. "I will, sir."

"Good. Peace be with you."

"And with you," I replied respectfully. I ventured a nervous glance at Michael and once again tried to decipher his mood. Hmm. Sadness, most definitely sadness. And for some unexplained reason I wanted to put my arms around him. Holy crap! Where was that coming from? I fervently prayed he wasn't anywhere near my crazy notions.

I decided a hasty retreat from the garden was in order. The sound of angry voices trailed behind me and I resisted the urge to run as I exited under the ever-watchful guardians. Clear of the gates, I hurled the half-eaten apple into the night sky, the full impact of what had transpired slamming into me like a speeding jet. My body shook uncontrollably. Drew! I needed him.

Chapter 19

I flashed home...fast. Too fast. A streak of light barreled through the doors and walls of Eccli Hall, landing in the garden. Totally against the "no flashing inside" rule. Damn, I was getting good at this rule-breaking. I nearly crashed into Drew. "Geez, Livy, slow down! And where've you been? I've been waiting over an hour."

"If I told you, you wouldn't believe me." My voice broadcasted weariness. His thoughts had been furiously assailing me, but I'd blocked them while immersed in a heated conversation with the Lord High Commander and his cohorts. In retrospect, I'd gotten off pretty easily.

Drew smirked, giving my sheath-clad body the once-over. "What are you wearing?" he asked, still attired in mortal clothing from earlier. In fact, most recruits wore human clothing rather than their uniforms. I guessed since we spent so much time on Earth lately we'd become more comfortable that way.

"Don't. I am the very definition of total dork."

"No, you look cute! Now tell me what's up."

I sighed. "Come on," I said, tugging Drew onto the garden pathway. "Wait until you hear this!"

We walked past a crowd of our buddies playing an otherworldly version of soccer under the lights in the back field. Several of them waved as we ambled along the flower-lined pathway. I found Drew's physical presence distracting and suppressed the urge to throw myself at him. His broad shoulders strained the seams of his white T-shirt, his muscular biceps filling his sleeves. When did he get so...big?

Continuing along the path, I let my conversation with the Scepters unfurl. I shared my dread about pushing thoughts to the Lord High Commander, which made us both smile. Then Drew frowned as I recounted the argument between Michael and the other Scepters. Drew reached out and put his arm around my shoulder, and the tension drained from my body. "There's definitely something out of the ordinary going on. They were pretty lenient."

"I know. What do you think they meant by Michael being overprotective of me?"

"I wish I had a clue. I guess, just forget about it, for now. What else can you do?" Drew gave me a squeeze around my shoulders before dropping his arm. A lock of his cinnamon-colored hair tumbled across his forehead, and his fingers brushed it back in place.

"What?" he said, peering down at me.

Contemplating his liquid brown eyes, I gushed, "You're so *beautiful*."

He chuckled. "You're pretty adorable yourself." He pulled me into his arms and kissed me. Hard. I feared I might combust and set the foliage ablaze.

We held hands, fingers intertwined, as the fragrant night breeze caressed us. In the distance the stars winked at me, and once again I anticipated a spark might spring from my fingertips. It didn't.

We arrived near the clearing and thankfully everyone had gone inside for the night. Standing near the back entrance to Eccli Hall, Drew released my hand and reached out to open the door. We stood at the bottom of the staircase leading to the women's dorm. I said, "I'm glad I had a chance to be with you."

"I'm glad, too. See you in the morning."

"Bright and early, as usual." He pulled me tightly into his chest, and I inhaled his honeyed scent. "I think I'm falling in love with you."

"Well hurry up, I'm already there," he whispered into my hair.

I gazed up into his chocolate-brown eyes. He bent his head toward me and nuzzled my neck, catching my earlobe in his teeth. I giggled as a ticklish rush pulsed down my spine. His hot breath on my neck made me shiver. He sealed his lips over mine, and I arched into him, my body curving against him like two perfectly matched puzzle pieces. His hand slid up my belly and settled on my breast, fingers caressing the tender flesh. I moaned into his mouth.

Our tongues danced to an erotic melody, a sweet expression of our love, and desire spread through me like wildfire.

Pulling away, Drew sighed. "I guess we better say good night." As we broke our embrace, our hands still held tight until eventually our fingertips slid away from each other. "Good night."

"Night." I watched him vanish into the shadows, exhaustion overwhelming me.

****

The assignment would have been comical if it hadn't been headed for tragedy. I managed to keep myself out of trouble for nearly two whole weeks and convinced myself I'd finally learned how to play by the rules.

Arriving at the small cemetery, an overwhelming sense of déjà vu hit me, and I asked Kadie if there might be some reason why this place seemed uncomfortably familiar.

"This is right behind the house where we met Dan and gave him the message from his dead wife."

Okay, so I'd been here. I scanned the landscape for some clue as to why my skin crawled. A large stone mausoleum sat off to the left with the surname *Vanderhaus* imprinted above the filigreed, ebony metal door. The ironwork formed tiny images of angels and a giant stone rendering of a magnificent winged warrior stood guard above the door. I theorized these might somehow represent the Travelers.

A chill invaded me as I surveyed the area. I half expected to see a crow or an owl swoop down. It felt like a bad dream.

Mrs. Iannello tottered toward her husband's gravestone to deposit her posies. A group of youngsters loitered nearby, their bikes flung on the lush green grass. They crept up behind her and yelled, "*Boo.*" Kadie and I caught the elderly woman just before her head would have hit her dead husband's tombstone.

Gathering up her daisies, we steadied her on her feet. Seth and Drew pranked the boys by riding two of their bicycles out of the cemetery while invisible. The kids spazzed. Kadie and I shook our heads and tried not to giggle. We'd have to leave this part out of our report to Aidan.

Leaving the tiny country graveyard, we ambled through town and headed homeward past modest shingled houses and people going about their chores on this typical weekday afternoon. We encountered a woman raking leaves. About twenty feet away her toddler attempted to kick a bright red ball around the neatly manicured front lawn. Apparently he hadn't fully mastered the art of walking upright as he wobbled around on his tiny legs. He seemed so proud of himself.

Their large black Labrador retriever appeared to be resting, but its eyes never left the child. The house bordered a two-lane highway. Lots of cars whizzed by, and it reminded me of the roadway in my neighborhood.

The woman's cell rang on the top step by the front door. Walking over to it, she had her back to the child for half a second. The boy chased the ball into the street. A silver Mercedes sedan sped into view. The mother turned, but she could never have reached the child. She screamed the child's name.

I hurled myself into the dog. It bolted after the child, grabbed it by the hood of its sweatshirt, and dragged it to the safety of the curb. The car zoomed by, the driver engrossed in a conversation on his phone, unaware of the near miss. I exited the dog as fast as I'd entered. I shuddered. It felt humid, slimy and dark in there, like being buried in warm mud. Examining my body, I fully expected to be covered in some kind of brown ooze. Oh my God! What had I done? I smacked my forehead. Just this morning I'd praised myself for avoiding trouble.

Seth yelled, "Are you out of your friggin' mind, Liv? You could've been killed if that dog had gotten hit by the car!"

"I know, I know, I don't know what came over me. It was stupid, really stupid. I'm sorry."

"There you go again," Drew said, his rage escalating, "acting without thinking about consequences!"

Drew was only concerned for my safety, but I didn't appreciate being yelled at. "It turned out all right. Let's forget it."

"You could've done a million things other than what you did!" Drew said, simmering in his anger. "Were you just showing off?"

"Of course not! It just seemed like the fastest solution."

"Whatever," Kadie said. "When we report back to Aidan, he's going to be furious."

I huffed. "I'll take full responsibility. This conversation is over."

"Never mind Aidan," Drew added. "Michael will definitely ground you this time."

Drew needed to shut up. I'd neglected to tell Kadie and Seth about having to answer to the Scepters for saving Peter. In fact, I hadn't mentioned Peter at all.

I turned on Drew. "You've got a big mouth."

"Truth hurts?"

Everything hurt right about now. I dashed away to avoid saying something I'd regret.

Trouble. Not only with my best friends, but also with Aidan, and I couldn't even imagine what Michael might do. And the idea of what could have happened...of being joined to the soul of a dog for all eternity...made me recoil. What was I thinking? Was I thinking at all?

The guardians immediately intercepted me upon my approach to Eccli Hall and ordered me to report to Aidan's office. A change of venue. Usually, I had to answer to the director, or the Scepters. I was apparently making the rounds. Soon everyone would know I was an idiot.

Aidan greeted me at the door to his chamber. "Walk with me."

I found this odd but respectfully agreed. We exited the campus and started out in the opposite direction of the Astral Plane, unfamiliar territory to me. "Olivia, I'm fully aware of what transpired today, and we need to talk about your use of animation. No doubt you're quite capable of performing such a deed with little risk to yourself. Your skills are far superior to anyone we've seen here in eons." Aidan paused briefly and then lowered his voice. "I don't want to alarm you, but there are still many things you don't know yet. About where you came from and where you're going. I'm not at liberty to discuss it with you, but I need you to understand your existence here in the afterlife is vital to our future."

Where I came from and where I was going? What did he know? Why wasn't he just meting out my punishment and sending me on my way?

"What caused you to enter the body of the dog as a means of intervention today?"

I searched my mind for some rational explanation. "I don't know how to answer that. From the first time I intervened with the old man on the bench, I can't swear that conscious thought was involved. It's more of a feeling, as if some force has control of me. I can honestly tell you sometimes I don't know why I do these things. I don't even realize what happened until it's over. I guess I'm just impulsive, or reckless."

As we continued to traverse this unknown pathway

I began to think Aidan wasn't angry with me, not really, but instead imparting some cryptic message.

"Olivia, I'm not as concerned for your safety as I am for your companions. They don't have your strength or skills. If they follow your lead, there may come a time when they won't be able to keep up."

I hadn't considered that. Up until now I'd only been concerned about what an ass I kept making of myself.

Aidan continued, "It's important for you to remember this as you work together. On the other hand this force, or impulsivity, you're experiencing isn't reckless so put your mind at ease. In truth, once we're at our highest evolution point this force is responsible for much of the service performed for the City of the Sun.

"New apprentices don't usually experience it, but it appears you've already begun to develop this skill. Think of it as being on autopilot. It's almost always accurate, but you need to keep an eye on it in case there's a glitch. The best explanation I can give you is there's a certain synergy to energy. In essence, a force of great magnitude takes on a life of its own and can actually compel movement without conscious thought. It just requires a catalyst of some sort." Aidan stopped, his expression grave. "Is this making any sense?"

"Not entirely, but I'll take your word for it."

"I can accept that for now. Someday you will see this clearly."

I'd no idea how long we'd been walking when I realized we'd made a full circle around this unfamiliar territory, and I sensed our conversation had come to an end.

Having returned to the front entrance of Eccli Hall, Aidan said, "Please keep this conversation between us. You must learn to control your actions until such time as you're given permission to venture into more dangerous situations. Agreed?"

"What I can promise is I'll try my very best."

"Fine, that's all I ask." He hesitated for a string of moments. "You seem worried?"

"What's going to happen when Michael finds out about this? He nearly grounded me the last time I screwed up." I shuddered to think of having to face the mighty Scepter for another rule violation.

"I've got that covered. He's away on important business, and I've taken great pains to make sure this information won't reach him."

I exhaled. "Thank you, Aidan. I really truly mean it."

"Now that that's settled, I'll bid you good night. Peace be with you."

"And with you."

Inside Eccli Hall, my three buddies sat waiting on the steps to the women's dorm and immediately rose at the sight of me. I made a beeline for them, prepared for interrogation.

"How bad?" Seth demanded.

"Let's just say I got a good talking to." I tried to appear contrite.

"A slap on the wrist?" I couldn't decide if Kadie was happy or annoyed that I'd gotten off so easily. *Again.*

"Yeah, for now," I lied. Or rather bent the truth, somewhat. "But every time I get myself into trouble, someone reminds me the real consequence of my behavior is putting those I care about at risk."

Drew shuffled his feet, and I worried what might be on his mind. "Look guys, I need to talk to Olivia alone for a minute. We'll meet you in the dining hall."

Kadie and Seth departed with, a sure-no-problem response. Here it comes. I hated when Drew was upset with me.

"To be perfectly honest with you, Liv, you pulled this whole thing off perfectly. I guess it wasn't that big a deal."

Drew's complete turnaround took me by surprise. Fury had turned to acceptance? "Why am I forgiven so easily?"

He hesitated before answering, "Look, I was only angry because I was afraid for you. But the more we work together the more I realize you're exceptionally gifted. I've decided you can take care of yourself just fine and you don't need us second-guessing. I think you're special in some way. I'm not sure how, or why, I just feel it."

Heat flushed my face at Drew's over-the-top praise. It almost sounded as if he'd been eavesdropping on my conversation with Aidan. "Thanks for the vote of confidence, Drew. You're being too nice to me…I'm sorry I acted like such an ass."

"We're even," he said, followed by a wink. "Or maybe we can find a way to make it up to each other?"

Grinning, I smacked him on the chest. "Deal."

Chapter 20

The next evening after dinner I decided on a solo trip to Earth to meet Peter. I'd checked on him a bunch of times and everything seemed on point, but I still felt a twinge of anxiety at being unable to monitor him more closely. And I didn't know how much longer I could keep my secret excursions from discovery.

Arriving early at our usual rendezvous spot, I strolled through the bucolic tree-lined roads, finding it reminiscent of my old 'hood. I passed the local high school and wondered what my former friends were doing right now? My family? How much had Tyler and Keith grown? Was Carrie still flying fighter jets?

Sadness blackened my mood. Bad line of thought, I told myself. Forget about that life, all your lives on Earth. I returned to the meeting place, but Peter still hadn't materialized. Hmm.

I wandered about, not paying much attention to where I was going, and found myself behind a supermarket. One lone streetlight lit the desolate parking lot, the others having been shattered by apparent vandalism. The lamp's bright circle of light fell on a large Dumpster sitting in front of a six-foot-high stockade fence. Great. I'd managed to maneuver myself into a dead end. Story of my existence.

Loud angry voices came from behind the metal trash bin, and I went to investigate. Two women had a young man of about twenty cornered against the fence. One had her hand wrapped around his throat while the other had hold of his belt buckle. His feet weren't touching the ground.

They both let him go, and the redhead turned toward me. The guy fell to his knees, but the dark-haired woman bent down and grabbed hold of him by his long blond hair, jerking his head back. Terror wafted off him like noxious fumes.

The redhead displayed a badge. "Police, Sex Crimes Division. We're questioning a suspect."

"Sorry," I said. "Didn't mean to interfere."

The dark-haired detective pulled the man to his feet by his long locks and then told him to beat it. He bolted.

"Hello, Olivia," the surly redhead said.

She knew my name? I should probably flash out of there at warp speed, but my curiosity kept my feet firmly on the ground. "Do I know you?"

The flame-haired beauty said, "We're actually third-termers on special assignment, trying to set that troubled guy on the road to redemption. A little persuasion detail, as it were."

"How's your training going?" the dark-haired, fake-detective asked.

Puzzled, I asked, "Third term? Haven't heard of a third term, or a second one for that matter."

She answered, "You know how it is at Eccli, they never give you much advance notice about anything. You have to figure everything out for yourself."

True. Yet, other recruits from Eccli? That would explain why they could see me.

They teleported in front of me. Too close. I stepped back. The redhead grabbed my arm, preventing me from further retreat. She sighed, mightily. "Look, Olivia, we're running out of time, and we're just about out of patience with you."

Her partner added, "Your destiny is to be with us. We need you to change the course of history and end this war between us once and for all. Then we can live in peace. You have to accept you belong with us. No more games. Come with us now, and all will be forgiven. Assume your rightful place alongside us. Come home, where you belong."

Fear seized me. Could I escape? I had no idea of their true motives, but obviously they weren't fellow recruits. They belonged to the Dark Side, a place I had no intention of calling home. "Leave me! I'm not going anywhere with you! And…you'll be sorry if you make me angry!" I poked my finger in their direction for added emphasis, hoping to sound fearless, although the redhead still clenched my arm in a death grip.

"That the best you got?" the redhead said, her green eyes icy. "I'm done trying to cajole you. Either come now or face our wrath. And believe me, you'd rather be our ally. Although we cannot kill you, we can certainly set acts in motion that'll reveal your abilities are fueled by black magic. Like it or not, you belong to us…Vana, hit her with your usual so she doesn't remember this little chat."

My lips parted to respond, yet my mouth burned with crimson light. Snaky tendrils of fog trapped me in a chilly embrace. Had I returned to the Astral Plane?

The stockade fence pressed into my back. My hands grasped the wooden slats. The light cast by the streetlamp formed a halo around my feet. Anger strangled my throat, but I didn't know why. I couldn't breathe, my head throbbed, my mouth dry as a desert, queasiness roiling my gut. I struggled to recall how I wound up in the alley. Peter, I'd been searching for Peter.

Sinking to my knees, I attempted to regain my equilibrium. Shivers wracked my body, like I had a fever, my skin clammy. How? Travelers never got sick. I needed to go...*Home*. Peter would have to wait.

As I walked past the Astral Plane on my return to Eccli, someone called my name. Thomas, my soul collector, emerged through the fog. His longish brown hair appeared windblown, and he wore just a white T-shirt, raggedy jeans, and his signature blue Nike sneakers. I smiled. He was still the hottest soul collector I'd ever beheld. "A sight for sore eyes," I said. As he neared I noticed the artwork adorning his arms. He wore full tattoo sleeves. How come I'd never noticed that before?

Thomas's blue eyes hinted he wasn't particularly glad to see me. But then his expression changed, his eyes narrowing. His index finger lifted my chin. "You look awful."

The intensity of his gaze made me squirm. "I...I don't feel well."

Thomas finally dropped his hand, releasing my face. Someone stood behind him. My jaw dropped. Peter?

"Is he yours?" Thomas said harshly, his frown tightening. I gave the little guy the once over and decided he'd retained his transformed state. Perhaps the situation wasn't as perilous as I'd thought.

"I claimed him," I said, feeling a bit anxious.

"Excellent, because he keeps asking for you." Peter

skulked in the shadows behind Thomas. He wouldn't approach. Did he trust me?

I asked, "How did he wind up in your care? Is he in trouble?"

"Technically, no, but he's not on anyone's list, and as a ghost he's supposed to belong to someone. We periodically check on the ghosts in our care. I found him hanging around with one of my charges. Honestly, I didn't believe his story at first, but then I remembered hearing about your involvement with a damned soul."

Thomas's patience wore thin. He'd always treated me with the utmost kindness, and such tenderness. I said, "I'm embarrassed that I overstepped my authority getting involved in this, but the Scepters gave me a reprieve. I've been keeping track of him, but I couldn't find him today."

Thomas's brow knit. "You're going to Earth alone?"

"Yeah, I just told you I was looking for Peter and—"

"Never be on Earth without your team! Who authorized this?"

"Nobody. What's the big deal?" His strong hand circled my arm. I grimaced.

"Don't go to Earth alone, ever. Never, Olivia. Promise me."

"Why?"

"I don't owe you a reason."

"Okay, okay." His hand gripped me too tightly and anger rose in my throat. "Please let go of me, Thomas."

He released my arm. "Give me your hand."

I slowly outstretched my palm obeying Thomas's order. He laced his fingers through mine and our palms pressed together. I expected sparks, like I had experienced with Michael, but no.

"This signifies your promise," Thomas declared.

He released me and moved backward. I waited for his temper to calm. At last, he spoke in a quieter tone, "What's your plan for Peter?"

"Guess this is the part where I seek your wisdom."

"Honestly, you shouldn't be responsible for him while in training. The best course is for me to take him off your hands."

"But the Scepters said—"

"I'll handle the bosses. You just do what I say."

I approached Peter. "Give me your hand," I said, mimicking Thomas. I'd seal our bond with his promise. He extended his palm and I froze, horrified. We had identical birthmarks! How could that be? Had it been there when I first encountered him? I recalled Elijah's reaction when he saw the mark on me before my transmutation, which only enhanced my apprehension.

"What's wrong?" Peter said. "I've been good, I have. Don't send me back."

"All is well," I lied, then pointed to the red crescent scar. "This mark on your wrist, where did you get it?"

"I don't know. I think it's a birthmark. Why?"

I pivoted to Thomas, brandishing the identical mark on my wrist. "Does this mark mean something?"

Thomas focused on the matching images, yet didn't answer.

"This cannot be coincidence," I said.

"There is no such thing as coincidence." Thomas sauntered closer to me and leaned in, landing a sweet kiss on my forehead. "Don't forget your promise."

With that, he hurried away with Peter in tow.

Chapter 21

As a mortal, I found discussions of demons somewhat fascinating, but they had nothing to do with reality. I likened them to thoughts of vampires, witches, and werewolves—interesting to contemplate or make scary movies about, but nothing I believed in or feared. Yet now it turned out these devilish creatures existed, and I had limited knowledge of their power.

Aidan displayed nasty pictures on the screen as he described the various species of demons as well as their hierarchy. "I want to call attention to the two dark princesses who rule the Underworld alongside Lucifer, his two wives. Of course he has limitless sex slaves at his disposal, both male and female, so I'd interpret the term *wife* rather loosely."

I glanced over at Kadie and rolled my eyes. So Lucifer was a player? How surprising.

"Lilith is his oldest wife and has been around since the dawn of time. She is a demon of the night and mostly preys on newborn souls. Additionally, she steals semen from sleeping men in order to produce demon sons." Yuck! Now that was totally creepy.

An image of Lilith appeared. I recognized her from our first trip to Earth. My chest tightened. The unmistakable red hair, not an orange-red like humans, but a deep neon red. Emerald green eyes, speckled with tiny sparks of crimson, hinted at a powerful and dangerous aura. A scarlet, velvet gown cloaked her trim frame, her full breasts. Six thin silver chains hung from each earlobe, ending in an icon of the crescent moon. I nearly choked. The same shape as the scar on my wrist, and Peter's too.

A corded black rope with knots at regular intervals surrounded her swanlike neck, each knot guarded by a pair of shiny red gemstones.

Wait! That necklace! I could swear Gabriel had one like it wrapped around his hand the day he showed up at Chrism Center. The day he talked with Margaret, and I first heard Lilith's name. Had Lilith really been near the Center that day to steal a baby? I focused on the picture. Lilith's berry-red cheeks and alluring pink lips hinted at innocence. Evil had many disguises.

"As you can see," Aidan said, "Lilith's favorite color is red, and thus she's been branded the original 'scarlet woman.' She usually appears in this form, except when she chooses to shapeshift. Then, she most frequently takes the form of a screech owl. And she certainly is a screecher! The resonance has been known to make both the City of the Sun and Earth tremble. She's also known as the Lady of the Beasts as she has an uncanny thrall over earthly animals. But make no mistake...she's no lady."

That night, behind Dan's house, when the screeching owl flew past me. My anxiety throbbed in my body, pulsing through each limb.

"The only creature known to escape her dominance, and which we believe can offer protection against her wickedness, is...the frog." Everyone chuckled. Was this why the frog was so influential in fairytales?

"Behold," Aidan said, "the other dark princess—Ravana. She's only come to power in the last two centuries. We do not know the extent of her abilities yet she calls herself the Immortal Queen of Witchcraft. Her primary goal is to bring souls into servitude as witches and warlocks. At death these souls are easily claimed as they are already on the list of the damned, and have been banished by us. Ravana's first officer is a formidable witch named Diana. Of the two, Diana is the one you'd most likely encounter in your dealings with humans. Ravana's aura is considered exceptionally strong, although untested, so be forewarned."

And I'd witnessed her also! She'd been with Lilith on Earth that day. And she was beautiful, more so than Lilith even. I found myself mesmerized by her raven hair, dark eyes, and bold blood-red lips.

Aidan continued, "It's of the utmost importance you take away one important message. You need not fear these dark forces if you maintain the strength and integrity of your aura. The threat of danger exists only when you are on Earth. Although it is forbidden for us to kill each other, we can inflict untold pain and suffering."

Aidan dismissed class and intercepted my team before we could exit. He shut the door and directed us to sit at the front table. One of our reports beamed onto the display. The assistants sat directly behind us. This couldn't be good.

"I've asked you to remain because I've something to show you. It's become apparent that both Lilith and Ravana have been following you." Aidan confirmed what I suspected, and I eagerly awaited his explanation. He scrolled through several reports we'd logged from our missions.

"Look closely because they aren't always visible to the untrained eye." I examined it carefully, but it resembled one of those Waldo puzzles. I couldn't form anything recognizable.

Aidan explained, "As I mentioned earlier, Lilith is a shapeshifter, a talent only the most powerful demons possess. We don't know if Ravana has developed the ability to shapeshift. But she is capable of casting potent spells we find difficult to thwart. The two wives working together are forces greater than nature, rivaling even Lucifer. Often, they take the form of shadows, manifesting in the corner of your eye. You see something, but then nothing. Malachi first sensed their presence and alerted me."

I gazed over my shoulder and acknowledged Aidan's assistant for detecting this unwelcome threat. My attention returned to the screen where Aidan pointed out their elusive forms during various interventions. At Dan's house, as we delivered the message from his dead wife, I thought I'd seen something as we left the premises. No one mentioned an appearance on the first trip to Earth. Apparently only I had observed them on that occasion. And they were there when I was with Peter, when I *kissed* him back into the Light. Peter had accused me of talking to someone. Hmm…

At least I hadn't been imagining all this. And had Lilith been lurking around Chrism Center searching for me instead of trying to snatch a baby? Were the women following my team or…*me*? And if so, for how long? While I was still mortal? And…the million-dollar question: Why?

The next image sent stabbing pains into my chest. Only a shadow at first but, there! Ravana lurking near a tree when I'd leapt into the black dog. I quailed. That could've gone so bad. What an incredibly stupid thing to do. I'd put everyone in danger that day.

"We've reason to believe it's Olivia they're watching," said Aidan, confirming my suspicions. Now I understood why Thomas was livid about me going to Earth alone.

"Are you absolutely sure?" I said.

Aidan said, "I can't fully explain this presently, so I'm simply asking the four of you to be careful. If you see them again, or if you have any interactions, you must alert someone immediately. For now, the worst they can do is complicate your interventions. All right, you may go, and until further notice I suggest you keep this to yourselves. The more credence you give it, the more energy it'll absorb."

As we rose, chair legs scraped across the gray-tiled floor. The door swung open, and a massive frame filled the doorway. Nobody moved. He entered, clad in a long, close-fitting, white robe with silver buttons down the front, the garment snug over his broad chest and shoulders. A starched, priestly collar encircled his neck. I'd never seen him dressed like this, not that I'd had an audience all that often.

In an authoritative voice, the Lord High Commander said, "May I have a minute, Aidan?"

"With me?" Aidan thumbed his chest.

"No...with your recruits."

"Certainly, I'll leave you to speak with them."

"This won't take long." The Lord High Commander pivoted, commanding, "Sit." We sank into seats, while Aidan and his assistants shuffled out of the room.

Michael appeared angry, and I wondered what I'd done to annoy him this time. On second thought, perhaps I was overreacting. Aidan had seemed rather blasé about the circumstances. Maybe he'd come for some other reason? Maybe.

"I have concerns," Michael said, his voice deep, ominous. "I don't like the fact that Ravana and Lilith have been surveilling you." He averted his eyes and began to pace. "This is most unusual. Occasionally they amuse themselves by following apprentices but not to this extent, and there have been far too many sightings to consider this random."

I sat there, stone-faced. The Prince of the Seventh Kingdom came here to talk to our insignificant quartet of apprentices.

"Olivia." The sound of Michael uttering my name shot quivers through me. I stood at attention and my elbow accidentally brushed against his arm. A spark erupted. I stepped backward and pretended nothing happened. He continued, "I'm alarmed Lilith and Ravana have taken serious interest in you. I need you to remain vigilant during your assignments."

"I don't understand," I said. "Why are they—"

"You don't have to understand why!" the Lord High Commander bellowed. "Just follow orders."

Five seconds became a lifetime.

"Y—yes, sir," I said like a good little soldier. Yet I didn't feel like such a good soldier.

The mighty Scepter said, "I'm deadly serious, Olivia! I've given you latitude in the past, but not this time. The stakes are too high."

Why was he yelling?

Anger hissed inside me like a rattlesnake. My insides seethed. I had no intention of letting him anywhere near my thoughts. The room grew too warm. My face heated. I had to get out. Venomous anger vibrated within. Compelling me to do something I'd regret.

"Olivia," Michael said. "Get control of your aura!"

Oh my God. He saw it. He could tell. Was he reading my mind? He promised he wouldn't do that. Then again, if I resisted him he couldn't get in. I locked my thoughts safely inside my head. I didn't answer him as I submerged my aura in the safety of my imaginary lake. A cool breeze fanned me. I took a deep breath.

"In the event," Michael said in a quieter voice, "that you see these women again, I expect you to report it to either the director or your commander."

"Yes, sir," Drew answered, my white knight. "We'll be on the lookout."

"Good." The Lord High Commander exited without further comment.

My legs morphed into jelly, as if I'd run a marathon, and I sank back into the chair, burying my head in my hands.

"What the hell, Liv?" Seth sounded pissed. I looked up. They surveyed me as if I was some sort of circus sideshow. "First that crazy light thing when you touched Michael. Then, you started to glow! The only time I saw you glow was the day you blew those ministration dudes across the room!"

"I'm so lost," I confessed. "And I didn't mean to touch Michael. Believe me, I avoid that at all costs. And then he made me furious ordering us around."

"I don't like this," Kadie said. "Downright scary." She swiveled to Drew. "Truth. Have you ever seen her do this stuff before?"

"I was there the first time she came into physical contact with Michael. But no, I've never seen her light up like that."

Seth said, "Geez, Livy, remind me never to piss you off."

"Listen, guys," I said. "If you want to ditch me I'll understand. I've long suspected I'd cause trouble, and my worst fears are coming true."

No one said anything in response to my offer and the silence started to eat at me. Seth finally spoke, "I ain't afraid of two measly girl demons. How 'bout the rest of you?"

"Not me," Drew said.

"Me either," Kadie agreed. "But I *am* afraid of Michael."

Their loyalty touched me, but I didn't deserve it. "Really, guys, I don't want to place you in harm's way."

Drew said, "That's our choice. Not yours. Not open for discussion. Now let's go, I need a cookie, or maybe ten." He stood to leave, and Kadie and Seth followed. Their willingness to spit in the face of danger warmed me.

Refueling pointed me toward the dining hall. But the mighty Scepter remained on my mind. Boy, I'd really gotten under his skin. And he was keeping something from me, something terrible.

I decided I had some digging to do, even if it might send me to an eternal grave.

Chapter 22

Several days passed and our assignments were uneventful, but still truly satisfying: saving a baby from abuse, rescuing a fireman from a heart attack at the scene of a raging inferno…I'd lost count of the number of lives saved. I loved this fucking job.

Drew and I hung out together most nights, in either the garden or the common area since we weren't allowed in each other's rooms. I wondered where this relationship was headed.

We finished dinner and most evenings played poker or chess. Jesse had become my rival at chess although he'd recently beaten me three games in a row. I vowed a comeback. I didn't think Drew was all that fond of the time I spent with Jesse, but Jesse's girlfriend, Rachel, was outright irate. What else was new? But I liked playing against Jesse better than I did Drew. For some reason I always played poorly with Drew.

Ten o'clock arrived, and Kadie and I glided upstairs to our dorm. We slipped into nightclothes, read for a while, then turned out the lights. Quiet blanketed the room, and I blissfully imagined how much I wanted Drew here beside me.

"Did you hear that?" Kadie pushed into my mind. *"Aidan wants us downstairs immediately."*

"Yes!" My aura raced.

"Come as you are!" He shouted in my head. I covered my ears, as if that would quiet his booming voice.

"We've never been called out in the middle of the night before," Kadie said. "Bad omen."

We scurried downstairs, barefooted and clad only in tank tops and pajama pants. Aidan waited at the bottom of the stairs along with Bath Qol, Drew, and Seth. The guys were clothed in only their pajama bottoms. Having never seen them shirtless before, Kadie and I gasped at their smooth skin, toned pecs, and rock-hard biceps. Did they work out somewhere? We had no gym. They both had that sought-after V marking their hips, like a road sign pointing to their…Geez! Get your mind out of the gutter, Olivia, before Aidan or Bath Qol…or the guys, read it!

Aidan interrupted my sordid thoughts. "You four are the fastest I have, and we need a team. This can't wait until morning. Here, get dressed." Bath Qol tossed clothing to us, and Aidan did the same for the guys. We swapped our sleepwear for jeans, sweaters, and sneakers, Bath Qol and Aidan respectfully turning their backs on us. We shot furtive glances at each other as we dressed. Awkward.

"Here are the coordinates." Aidan handed Drew the paper. "You have less than an hour to intervene. The entire family will be massacred if you don't get there in time. This man has despaired to the point where he'll murder his entire family, then kill himself. Now, go, go!" Aidan shoved us out the front doors.

Entering the master bedroom of the two-story, white colonial, we discovered the man straddled over his wife, pinning her to the bed, her face bloodied. She whimpered.

Fear snaked its way along my spine. An ice-cold draft wafted through the room. Someone was here with us. I glanced toward the bedroom door for intruders. Nothing.

I ran to the baby's room, pushing the door slowly open. Nobody there, but I couldn't shake the feeling of being watched.

I crept toward the crib and peered inside. The baby didn't move and I worried maybe she wasn't sleeping. Lilith preyed on the souls of babies, maybe the baby was…dead.

Goosebumps erupted on my skin, the little hairs on the back of my neck raised. Rotating, I faced two dark shadows framed in the doorway behind me. They didn't move. Neither did I.

Aidan said I needn't fear them but his words weren't enough. I didn't push thoughts to my pals, worried that the two evil women might hurt them. Turmoil rumbled inside my head. Should I confront them?

"Hello, Olivia," Lilith said, stepping out into the moonlit room, Ravana mute alongside her.

"The Scepters don't give a damn about you. They're only interested in using you. And when they're done, they will toss you out."

Ravana mumbled some words under her breath, and a warm sensation trembled through me. The air in the tiny room grew thick, and my eyelids drooped.

Lilith's words reached me yet sounded garbled, as if I were under water. "If you stay under the spell of the Scepters they will force you to do their bidding, they'll abuse you. If you come with us, you will have the choice to achieve greatness."

My brainwaves swam in oil, in sluggish, irregular circles. I opened my mouth to say something, but my lips felt numb.

Ravana's deep voice penetrated me to my core. "Enough, Lily, we need to tell her the truth. No more spells."

Lilith said, "I vote that we take her against her will."

"That would break the Covenant between Michael and Lucifer. We'd most likely start a war to end all wars."

Lilith's voice shot up several octaves. "She mustn't become who they want her to, and we can't let Lucifer have her, either. Not another woman in my bed."

Ravana said, "You're right, of course."

Lilith sighed. "So, it's up to us to neutralize her."

Words, nothing but meaningless words. It felt as if my eyelids were glued shut. I struggled to open them...to clear my vision and awareness.

Alone in the tiny bedroom. What was I doing here? I shifted to the baby again and, leaning into the crib, gently placed the palm of my hand on her warm chest. The hummingbird rhythm of a baby heart thumped against my hand. Relief.

The bloodied woman flew past me and scooped up the slumbering baby. Her cell phone at her ear, she shrieked her plea for help to the 911 operator, then sped into her other children's bedroom slamming and locking the door. I returned to the master bedroom to find the man cowering on the floor, the gun in Drew's hand.

"A lot of help you were," Kadie said.

Drew confronted me. "Were they here?"

I met his gaze with consternation. "Who?"

"You know who," he said.

Kadie said, "You mean Lilith and Ravana?"

I rubbed the back of my neck, tension knotting my shoulders. "I think you might be right, Drew, but I can't say for sure. I swear."

"Crap," Kadie said, "it seems like they're showing up more and more often."

"We have to tell someone," Seth said. "Michael told us to report any incident."

Nobody spoke. For some reason, I didn't want to tell anyone about this. It could've been a false alarm. Michael's attitude still annoyed me. I didn't like being told to follow blindly. I wanted to know what was going on. If anyone had a right to this information, it was me. And if he wasn't going to trust me, then I wasn't going to share anything.

"Why can't we keep it between us for now?" I asked. "It's probably much ado about nothing anyway."

"If Michael finds out, we'll all be in hot water." Kadie's voice was shrill.

"Personally, I don't really care," said Drew. "The wives don't scare me. They can follow us around all day. They're no match."

Blaring sirens shattered the night's stillness. Help had arrived.

I couldn't say I totally agreed with Drew's assessment, but I'd no intention of communicating my fears since I'd just asked them to ignore the entire incident. However, something had to give. And soon.

Seth said, "I agree with Kadie. I don't want trouble with Michael."

I laced my fingers together behind my neck and exhaled slowly, glancing at the ceiling. I squeezed my elbows against my ears and then relaxed. "I don't want any of you getting in trouble because of me. Just this one last time and if there's a repeat performance, I'll report it myself."

Thoughts abounded, but I couldn't read them.

"Promise?" Kadie said.

"Promise."

"Agreed," Seth said, followed by assent from Kadie and Drew. "But this is the last time."

Drew urged us home. "I'm sure Aidan is anxious to hear the outcome of this intervention. Let's go."

****

The dimly lit foyer welcomed us. Bath Qol's door stood ajar, her light on. Seth knocked, and the director glanced up from her paperwork. We'd already pushed our thoughts to her so she knew the outcome. True to their word, no one mentioned the possible visit from the evil princesses. Commitment honored.

"All's well that ends well," Seth said.

"I'm pleased," Bath Qol said. "Especially since we threw you into this without any time to prepare. We'd no one left to send and normally I wouldn't burden apprentices. But your record has proven exceptional. Aidan is terribly proud of your team."

Our eyes stayed locked on our feet. No one spoke. Hearing such lavish praise from the director made me uncomfortable, especially since we'd just lied. Okay, we hadn't technically lied, just hadn't been forthcoming. Confession wasn't always good for the soul.

"I'd like you all to take the day off tomorrow," the

director said, to everyone's surprise. "Go out and have some fun. You've earned it. Kadie and Drew know where the nearest colony can be found. Explore. If we need you, I'll find you. Now you're excused. Go and get some rest. Peace be with you."

In unison we responded, "And with you."

We filed out of the office and loitered under the foyer's subtle radiance.

"Wow," I said. "Wasn't expecting a vacation."

Seth said, "Me either. I've never been to a colony, have you, Liv?"

"Nope," I said. "But how can we think about fun with so much going on?"

"Change of heart?" Seth said, "Because if we don't go and at least try to enjoy ourselves, they'll know something's going on."

"No, you're right," I said, turning to Kadie and Drew. "We've been showing you Earth. Now you get to return the favor."

Kadie stood on tiptoes and clapped. "Yay!"

Drew broke into an impish grin. "Be careful what you wish for."

Chapter 23

The morning found me unsettled, thoughts of the evil princesses haunting my psyche. I considered if we'd meet either Kadie's or Drew's family on our sojourn today. I only remembered vague bits of what I'd learned about the colonies. A hint of excitement and adventure loomed large. How much like mortal society would these otherworldly towns be?

Kadie interrupted my thoughts. "Time to get going, missy."

"Right," I said, jumping out of bed. "What to wear?"

"Definitely something that identifies Eccli Hall, because we'll sort of be celebs."

"Really?"

"There isn't anyone our age still living in the colonies. By the time we're nineteen, everyone is placed in some type of service. And Eccli is the most prestigious placement you can get."

"Wow, I had no idea." I'd caught on to the fact that Eccli was sort of the otherworldly version of Ivy League schooling, but I hadn't thought about what other types of assignments there might be.

"So I'm wearing the flight suit," Kadie announced.

"Great choice." We grabbed clothes from the closet, and I tugged a brush through my hair and fastened it with an elastic band.

"Throw me one of those, will you?" asked Kadie. I shot it her way; it smacked her head.

"Ouch! What's wrong with you? Suddenly ten years old again?"

"Feeling playful." I flashed Kadie my best adolescent grin.

Kadie shook her head in mock disgust. "Idiot."

"Yeah, we know." After a short pause I asked, "Will we be meeting your family today?"

"Unh-uh. There are thousands of colonies, and mine is far, far away. When I do go home during break, it'll be huge. I'm the only one from my colony here."

"That's awesome. Your family must be doing cartwheels."

"Yeah, especially since neither of my older brothers got in." Kadie smiled with well-deserved pride.

"What do they do?" I inquired.

"They're musicians." And where do they play, I wondered.

With a loud thump, the book Kadie had been reading all night slipped off her bed. I picked it up to return it. Grinning, I said, "How many times are you going to read this?" She'd "borrowed" it from a public library on Earth. Kadie cherished libraries.

"Why do you care? I love Bella and Edward. Mortal love is so maddening."

"Kadie, this isn't mortal love. The guy's a vampire!"

"Sounds just about perfect to me."

"There's no such thing as vampires!"

"You didn't think demons existed either. Or us, for that matter."

I sighed. "You're such a romantic."

"What's wrong with that? I think you're somewhat jaded, actually. Besides, you've had sex before and I haven't."

"Yeah, well, it's not all it's cracked up to be, trust me." Kadie bent over to fasten the strap on her sandal while I rummaged through the jumble of shoes.

"Livy, please. Don't ruin this for me."

I selected sandals and sat down on the bed. "I don't mean to. It's just that…with the right guy it's great, but with the wrong guy it can be awful."

Kadie threw her hands up in a give-up gesture. "Whatever. Let's just drop the subject."

"Fine."

****

A giant crimson sign with gold letters announced the colony entrance. Tiny baby faces rimmed the border and my mind immediately recalled the images of mad baby faces etched on the Fountain of Lost Souls. I blanched at the horrid memory.

We crossed a small town square where quaint little buildings displayed signs for food and clothing. To the right, a large park with a sparkling lake enticed me. Children romped on the playground. The adults perched on stone benches, reading or talking with others and dressed alike in the traditional sheath. Trees and gardens dotted the landscape, analogous to those in the Lord High Commander's garden, shimmery, in bright primary colors, and a mood of contentment danced in the warm, fragrant air.

Musicians performed in a nearby courtyard. The tuneful little ditty, jazz *à la* Thelonius Monk, had my attention when a noise rustled from behind. A gaggle of toddlers fluttered around my knees, emitting sparkles of white light as they jumped up and down.

"Oh my!" I exclaimed, feeling like a nursery school teacher. "Hello!"

The excited little ones nudged my legs. "You're pretty!" one of the boys said. Giggles abounded. They poked and pulled on my clothing, making me a tad nervous.

"Why are they all sparkly?" I asked Kadie.

"They haven't learned how to flash yet, but feel the urge. And apparently your aura is attracting them."

"What should I do?" A tinge of panic rose in my voice. This reminded me of the swarming monarch butterflies at the Seventh Kingdom. Why did stuff like this keep happening to me?

Before my friends could respond, one of the children asked, "Are you here to save us from the Jinn, miss?"

I asked Kadie and Drew, "What's a Jinn?"

Concern scrunched Kadie's face. Drew stared ahead at seemingly nothing, while Seth shrugged.

"What?" I pressed. "What's the matter?"

But Kadie focused intently on one of the mothers. "Have the Jinn been here?"

The distraught woman wrung her hands. "They've been sighted recently. But no children have been abducted, yet."

"The Jinn are crazy," Drew said in an attempt to educate me. "There are many species, Livy. These probably belong to the clan that haunts the colonies, and they can never actually leave. The Jinn, whether they live here or on Earth, usually remain secretive, but when they get bored they sometimes cause trouble."

"What kind?" I asked.

"On Earth they're given credit for performing magic," Drew said. "They have no connection to us and they're not immortal. They often steal either our young or human babies to play with. Usually the babies are returned after a period of time, but sometimes not."

"Do they belong to the Underworld?" I asked. "And if they do, why are they here?"

"No one's really sure how they got here," Drew said. "Some believe Lilith failed in her attempt to create something truly evil, but instead they turned out to be silly pranksters. Not one of her proudest moments, I guess. But they aren't dangerous, just a nuisance."

I shook my head, bewildered. Stealing babies on Earth is a major crime. Why were they so cavalier about this?

The mothers collected their children, freeing my feet and easing the awkwardness.

Kadie addressed the concerned mothers. "We're only here for a day, but if you have another sighting, let us know and we will try to help."

The woman seemed perplexed. "Am I mistaken? You're the warriors of the universe. The true vanquishers of evil, yet you can't help us prevent the Jinn from attacking us?"

"I understand your thinking, however we are never permitted to intervene without a direct order. I know this is difficult for you to comprehend, but—"

We extricated ourselves from the mob of mothers and babies and walked off toward the park.

"I feel bad about not helping them," I moaned.

Drew attempted to placate me. "The Jinn don't hurt anyone. It's mostly mischief."

He and Seth broke into a run, and Kadie and I struggled to keep up. As we reached the shore of the glistening lake, Drew yelled, "How about a swim?"

Flight suits on the ground, only in their underwear, the guys shattered the water's calm blue surface. Kadie and I exchanged surprised expressions, and I suppressed the urge to giggle. I couldn't remember the last time I went swimming and found the idea both inviting and exhilarating.

"Come on in, the water's awesome," Seth called out.

"Yeah, come on, you wimps," Drew said.

I immediately thought about Seth's death. That was probably the last time he'd gone swimming. I guess no aftereffects lingered as he seemed to be thoroughly enjoying himself.

We stripped to our underwear too, and sprinted for the lake, screaming and hooting. We dove under the glassy lake's surface releasing our long locks from elastic bondage.

I rose and floated aimlessly, mesmerized by the beautiful blue sky above. The slightest breeze washed over my wet face, and I closed my eyes and soaked up the warmth of the bright sunshine.

My whole body was a smile.

Time seemed suspended, but in a good way, not like on the Astral Plane. Suddenly, a hand grabbed my ankle and pulled me underwater, then released. I swam to the surface again and found myself face to face with Drew.

He teased, "Did I break your mood of transcendental meditation?"

In mock anger, I said, "This day is about de-stressing and now you try to drown me?" Uh-oh, I hoped Seth didn't hear me say that. I glanced in his direction as he blissfully floated alongside Kadie.

I couldn't hide my smile, and we playfully splashed water in each other's faces, childlike laughter dominating the scene.

Drew grabbed my hand and dragged me farther out into the lake. He said, "Race you to the other side!"

I dogpaddled furiously, determined to win, but finished a few feet behind. Arriving at the opposite shoreline, we collapsed onto the sand.

I felt more alive than ever! My heart pounded, breath filled my lungs, blood pumping though my veins. Illusion or reality? I didn't know and didn't care.

The warm sand on my bare skin calmed me, and for a moment I forgot I wasn't alone. Turning my head, Drew stared at me with his liquid brown eyes. Water droplets danced on his long dark lashes, sparkling with the glint of the brilliant sunshine. I said, "Swimming is the best idea you've ever had. I'm enjoying myself so much."

"I'm glad," he said, hoisting himself up on one arm. "It's nice to see you so happy." His hand settled on my stomach, his touch hot on my bare skin, and his wicked smile ignited a familiar spark. I shivered. Drew frowned. "Cold?"

When I didn't respond, he reached across my chest and clutched my arm, pulling me on top of him. Heat shot through me. Beads of water in his hair reflected tiny rays of sunbeams. My wet hair fell on his chest, and he reached up with both hands and tucked it behind my ears. He wrapped his arms around me, pressing me firmly against his chest. "Better?" he whispered, our faces close.

I crossed my arms over his chest and leaned my chin on my forearms. "Yes," I said with hesitation. "And no."

Drew furrowed his brow. "That makes no sense."

"I'm afraid," I whispered.

The lines between his eyes deepened. "Of what?"

But then a vision of loving him blossomed, and my feelings for him overwhelmed me. I'd been in love many times as a mortal but not like this. "Never mind," I murmured, the strain in my voice gone.

I sighed quietly and nestled my elbows in the sand on either side of his head, the weight of my body pressing down on him. For a moment, neither of us moved. Running my fingers through his wet hair, I gazed into his beautiful eyes. His warm hand caressed the small of my back, the other slipping behind my neck. He tugged me to his chest and kissed me, deeply, and I found myself responding a little too eagerly. Our kisses became urgent, and I let myself melt into his body.

Somehow the clasp on my bra had magically opened. An impishness played in Drew's face. I said, "Tricky little devil!"

"Who, me?" he said. He slipped the straps down my shoulders and tossed the undergarment aside. My breasts filled his warm hands and he pinched and prodded my nipples into hard peaks, his lips sucking, his tongue licking until I writhed.

"Feels so good," I moaned. Suddenly, I backed away and let my body roll onto the warm sand, my breathing labored.

Gazing up at the huge sun, a shadow loomed

above. Drew's silhouette framed itself against the brilliant blue sky as the weight of his muscular body pressed down, our bodies plunging into pleasure. He kissed my neck, my shoulder, my cheek, then plundered my mouth for another endless interlude. Another wave of passion trembled through me. Scalding desire. I rose up so my lips met his again. I wanted him, and clutched him to me.

Chapter 24

Drew's voice vibrated in my mind. *Although I could spend the rest of eternity right here with you in our own little Eden, we better start heading back.*

"Oh, if we must..." I groaned, quickly redressing.

Our smiles merged into one last kiss. He stood and held his hand out to help me up. "I'll race you back!" I instantly protested, asking if we could swim back at a leisurely pace so as not to totally destroy the mood.

"I'm here to make you happy," Drew said.

We slid effortlessly into the cool, clear water as my pulse slowed. The swim back sobered me, but still felt luxurious. Seth and Kadie sunbathed on the sand as we materialized from the water. My shadow crossed Kadie's motionless form, and I sprinkled her with water from my wet body. Kadie opened her eyes. "I thought maybe you two drowned or *something*."

Sitting up, Kadie eyed me, then Drew, and even without telepathy I guessed Kadie had a good idea what we'd been doing. Politely, she said nothing.

Dressed again in our uniforms we walked back to town to get something to eat. A variety of confections filled the local eatery's display cases. I asked Kadie, "How come we don't get anything like this at Eccli?"

"They don't want to spoil us. It's sort of like we're in the army, you know."

"Armies eat better," I said. "Trust me."

Making our way back to the square we once again encountered the gaggle of mothers who promptly reported a kidnapping, of not one but *three* babes. So, as promised, we set out to catch the culprits.

"Shouldn't we ask for permission?" I said to Kadie, following her into the woods.

"I don't think this would be considered an unauthorized intervention, since the Jinn aren't humans." Made sense.

"Let's split up," suggested Drew.

Off in the distance the laughter of a small child caught my attention, and I furtively crept in the direction of the sound. My hands and knees fell on hard earth, pebbles biting into my flesh. I separated low-hanging branches of prickly holly bushes and spied the three babies in the grass, giggling and clapping their hands together in unrestrained glee. A creepy version of an otherworldly cartoon character jumped up and down on one foot, his face contorted into a silly expression. I immediately thought of Rumpelstiltskin, one of my favorite fairytales, and reveled in the hilarity of the creature's performance.

Before I could decide what to do, the Jinni turned toward me, his face suddenly threatening and I braced myself for a possible attack. He promptly flew at me and bound himself to my thigh. His scaly green wings flapped furiously, but he couldn't manage to dislodge. He screamed at me to let him go.

"I'm not doing anything!" I said, holding my hands in the air. The Jinni scrunched his tiny elfin face into a grimace, a feeble attempt to appear fierce, but instead he just looked silly.

I pushed a mental S.O.S. to my team and they

appeared. Kadie bent down and scooped up one of the children into the safety of her arms, Seth and Drew grabbed the other two.

Three more Jinn flew out of the bushes and slammed into my legs, their wings flailing wildly in a futile attempt to flee. I freaked. How many more were there? "Oh my God. Somebody help me get these things off me!"

But my buddies didn't share my concern as they attempted, unsuccessfully, to suppress a laugh. Only Seth appeared a bit bewildered, but eventually joined in the merriment, too.

Furious, the curses flying out of the Jinn's mouths would have made a prison guard cringe. Since nobody seemed inclined to jump to my aid, I bent down and tried to pry one of the little fellows off my thigh. Unfortunately, I must have squeezed him too hard because he exploded and green goo splattered the entire lower half of my body. Horrified, the other three Jinn gawked at me. I gaped at my hands dripping in gooey green...*Oh my God*...could it be their...*blood*?

"Ick. What's happening?" I couldn't control my rising hysteria.

Drew came to my side. "Your aura is way too strong for these little guys, and they can't escape it. Usually they're easy to shoo away, but they are spontaneously exploding. Don't worry they can't feel anything."

Sure enough, before I could even wrap my mind around the meaning of Drew's words, the other three Jinn erupted, covering me in gobs of glistening emerald slime. Drew recoiled, barely escaping the slimy goop. It looked like somebody had dumped a bucket of neon-green pea soup over me. I screamed. "Did I kill them?" The disgusting mess smelled like rotten eggs. I wiped my hands on my jumpsuit and buried my mouth and nose in the crook of my elbow to keep from gagging. Everyone covered their noses.

"I think I'm gonna puke," Seth muttered through his fingers.

"At least you're not wearing it!" I screeched.

I didn't like the fact that I'd just disintegrated four living creatures, no matter how devilish they might be. I mumbled into my sleeve. "How do you know they don't feel anything?" I dropped my arm and tried to ignore the sulfurous stench. "Never mind, I'll take your word for it. What now?"

Kadie stepped forward. "Let's return the children, then we should go back. You'll have to wait until we get home to get that junk off you. It's pretty vile."

We returned the babies to the mothers, who expressed their relief and thankfully ignored my revolting presence. The children appeared to have no idea they'd even been missing.

Arriving at the front doors of Eccli Hall, I noticed the guardians raise their eyebrows at the sight of me. I returned their stare with disdain, projecting, *Don't even ask!*

But apparently they couldn't restrain themselves, and a mocking voice inside my head said, *Had a little encounter with the Jinn, Olivia?* I'd never heard a guardian laugh before and a smile snuck its way across my lips.

Entering the foyer, I had an epiphany. Had Bath Qol sent us to the colony knowing the Jinn would be there?

The director stood in front of her office. "I'm afraid you're on to me," she said as she strode toward us. "My goodness, Olivia! You look a fright!" I didn't respond at first, because I feared I might say something disrespectful. "Apparently the Jinn weren't pleased to see you?"

"Actually they threw a welcome party," I replied as politely as I could muster.

"I didn't send you there with the intent of making you work, but I thought if you happened to stumble upon the Jinn while enjoying some free time, you might be able to dispel them."

I put my hands on my hips, fully intending to give her a piece of my mind, but what was I thinking? She was the boss and if she told me to jump off a bridge my only response should be *Yes, ma'am*. On the other hand, I never seemed able to adopt this attitude around the Scepters, and specifically Michael.

"I'd no idea what I was getting myself into," I finally said. The layer of thick green slime on my clothing had seeped through to my skin and started to crust, making me all itchy.

The director made a weak attempt at a smile. "I appreciate what you did for the colony, and I hope it didn't ruin your day."

My buddies apparently had a collective case of lockjaw. At least they could keep their mouths shut. That definitely came in handy.

"No," I said through gritted teeth, "our day was very nice and the tangle with the Jinn merely an inconvenience. As always, we were glad to help."

"I'm glad all went well," Bath Qol said. "Off you go then, back to the grindstone in the morning." And she spun on her heels and left us standing in the dimly lit foyer.

It took me nearly an hour in the shower to de-goo and I had to resort to scraping most of the vile mess off with my fingernails. I looked like I'd gone ten rounds with a family of alley cats and the felines won.

That night as I settled into bed, Kadie said, "I probably should have told you this before."

I eyed her suspiciously. "What?"

"You and Drew seem to be getting kind of serious. You should know the only place you can get pregnant is in a colony."

"Excuse me?" I said.

"We're not mature enough to actually conceive yet, but just so you know for the future. You go to a colony when you want to have a baby."

"Are you kidding? You think this is something you should've told me before today?"

"I wasn't really worried. Drew knows how things work. He wouldn't get you pregnant. Besides, you both have to wish for a baby."

Totally overwhelmed, I prepared to interrogate my new health teacher. "Let me get this straight. If only one of you wishes for a baby it won't happen?"

"You have to do *the deed*, too. And at that special moment you both make a wish."

I swallowed hard. Ridiculous. Words escaped me, which for me was unheard of.

"Don't look so shocked," Kadie said. "I'm just trying to be helpful."

"Just so we're clear, I didn't have sex with Drew." Well, we'd almost gone there, but at the last minute I chickened out. I wasn't sure why. I knew I loved Drew, and yet something held me back. And Drew wasn't pressuring me either, not like so many other guys I'd known over twelve lifetimes. "There's no rush," he'd said, allowing me a graceful escape. "We have all of eternity."

"Whatever you say." Kadie put up both hands in surrender.

"I'm telling the truth!"

I threw myself forcefully back onto the bed. Releasing a giant sigh, I covered my face with a pillow. Oh my God, I already had too much to think about. Divine conception lesson aside, the absurd encounter with the Jinn totally unnerved me. I could only hope they went painlessly.

Chapter 25

Dressed for work, we flitted off to an all-night fraternity party to avert a case of alcohol poisoning. Arriving in the small-town college in rural upstate New York, the dreary, cold weather dampened my enthusiasm for this mission as we trekked through mounds of dirty gray snow and ramshackle houses. What a depressing place. We landed too far out, seemed like we weren't at our best today.

The opportunity to play college students for a few hours proved amusing. We even drank beer, although alcohol had no effect on me anymore.

Mission accomplished, we exited the fraternity house, ready to flash home. Standing near the darkened roadway, uneasiness crept over my skin. "Do you feel that?" I said.

"What?" Drew said.

"I don't feel anything," Kadie said, and Seth quickly agreed.

"I'm not sure. It's like there's something lurking around, something dark and cold." I veered off into the forest of scrub pines searching for the source of my anxiety. I didn't know where I was going, but I was traveling fast. My friends followed, albeit without much enthusiasm.

Seth called out, "Livy, slow down, where you going?"

Drew spoke next. "Livy, c'mon, wait for us."

Now came Kadie. "Liv! We can't separate, if it's something bad we should be together!"

"Shush!" I hissed. "You're making too much noise, I can't hear." I skulked through the brush, unheeded by my friend's warnings. A small dark creature stepped out from behind a nearby pine tree. He resembled a Jinni, but he wasn't green and stood about a foot taller, grotesque looking, yet dressed in formal attire.

"Hello, Olivia," he said in an oddly deep voice for such a small body. "I was confident you'd find me as your instincts are far superior to the others."

"The others?" I insisted, taken off guard. And he knew my name?

"The other guardians of the Light." His foot, actually more of a hoof, tapped up and down convulsively. He tugged at the too-tight collar of his starched white shirt and grimaced. He exhaled loudly. "You may still be trying to deny it, but we know."

"What do you want?" I demanded.

"I've a message for you." The demon-like thing held out his grimy, scaly hand, his long, dark fingers clasping a scroll of white parchment tied with rawhide string. "It's from Ravana. I am to give it directly to you and no one else. I must wait for your reply."

By now my buddies were in full force around me. Taking the scroll from his filthy hand, I untied the string and unrolled the thick paper. As I read, every fiber of my being tensed.

"What's it say?" Drew asked.

I swiveled to face the three of them. "Ravana's requested a meeting. With me. She said to join her at the top of this mountain in northern Canada at midnight, tonight. The coordinates are here. It says I may bring my lieutenants, but not my legion. She'll do the same."

I peered down at Ravana's sinister little messenger. "I don't have any lieutenants, and I definitely don't have a legion."

"That's not what we see. Aren't these guys your lieutenants?"

I would've laughed if this situation weren't fraught with danger, so I decided to play along. "All right, I will bring them and no one else. Tell Ravana I will honor her request."

"Excellent," the creepy demon said. "I'll tell the Queen." In a flash, he vanished.

"Are you crazy?" Drew yelled. "Why would you agree? And especially on her terms?"

"Why shouldn't we go? She's no match for us, especially if we're prepared. At least she's not trying to ambush us."

Seth said, "That's ridiculous, of course it could be an ambush!"

"And besides," Kadie said, "Michael would never allow it."

"Everyone take a breath," I said. "Honestly, I'm sick and tired of Michael bossing me around. Let's head home. We have plenty of time before midnight. We'll discuss it further back at Eccli. If you don't want to go with me, fine, I promise not to hold it against anyone."

As we approached the front entrance to Eccli Hall, I spied Thomas and Johnny sitting tandem on the bottom step. Their body language told me they were pissed, really pissed. Crap, they already knew. Who'd betrayed me? I looked to Seth and Drew as my two protectors marched in my direction.

Johnny went first. "What the hell are you thinking, Olivia!"

"Who told you?" I said.

"We have our ways," Thomas said. His blue eyes blazed with fury. "She's dangerous and you can't trust her, and there's no way I'm letting you go!"

Their verbal assault continued for probably two whole minutes. I stood with my arms crossed over my chest, lips pressed together in a tight line, trying valiantly to maintain my cool. But my anger threatened to unleash.

Finally, they stopped and glared at me.

"Finished?" I said, my indignation echoing in the warm, night air.

"Don't try my patience, Olivia," Thomas said.

"That's your problem." I huffed. "Patience. First of all, neither one of you is going to tell me what I can and can't do. Secondly, I've already made up my mind, so it's done. And thirdly—"

Thomas cut me off and poked his finger in Drew's chest. "*You*. Talk her out of this. You're her partner, and it's your responsibility to make sure you have her back."

"Back off, buddy!" Drew shoved Thomas, forcing him onto his heels.

Kadie lunged between them. Johnny grabbed Thomas from behind to restrain him; Seth pulled Drew away before a fistfight broke out.

Oh my God. All I needed. I screamed, "Will you two stop?"

I took a breath. Anger suddenly seemed like a communicable disease.

"Look, Thomas," Drew said. "I get that you're worried about her. And you're right, I'm her partner, and it's my job to watch her back. That's why I'm going with her."

Thomas appeared to consider Drew's words, but then: "You're all out of your goddamned minds! Totally reckless. Ravana's dangerous, and she's probably set a trap. You're naïve if you think you're going to waltz in there and have an uneventful chat with the Princess of Darkness."

"There won't be any dancing, Thomas, I promise." My joke didn't go over.

"This isn't funny, Olivia," Thomas said.

"Not to mention," Johnny said, "it's probably one of their Crossroads. They've got a ton of them up there."

"What the heck is a Crossroad?" I asked in bewilderment.

Johnny said, "You normally don't learn about them until second term because no one would send a first-termer near one. It's a sacred place for members of the Underworld, areas where their strength is at its greatest. Unfortunately it has the opposite effect on our power. If you don't have your wits about you, your aura could be weakened and your mind can become confused."

"I'll have my wits about me," I said, "so don't worry. Besides, the Covenant forbids us from killing each other."

"There are worse things," Thomas said.

"Like what?" I stepped close, our chests nearly touching.

"Like spending an eternity in Hell!" Thomas declared, inching closer.

Okay, I hadn't considered that. Captured? Spending forever in hell? Why hadn't that thought occurred to me? Was I overly impressed with my abilities?

Thomas backed up and rubbed his forehead with both hands. "Look, Olivia, we're supposed to stay out of each other's way, but it doesn't mean somebody won't cross the line. Another war is not an option."

Both of these guys cared for me, and I wanted to give credibility to their worries. "I've no intention of battling Ravana or Lilith, and I'm sure they don't want a fight either. But I need to know why they're so interested in me. Since no one is inclined to tell me anything, I've no other choice." A moment of silence hovered while they seemed to consider my argument.

"Listen," Thomas said more quietly, "aura for aura, you can probably overtake Ravana if it came to it, but you haven't got enough experience yet. She's been at this a lot longer than you. And you can't trust anything she says."

"I appreciate your concern for my safety, Thomas, I really do, but I'm going and you can't talk me out of it."

Johnny grimaced. "I don't want to undermine your confidence, but Thomas is right, you're too young, too inexperienced."

My two protectors made their final attempt to intervene in my rendezvous with the evil princess.

"Then we're going with you, too," Thomas said. Johnny nodded his agreement.

I decided to end this standoff. "I'll make you a deal. I'll tell Aidan and abide by his decision."

Thomas and Johnny considered my offer and

eventually conceded. "Promise?" Johnny said.

"Cross my heart and hope to die," I said, marking my fingers in an X over my heart. Now that was a stupid thing to say, and judging by the mass of frowning foreheads it landed as expected.

I ascended the steps with my lieutenants close on my heels and made for the stairs.

"Aren't you going to see Aidan?" Kadie asked from behind.

"No." I stopped and leaned against the bannister. My three lieutenants made an audience around me.

"But I thought…"

"I already pushed it to him, and he said I could go."

"You're lying," Seth said.

"I'm not."

Seth persisted. "Look, Livy, I want to believe you but—"

"You're going to have to trust me on this. All of you." Drew hadn't said a word and I wondered why.

"Didn't we agree that the next time the wives got near us you would report it?" Seth said.

"Well, technically, I just did. I'm sure Aidan checked with somebody higher up. Either that, or his authority is sufficient. I'm running with that."

"I don't want trouble with Michael. I clearly told you that already," Seth added.

Finally, Drew said, "I trust Livy. Nobody has been very forthcoming in explaining what the wives want with her, so I say, let's find out for ourselves."

"Well, then we better get ready," Kadie said. "I'll go and get us warm clothing, something good for snow. Seth, come with me."

"Everyone, let's meet back here at eleven-thirty," I

said.

Drew came close. I stood on the bottom step effectively making us the same height. He wrapped his arms around my waist. "Thanks for backing me up," I said.

"You're welcome." He kissed me. "We'll be fine. And I think it's time you got some answers."

In my room, I peered out my bedroom window at the darkening sky. The stars winked at me, and the moon peeked above the horizon. A full moon was expected, and I wasn't sure if that was good or bad.

Kadie returned with a full-length, white, hooded cloak lined with plush red velvet.

I said, "Going for the regal look?"

"We don't have summits with demons on top of mountains everyday. We might as well look the part. Try it on."

I wrapped the plush cape around my body. A chill invaded me, oddly. I pulled the hood over the crown of my head, the soft velvet caressing me. We faced each other, like seeing my image in a mirror, except for the blonde curls and green eyes.

"Looking good," I complimented her. "I'm going to try and relax a little before we head out." I hung the cloak in the closet.

"Yeah, me too," Kadie said, placing her garment alongside mine.

I pretended to read and acted as though I didn't have a big meeting with a powerful Princess of The Dark Side in a few hours. Somehow, I knew this night would change everything. I prayed for the better.

At 11:30 sharp we marched down the stairs to find Seth and Drew waiting in the garden in matching cloaks.

A butterfly flew past my face. And then another. My body tensed as I anticipated the onset of the herd. A third, then a fourth...they circled my head like a ring of shimmering orange and black stars. The halo of fluttering insects descended, circling my shoulders, my waist, my knees, my feet. My eyes searched the ground. Nestled in the grass near the hem of my cape sat four tiny, shimmering, emerald green creatures.

Frogs. "Peep," they chirped. Peeper frogs.

Chapter 26

The mysterious butterflies vanished into the shadows of trees. "What the heck?" Kadie said.

"It's a sign," Drew said, stooping and gathering the tiny otherworldly amphibians into his hands. He slipped one into the breast pocket of my cape, then placed one in Kadie's, Seth's, and his own. "Protection. Remember what Aidan told us?"

"You're kidding, right?" I said. "That's the stuff of fairytales."

"Why not?" Drew asked. "We are the stuff of fairytales."

The absurd truth of Drew's comment hit hard. I *was* living in a goddamned fairytale, complete with evil princesses, magic, telepathy, time travel...the works. Perhaps this was just some stupid dream, like Dorothy had. I'm in a coma somewhere and about to wake up.

I peered down at the red amphibian eyes staring back at me, the tiny three-fingered forearms curled around the edge of my breast pocket.

"Peep," the frog chirped.

"I guess you're coming along for the ride, little guy," I said.

"Peep," it squeaked again and almost seemed to smile.

****

We arrived first and stood atop the mountain. The

full moon shone brightly, casting a bluish hue over the crusty, white snow. Stunted pine trees dotted the landscape, flora struggling to survive in the frigid tundra of the northern latitudes. The brisk wind whipped our majestic white cloaks into swirls of dancing velvet.

My aura churned inside me as I pondered the meaning of this summit. Was I afraid? I didn't think so. Was I strong enough to defend myself if I had to? I wasn't entirely sure.

The sky erupted with crimson light, the air crackled. Blinding threads of red laser beams intersected in a spider-web pattern of dancing photons. A small explosion ignited. I jumped. Four tall figures clad in hooded black capes emerged from a cloud of ruddy smoke and marched forward. *Geez, talk about making an entrance!*

The bright moon, pale as a corpse, hung low on the horizon behind the approaching gloom, the evening's icy chill inescapable. The air smelled of rotten eggs. Tension hung between us like a fiery nebula that might explode with the tiniest spark. I quickly identified Ravana, her long, jet-black tresses dancing in the howling wind, her blazing scarlet lips taut. Lilith alongside, her poppy-red hair peeked out from beneath her hood. Two men flanked them and I found them quite attractive, both with blond hair and devil-blue eyes. I'd expected something entirely different. Evidently, I'd watched too many horror movies in my human days.

I waited. Ravana took a step forward, leaving only a short space between us. "You're in denial, Olivia. Your charade is over. Your crimes place you squarely in the realm of the Underworld. Fess up. Confession is good for the soul."

Crimes?...What crimes? Thoughts tumbling around in my head. I didn't—no, *couldn't* respond, trying to make sense of Ravana's words.

Ravana mirrored my bewildered expression. "I almost believe you have no idea what I'm talking about." Her frown vanished and a sinister grin commandeered her blood-red lips. "It's true. They haven't told you?" She laughed, yet her dark eyes stayed serious. "This is going to be quite pleasurable."

Finally finding my words, I said, "The only reason I agreed to meet is because I demand to know why you hellish creatures are following me."

Ravana laughed. "Oh my," she said, struggling to regain composure. "Apparently your precious Scepters have kept you in the dark. So like them. They're using you for their own greed. When they're done with you there'll be nothing left but ashes. They'll never let you think for yourself. There's no free will in the City of the Sun. No one questions Michael's orders."

"Not true, I saved—"

"You mean your silly attempt to rescue Peter?" Ravana said. "A waste of time."

She knew about Peter? "I did save him. I explained to the Scepters that I believe all souls can be saved if they wish to be. No one has stopped me so far."

"My, my, disobeying the Scepters. I'm impressed," Ravana said. "So very much like you." She stepped closer and my lieutenants closed in around me, yet I put a hand up to prevent them from interfering.

Lilith's voice came from behind Ravana. "Get it over with, Vana. Tell her."

"I suppose so," she said, hesitating for an agonizing moment. "You, my sweet Olivia, are my blood, my sister."

The words punched into my chest, a dagger slicing through my core. Revulsion bubbled up, and I swallowed it back before it choked me. "Ridiculous! You and I share nothing."

Ravana's visage grew dark. "We were twins once, a long time ago. Our mother died in childbirth, and we were left with a pathetic excuse for a father, a penniless drunkard, and a cruel one at that. You criticized me for stealing food and for defending myself from the terrible mortals who abused us. One boy in particular delighted in taunting me, so one evening I followed him to the pier. I only meant to threaten him with the knife. But when he laughed in my face, I saw red, and yes, I killed him.

"I saw you standing there, having witnessed the entire incident. You were always the righteous one, always helping people, saying my misfortune was my own fault. We got angry at each other, like always, but this was different."

"Don't listen to a word she says," Drew interjected.

"I can speak for myself," I said.

Ravana slid the sleeve of her black cape up her arm and brandished her wrist. Behind her, Lilith and her two companions did the same. "He marked us as one of the damned! Both of us!"

I furrowed my brow, my eyes narrowing. The *mark*! A sign of evil? That's why Peter had it. Why hadn't anyone told me? And what did it say about me?

Ravana continued, "I'd never seen you so furious. You started to glow, and the light blinded me. A bolt of electricity struck me dead." Ravana's features contorted with rage. "You murdered me!"

Her words landed like giant hailstones, shattering my thoughts into dangerous shards.

Ravana inhaled, exhaled, seeming to regain control. "He dragged me to Hell, my last chance for redemption forfeited. We're both murderers, kindred spirits, and it's time for you to accept your destiny. Collectively, we could rule both the City of the Sun and Earth. A force no one could reckon with. Not Lucifer, not Michael."

I actually laughed out loud. "Never going to happen."

Ravana's eyes darkened, and her sharp fingernails reached for my face. I blocked her hand and our wrists crossed in a perfect X, the cursed crescent marks making contact. Lightning streaked in a cloudless sky. Electricity erupted at the point of contact, my brilliant surge of blue and white sparks clashing with fiery red flashes from Ravana. The dark princess fell backward onto the snow-encrusted ground, smoke wafting up from her prone form.

The collective lieutenants stood at the ready, as conflict appeared imminent. No one moved. Everyone's attention stayed fixed on the motionless dark princess. I wrapped my hand around the mark on my wrist, my body still tingling.

Was she dead? My gut wrenched with dread. If I'd killed Ravana, I'd have broken the Covenant. Had I started the apocalypse? I never should've come. I should've listened.

Ravana's body jerked violently, and her eyes flew open. She struggled to her feet, aided by the two blue-eyed demons. They brushed the snow from her black velvet cloak. Her gaze fell on Lilith. "Come attend to me!"

"Peep," said the tiny creature in my pocket, promptly followed by a chorus from the others.

"I can't. I..." Lilith fainted.

"What the hell!" Ravana stooped before the redheaded princess. She slapped her face, hard. "Get up!" Lilith quickly revived, and their male comrades heaved her upright. Lilith's complexion had taken on a sickly, greenish-gray pallor, her stance unsteady, and the two blue-eyed demons secured her between them.

The tiny frog squirmed in my pocket and a little surge of heat warmed my breast. Thankfully, the errant bolt of lightning hadn't fried the little guy. Could he be the reason for Lilith's swan dive?

Ravana spun on me. "This is the last time we'll ask you nicely."

Nicely? If this was nice I couldn't imagine what *not nice* would be. Her own defiance surfaced again and although I couldn't deny the evil mark's existence, I still couldn't embrace Ravana's story. "I reject everything you've said."

Were Ravana's words just the ranting of a lunatic, or—? Heavy thoughts hung unfocused, uneasiness and anger dueling between us.

Ravana warned, "Mark my words, Olivia, you do not understand who you are. You've only begun to hear the truth, which I've planted like a seed inside you. Accept your fate, as even the Scepters have, even they realize your nature. I won't allow you to forsake your grand purpose."

I said no words in response to Ravana's threats,

even as Armageddon loomed.

After a momentary hesitation, the four demons rotated with military precision. Their black capes swirled around their feet, their boots crunching snow as they made their departure. The sky became crimson and a wave of heat bathed my face. The atmosphere seemed lighter, the sulfurous odor dissipated.

I gazed into the full moon and contemplated my options.

"Geez, Liv," Kadie said, "that lightning bolt? I mean we've seen you glow, but…"

"Did it hurt?" Drew asked, touching my arm.

"The least of my worries."

"Honestly," Seth said, "I'm impressed."

Kadie said, "As far as I'm concerned, you kicked butt!"

Not entirely sure I agreed with Kadie. I focused on Ravana's horrid revelations. Anger shrouded my aura like a freshly made casket. Fists clenched, I said, "Time for answers, *Michael*."

Chapter 27

I hit the foggy ground opposite the vaulted complex of the Kingdoms and nearly did a face-plant. I sped toward the imposing archway. From behind, Drew yelled, "Livy! Wait up!"

The guardians defended their post. A dangerous mental state consumed me, and they stiffened the second they saw me, shielding the gate with their bodies. I yelled, "Let me in!"

The one to the left answered. "You aren't expected, Olivia, and court's in session."

"I'm only going to say this once. If you don't move out of my way, I'll do it for you and open the gate myself!"

The guardians exchanged anxious glances as they weighed my threat. My overly charged aura might be something I could finally use to my advantage. Reluctantly, the guardians moved aside.

"Good choice." I marched through the gateway and did a repeat performance at the front doors and the guards threw open the heavy double doors. My three companions had caught up and witnessed me bullying the guardians. Not proud of my behavior, I pushed that thought in their direction and told them to wait outside.

I stomped through the two front chambers, passing the sword effigy and the garden doors, in search of the courtroom. The place appeared abandoned.

I navigated a maze of dark hallways when the din of voices caught my attention. A rendering of the Scales of Justice marked ornately carved doors. This had to be it. I shoved violently. The heavy panels' thunderous crash into the walls reverberated throughout the busy chamber. The white cloak churned around me, barely containing my fury as I struggled to control my aura. At least fifty people crowded the huge chamber. Icy stares shot my way.

Michael. He sat with the other ruling Scepters around a large table near the front. He stood as I approached. No one else even breathed.

"Time for a talk," I said.

Audible gasps resonated. No one spoke to a Scepter like that, especially not a lowly apprentice. But I remained firm in my resolve. We stared at each other, and I pelted his mind with a thousand furious thoughts. He winced at the onslaught of psychic energy.

The Lord High Commander addressed the crowd, his voice too calm. "Everyone out, leave us."

A maddening hush covered the room as I witnessed the clearing of the chamber. Slowly, deliberately, the throng of courthouse workers collected their papers and departed. The three ruling Scepters remained at their table. Michael said, "You also."

They left as ordered, and Gabriel shut the doors. Finally, alone with the Prince of the Seventh Kingdom.

Michael turned to face the stained glass window to my right, his snug white robe barely containing his muscular body. The multi-colored glass depicted an image of him with his mighty sword as he fought a great dragon.

"Sit down, Olivia," he said, softly. I braced myself.

I couldn't see his expression. He must be furious. But either he kept it in check, or he'd finally accepted that I intended to do whatever I damn well pleased.

"I prefer to stand," I said.

Michael's thick finger traced a dragon wing. In a grim tone, he said, "I warned you to stay away from Lilith and Ravana, but once again you have ignored my directive."

"It wasn't a secret. I told Aidan I was going."

"Ah, I didn't know. If I had, I would have forbidden it."

"Turn around and look at me when you're talking to me," I said rather impertinently. I'd anticipated anger, but instead his shoulders drooped, his arms hung loose at his sides. He seemed...deflated. His monotone and downturned facial features made him seem *sad.* "But I thought you made all the decisions around here," I said.

"I like to think I do, however when it comes to you, others believe I am overprotective and I should let you out on your own more."

"Maybe they're right."

Michael sighed. "What's done is done. And now, you've learned things from your past you should never have remembered."

"You mean it's true? She's my twin sister? And I...I killed her?" My mouth dropped open.

"Yes," he said, "on both counts." His expression changed, a grim twist pinched his mouth, an unfocused stare as if recalling a bad memory.

"Why did no one tell me?" I nearly screamed, my hands beseeching.

"We considered it, but agreed you'd find it too

difficult, and it would be better to wait."

"Difficult? I'll show you difficult! I want the truth from you, about everything."

Michael grew pensive. "There are some things you need to understand before you can accept what happened all those centuries ago."

But my patience was gone and I yanked up my sleeve and blurted, "This mark, have you seen it before?"

"Yes."

"What does it mean?" I said, terrified again.

Michael frowned, then took my hand in his and ran his thumb over the perfect red crescent. Electricity traveled up my arm, and I struggled to tamp it down. I yanked my hand away.

"I'm sorry," he said, his voice tender. "It is the mark of Lucifer. It signifies his conquest. Mortals cannot see it. Only we can."

"But I can't be…damned." Or could I? Was I? A sick feeling swam through me.

"Let me attempt to put your mind at ease. The easiest explanation is that it's wishful thinking on Lucifer's part. You must understand you'd be a tremendous asset to whichever side you choose. Think of it like the mortal race for nuclear weapons. Whoever possesses them can dominate others."

What? Had Ravana been accurate regarding the Scepter's desire to possess me? Was I merely equipment to be bought or sold, traded or captured?

"I know this sounds terrible," the mighty Scepter said. "I don't want you to think I view you as simply a chess piece."

I struggled to keep my thoughts to myself fearing

I'd think something I'd regret.

"Branding you with the mark was stupid of him—to think this would camouflage you from us. We've had you on our radar since your inception. In some ways, I guess Lucifer hoped you would follow Ravana's pathway. She also bears the mark."

"Yes, I saw."

"You have seen it on others?'

"Absolutely."

"You understand it claims souls who are to be taken, or who already belong to them?"

"Except not in the case of Peter."

"As you so aptly pointed out with Peter, it's not a foregone conclusion, more of a reminder."

Shaking my head, I tried to calm down for about the tenth time today.

"Olivia..." Michael's voice deepened. And suddenly I'd had enough. Frustration swarmed me like a human illness. How quickly could I make my escape?

He continued, "You and Ravana are powerful forces, the likes of which have not been seen in this universe since its inception." He pulled out a chair and sat down heavily, clasping his hands together on the table. "Sit."

I waited a few beats before taking a seat across from him. Michael poured a glass of golden water from a pitcher, pushing the drink in my direction.

"There are things you need to comprehend before you can accept what happened." He paused as if thinking of a way to explain the laws of the universe to a child. "We have no control over where a soul is placed once it's on its way to Earth. The soul makes that choice. You and Ravana had already lived many mortal lives. We'd been tracking both of you very carefully. But then, one day, both your souls headed toward Earth at the same exact moment and location. Usually twins, or other multiple births, are not cause for concern. But this was different. You see, Olivia, you and Ravana possess extremely powerful auras. Regrettably, rather than working in harmony, you two were rivals. That is because your aura is composed entirely of negative ions, which is extremely rare, while Ravana's aura is composed of positive ions like most auras. Normally, positive and negative forces attract each other and then discharge their energy, which serves to neutralize the attraction. But you two remain in a constant state of friction, defying physics. No one can figure out why, it just is. Are you with me so far?"

"I'm listening," I said.

"Good. It is important for you to understand that the negative aura is essentially composed of electrons, thus electrical in nature. Hence, the phenomena you've experienced." I feared what more he had to tell. "On the pier that night you came upon Ravana killing the boy. Your outrage was so great your aura virtually escaped from you temporarily, striking Ravana dead. The dark side claimed her immediately, and she was lost to us."

I found a moment of clarity. "*So, who am I?*"

"That depends on you. Your choices. You decide your fate, just as Ravana did."

Now he was being cryptic again. I hated when he did this. "Why doesn't everyone just leave me alone? All I want to do is save souls."

Yet Michael's grave expression frightened me. "Perhaps it would be best if I offered proof of what I'm telling you. Come." He stood, pivoted away from me and headed toward the doors. What lay ahead? I hesitated, then followed, wrapping my skepticism around me like a shield.

We arrived at a door that seemed to be a back entrance to one of the kingdoms. Michael reached into the pocket of his robe, retrieving a large silver key. It slid effortlessly into the keyhole and he pushed the door open slowly. Darkness greeted us, and I found myself unwilling to enter the unknown. Michael waved his hand, illuminating a cavernous warehouse. Dusty equipment littered the floor, and I glimpsed shelves piled high with boxes and peculiar machines.

The mighty Scepter beckoned me inside. Something in my pocket squirmed and then a tiny peep came. Crap, I still had that frog in my pocket.

Michael chuckled. "You brought a frog with you for your meeting with Lilith and Ravana?"

He reached over and plucked the tiny creature from its hiding place. It seemed to cower in the palm of his huge hand. A childlike smile captured his lips.

"Drew's idea," I offered. "I didn't believe it would offer any protection against Lilith, or Ravana."

"It is an old tale, but I wouldn't totally discount the effects. The truth is, we don't actually know much about witchcraft, as it is a skill only the demons of the Underworld have developed. We are somewhat lacking in that regard." Michael squatted down and gently tossed the silvery frog into the fog circling our feet. Its head popped up and down a few times as it hopped off into oblivion.

"This is the back entrance to the Sixth Kingdom," he said, rising. "I'm bringing you here to show you evidence of the day the universe shifted."

Chapter 28

The Sixth Kingdom's main chamber appeared deserted. I recalled Aidan saying this City of the Sun's Kingdom housed the Fountain of Life, the place where souls were processed for re-entry to Earth. It wasn't a fountain of water but a form of swirling luminous energy. I stared at it, and the longer I did, the brighter it became. Like staring into the sun, I had to avert my eyes.

Michael moved close to the foreboding vortex and stopped near the rim. "Come," he said.

I couldn't move. I'd no desire to get anywhere near that fountain. What if I fell in? Or worse, what if he'd brought me here to throw me in? Had I become too much trouble to keep around? Did I know too much? He could be jettisoning me back to Earth this very second!

"Olivia, you look terrified." Michael's voice yanked me from my horrific daydream.

"Uh…I think I'll keep my distance."

Michael smiled. "Nothing will happen. I'll keep you safe."

Like I had cement encasing my feet, I remained paralyzed. Before I could come up with an escape plan, he chuckled. "You don't believe I have any ill intention, do you?"

It did sound ridiculous now that he'd said it out

loud.

"I…I…" I swallowed.

"Olivia, regardless of what you might think, your destiny is not on Earth. Believe me, it has taken tremendous effort on both our parts to get you this far. I have no desire to start it all over again. Besides, I've grown rather fond of you."

Fond? Of me?

Michael extended his hand, but I still couldn't get my toes to even squirm.

"I simply want to show you something. It's very important."

Oh boy! I really didn't want to go over there. But then I had to assume he wasn't lying. I needed to trust him. Slowly, I put one foot in front of the other, tiny baby steps declaring my cowardice.

Michael gently grasped my hand. I must've been holding onto my aura so tightly that only the tiniest spark erupted.

"Here," he said, pointing to the thick marble rim surrounding the pool. I struggled to focus on the place he indicated, the spinning waves of energy making me dizzy.

"See this crack that's been mended?" Michael asked, running his thumb along the snake-like fault in the marble.

I peered intently at the gray fracture repaired with some type of filler. I nodded.

"There's another one on the opposite side."

"Yes, what's so important about it?"

Michael dropped my hand, his brown eyes fixing me. "A very strange thing happened on that historic day when your soul and Ravana's passed through here at the same moment. Can you imagine a tornado and earthquake striking somewhere on Earth simultaneously?"

I imagined what the effects of two natural disasters might be. "Chaos times infinity?"

"Exactly."

Oh my God!

"The sky became pitch black. Thunderclouds formed, and the floor rumbled. A giant inverted tornado of multicolored light exploded from the vortex's center. The fountain cracked wide open. The force tripled the size of the wormhole leading to Earth." He paused and I realized my mouth hung open.

"It took us several days to fix it. If you consulted our registers on that date, you would see no births recorded and for several days afterward."

My eyebrows knit together. "I don't understand."

"You must realize how powerful you and Ravana are. No other auras of this magnitude ever emerged before. It shocked all of us."

"I don't know what to say."

"I just want you to appreciate what I am telling you about the prospects for your destiny. Lucifer already has Ravana. If he was ever to possess you, all will be lost. The repercussions will be of a magnitude we cannot even imagine. So you must understand, you are extremely important to the universe's future. Stop, give pause to these possibilities."

Okay, now he was scaring me again and I decided I'd had enough. No…more than enough, I'd had entirely too much truth telling for one day. Just tell him what he wanted to hear and then go.

"All right. I understand and you don't have to

worry. I know which team I'm playing for, and I'll be careful."

"That's all I can ask of you."

We made our way back to the Seventh Kingdom, and Michael ushered me to the front exit.

"If you would like me to make a public apology for my outburst in the courthouse, I will."

"That won't be necessary. I will make any explanations warranted. If we're not angry at each other, it will be laid to rest. So go, restore your spirit, and we can talk again soon."

He slipped his strong arm around my shoulders. The heat from the nearness of his body calmed me. But then I feared if his touch lingered too long, I wouldn't be able to contain myself. It always seemed I was on the edge of losing control whenever he came close. The current surged between us, but as always, we pretended it wasn't happening.

My aura simmered. Michael's arm fell away, and the doors magically sprung open.

"Peace be with you, Olivia," Michael offered.

"And with you also, Michael. I could really use some peace right now."

On my way out, I apologized to the guardians, begging their forgiveness. They acted gracious, although they probably wanted to smack me.

Once through the gate, I discovered my three lieutenants waiting. Standing rigid, their expressions of shock beaming like neon lights.

Drew raced to my side. "Well?"

"Did you find answers?" Kadie said, with Seth mute alongside her.

"Yeah, pretty much. What Ravana told me was

accurate." I had no intention of telling them about how Ravana and I had cracked the Fountain of Life. Somehow, it would sound like bragging. "I'm beat. Let's go home."

But I couldn't put all of this away, not yet. I needed to tell them about the crescent mark. They should at least know that much.

"Listen, guys, there's something…" I explained what Michael told me in hopes it would alleviate their impression I might be cursed or some such.

"I honestly thought it was a birthmark," Seth said.

"Drew and I noticed it but didn't think much about it," Kadie said.

Greatly relieved by their loyalty, I trudged my way homeward for the night. I seriously hoped no mortal needed me tonight because all things afterlife disheartened me presently.

Kadie and Seth bid their goodnights and left me standing in the foyer with Drew. He grabbed my hands and pulled me into his chest. Wrapping my arms around his back, he pinned them there. He gazed at me, his dark eyes warm and soft, yet pain glinted in them. Releasing my hands, he framed my face with his strong grip, using his thumbs to stroke my cheeks. I shuddered. Our lips touched. The heat of his body, his firm hold, made me safe, warm, loved.

Suddenly, I wanted to cry, to unburden myself from my past, yet the reservoir holding my tears was empty.

"Oh, Livy," he said wearily, his breath on my neck. "I want to make it all better."

"Just you being here helps," I mumbled.

"You must be so upset, so…confused."

I sighed. "I'm so tired, Drew."

He pushed me away from his chest and kept me at arm's length. "There's no way I'm letting you out of my sight tonight."

I frowned. We weren't allowed in each other's rooms. Where?

"I know a place," he said, reading my thoughts. "My buddy is away for a few weeks on assignment, and we can stay in his room."

He tugged me by the hand until we were out of Eccli Hall. "Just hold tight, and we'll tandem flash."

We hadn't done this since I'd learn to transport on my own. And in a flicker we arrived on the steps of a huge multi-storied building. I gazed up, amazed.

"What is this place?" I said. Drew still had my hand secured in his, as if I'd flit away.

"This building serves as living quarters for those who work for the City of the Sun. Messengers, healers, guardians, or soul collectors. Ones who don't have families of their own. It'll be available to us after we get our commissions."

It reminded me of a housing complex on a bustling college campus. Lots of Travelers milled around, exchanging friendly banter as they entered and left the building. Drew led me up to the twelfth floor into a square room. Only one bed so I assumed his friend had no roommate. What now?

"I'm going to take a shower." Drew tossed his shirt on the bedside chair. The sight of his half-clad body sent my pulse racing. He headed toward the bathroom and shut the door. A sudden chill invaded me. I couldn't decide why I felt so cold, like someone had walked over my grave. I needed warmth, heat. I needed

The Wives of Lucifer

Drew's body against mine.

I sat on the edge of the bed and slipped off my shoes, then tugged the elastic band from my hair. My jeans came next. I wanted to join him in the shower, to feel his wet body. But instead, I slipped under the covers and snuggled into the gray flannel sheets, hesitant about giving myself to him—again. I couldn't understand why.

I lay on my side, watching Drew as he exited the bathroom, a towel around his waist, beads of water speckling his beautiful skin. "You okay?"

"I love you, Drew."

"I know. I love you too, Liv."

I lifted up the covers and urged him inside.

"I didn't bring you here to have sex," he said, slipping his boxers on under the towel. He then threw it on the nearby chair and finger-combed his longish locks into place.

"I want you, Drew. I want you so damn bad." I hesitated before adding, "No, that's not right. I want to make love to you."

I didn't get the response I was hoping for. "Look, Liv, I don't want to take advantage of you. You're obviously upset and, well, I don't think our first time should be when you're feeling so vulnerable." He walked over to the side of the bed, his hands on his hips. "Let's take it slow. I just want you near me." Accepting my invitation, he slid in alongside me and tucked my hand around his waist, squeezing me against his hard body. His finger chucked my chin up so his lips could find mine. His kiss drained the rivers of pain from my soul.

I pressed my face against his nipple, and it seemed

as if I floated on air, lithe and free. He said, "You're so beautiful, here with me, just like this."

I closed my eyes and just let myself feel his body. He filled me with a fire that threatened to consume every part of me.

I didn't want to let him go. *Ever.*

"I love you so much, Livy," he whispered. Tingles slid across my skin, and I almost giggled, clutching him to me. We stayed that way for a long while, but then he pulled my hand up and studied the brand on my wrist. I winced. What was he thinking? Did he truly believe it had no meaning? Running his thumb back and forth over the soft flesh, he brought it to his mouth and placed a gentle kiss on the raised red crescent.

"Pretend you're sleeping, my beauty," he said. "We'll await the sunrise together."

I smiled, contented. I loved him so much. It had been an awful day, and I closed my eyes and wished for sleep.

I should have wished for something else.

Chapter 29

Scalding water seared Ravana's skin, the bloody scratches on her back pulsing to her wrathful heart's rhythm. Rage consumed her. A rage buried under a thick layer of humiliation. She thought revealing their sisterly bond would force Olivia to see her as a kindred spirit, while at the same time fostering distrust in those arrogant Scepters. But her plan backfired, and then she lost her temper, making things worse. She'd hoped her threats would scare Olivia, but they had the opposite effect. Olivia left angry rather than fearful and might be realizing her true power. Ravana needed to regroup.

Stepping from the shower, she wrapped her supermodel-worthy torso in the thick black-and-white striped bath sheet, tucking the corner between her ample breasts. Steam clung to the bathroom mirror, and she blew her warm breath over the glass surface, the moist film evaporating. Emotionless green eyes stared back at her. She startled.

"Damn it, Lily! Don't sneak up on me like that!"

"You *are* the Immortal Queen of Witchcraft. Don't you have a protection spell or something around here?"

Ravana stared at Lilith's reflection. "Not in my bathroom!" She faced her sister-wife and huffed.

"I'm joking, dear," Lilith said.

"When did you develop a sense of humor? And what's so damned important you had to come to my room? I don't have time for chitchat." Ravana pushed past Lilith and stood in front of her vanity. She dragged a sterling silver, wide-toothed comb through her long, dark locks and let them fall down her back.

Lilith eyed the shiny implement as Ravana placed it atop her dressing table. "Don't even think about pilfering my comb," Ravana said.

Lilith arched her eyebrows innocently. "*Moi?*"

"Yes, you."

Lilith guffawed, then stared at the rumpled bed sheets. "Hmm, looks like you two had a wild ride last night. The sheets are shredded. And your back has some lovely scratches. I'm jealous."

Ravana slumped into the overstuffed chair in the corner and splayed her legs in front of her. "L was...*in a mood.* Just got him out of here a few minutes ago." Ravana sighed heavily. It had been a rough night, as usual with Lucifer. "You'll get your turn. Be prepared, he's seriously horny."

Lilith roared with laughter. "Hysterical!"

"What is?"

"The double entendre. Horny? Lucifer? The Devil? Get it?" Lilith leaned against the massive mahogany bedpost, crossed her feet and her arms across her chest.

"You're an ass." Ravana frowned. "You didn't come here to socialize, Lily. Get to the point."

Lilith huffed. "Well...the other night, on the mountain...Hell, a total disaster. She nearly killed one of us. And if I cease, dost think thou shalt survive?"

"You're doing it again," Ravana declared. "Speaking in the old tongue."

Lilith averted her eyes, and Ravana was glad, yet she knew Lilith's observation was accurate. "That's the understatement of the century, Lily. Actually, a century and a half to be exact." She paused. "What made you faint?" Ravana struggled to keep her voice under control. She still needed Lilith's help. But this frog phobia frayed her last nerve. She worried Lilith had lost her edge and might not have enough power to do what she required.

"I wouldn't talk if I were you," Lilith said. "The little twerp knocked you on your ass. We both looked pathetic." She obsessively bit at the skin around her fingernails like she always did under pressure.

"You're ruining your lovely manicure again," Ravana said.

"You always try to distract me." Lilith shoved her hands in the back pockets of her black jeans.

Not that difficult... Ravana thought.

"What's *your* excuse?" Lilith demanded.

"I didn't anticipate the lightning." Ravana heard involuntary dejection in her own voice.

"It's the same damn thing she did to you on the pier that night."

"I was ten!" screamed Ravana. "How the hell was I supposed to know what was going on?"

"Whatever. She's hit you with it twice so far. When are you going to smarten up?"

Ravana had hoped she'd have more time before Olivia embraced her dark talents, but now...

"Personally," Lilith said, "I don't think she realizes she can summon lightning. She assumes it's a fluke, and I doubt the Scepters want her to know how powerful she is...not yet. It's too dangerous, and I'm surprised she's even able to survive it with so little experience."

Ravana let out a deep breath. Her vile temper pricked at her, like metal spikes across her skin. "Why are you here?"

"We need to talk. Formulate a new plan."

"We could have arranged to meet somewhere like always. You didn't have to come to my room. I cherish my privacy."

"Stop whining," Lilith said. "It's unbecoming."

Ravana's patience had nearly evaporated. But she had an idea that inspired her all night, which had angered Lucifer. She'd seemed distracted, he'd said, unresponsive, and made it clear he expected more in the future.

"Okay, you're right. It's time for something drastic. We've tried to lure her in with offers of sharing our kingdom, we've threatened her, hit her with spells and nothing works. I thought tricking her into saving Peter would get her into serious trouble with the Scepters, and she'd start to grow tired of their authority. Yet they were way too lenient. We have to hit her where it hurts. Make her see she doesn't belong in the City of the Sun because they don't want her." Ravana paused before continuing, "I have an idea."

"What?" Lilith said, hopefulness coloring her voice.

Ravana rose from the chair and paced. Lilith had the weapon she needed. She just had to point her in the right direction and wait for Lilith to pull the trigger. "I've got a plan that will send her over the edge, she'll kill herself."

"We should be so lucky."

"If she surrenders her will to live, then we can grab her. She'll be a free agent."

Ravana stopped pacing and Lilith leaned in. "Sounds too good to be true. How can we pull that off?"

Heartened, Ravana grinned. She'd set Lilith up as the foil and keep her involvement under wraps. Ravana asked, "You can control the beasts of Earth?"

"Mostly, except for...you know..." Lilith swallowed hard.

Ravana knew visions of web-footed amphibians taunted Lilith. She'd tried casting a spell once to rid Lilith of her ridiculous phobia, but it never stuck. The image of them both momentarily immobilized by the little Lightning Girl sickened her. She'd been mortified and knew Lilith felt the same. Lilith was right. They needed to make sure Olivia suffered the same pain and humiliation.

"I'll tell you what I have in mind, but we're going to need help from your spy."

"Like what?"

"We need to know a time and place where we can get to Olivia, and she needs to be with her posse."

"Done. But just so you know," Lilith said, followed by a wicked smile, "if this doesn't do it, I might resort to releasing my favorite little pet from its lair..." Lilith's entire form glinted with her aura's energy, and it warmed Ravana's soul.

"You wouldn't?" Ravana said.

"*Au contraire*," Lilith said, folding her arms.

"Lucifer would be furious if you did that without his blessing!"

"I'm looking forward to it. He'd definitely punish us, and his torture can be incredibly gratifying."

"I'll say," Ravana said.

"How fast can you get ready?" Lilith asked.

Ravana twirled herself around like a blurring dervish and then stopped. "Ta-da!" She threw her hands up like a medal-winning Olympian. "Do you approve?"

Lilith whistled. "Now that's a trick." The hooded ebony velvet cape covered a black cat-suit tucked into knee-high patent leather boots. A silver-buckled belt trimmed her thin waist and multi-carat diamond studs adorned her earlobes. Ravana tied the laces of the velvet cape around her neck into a perfect bow.

"Give me your jacket, darling," Ravana said. Lilith slipped off the red leather coat, handing it over. Ravana's index finger pointed at Lilith and glowed. Bright red light flooded the room and when it dissipated, Lilith found herself in a matching black cape. "There," Ravana said, satisfied.

"Very nice," Lilith said. "Dust off your broom, sister, let's book."

Ravana laughed. "Brooms are so Salem, circa late sixteen hundreds."

Lilith shrugged. "A detestable era. A few of my most ardent followers were burned at the stake, and I wasn't ready to let them go yet."

"Well, let's go...and, oh, put the comb back," Ravana said. Chagrined, Lilith plucked the silver implement from her back pocket and slammed it on the tabletop. The room erupted in a spider-web of red light as they tandem flashed to Earth.

Chapter 30

Late for class, I hustled into my seat. Drew sat close, and his tempting lips and gorgeous everything made it difficult to concentrate on the day's topic. We exchanged playful glances and tried to refrain from pushing thoughts to each other. I arrived back in my room just before dawn. Kadie pummeled me with questions as to where Drew and I had been last night. Since thoughts of being wrapped around Drew danced in my head, it didn't take her long to figure things out. "Oh, you wicked woman," she'd said. "So jealous."

I didn't have the heart to tell her that Drew and I didn't have sex.

Yellowstone National Park in Wyoming would be the destination today. Even though we'd be encountering a grizzly bear, it seemed like a pretty tame task.

"All of you will be encountering animals in this assignment," Aidan said. "And I remind you again, no possession. In the event the animal is killed while you inhabit it, your aura will be trapped inside, along with the creature's soul. Forever. You will cease to exist. Total *nihility*. That applies to all apprentices. Only a few of the more advanced are skilled enough to engage in this practice and make it out alive."

Everyone knew I had performed an unauthorized animation. Thankfully, only four glanced my way. I'd made a promise to myself after Aidan's last warning that I wouldn't do anything that stupid again, especially not with a grizzly!

****

Drizzle frizzed my hair, and we found ourselves alone on the trail. It was not the kind of day that attracted huge crowds in the park. Drew put his arm around my shoulder as we trekked into the woods. It felt nice.

The lone camper chose to hike the three-mile trail alone and must've considered the chance of having a dangerous encounter with wildlife unlikely. He toted a large backpack as he ascended the rocky trail. Fresh pine scented the air on this beautiful day, invigorating us as we walked quietly beside our mark. His step almost a dance. Of course, this man had no idea a dangerous encounter with Mother Nature loomed in his future.

He staked out an area for his campsite, erecting his bright orange tent. Drew settled on the ground, lying back, his head cradled in his hands. I sat nearby, cross-legged, my knees pressed against his thigh. I pretended the pine needles were pick-up sticks, crafting them into precarious mounds and then trying to remove one without disturbing the pile.

The sun dropped low on the horizon, and Kadie commented on the spectacular beauty of the setting sun. Seth flipped a twig over and over again between his fingers as if trying to make it disappear. It didn't. No Traveler magic for such a simple task.

The hiker ignited a campfire and heated canned beef stew. His simple meal finished, he dutifully cleaned up his dishes, and as every good camper knows, suspended his trash on a high branch to avoid attracting bears.

He should have hung it higher.

The sun finally set, he climbed into his tent, zipping it shut. His silhouette illuminated by the lantern inside, he settled into his sleeping bag and opened a book before drifting off to sleep. A rustling in the woods alerted us to the approaching danger.

The huge brown bear ambled toward the campsite sniffing around in search of the source of the delectable smell. Rising up on its haunches, it swatted wildly at the trash and stayed at it until the sack finally crashed to the ground. The camper startled and flicked on the lantern. We rolled our eyes with the same thought: Now, that was dumb.

The bear sauntered over and sniffed the tent.

Drew stood. "I've got this." He confronted the bear. "Come." The animal ignored him. "Come on, come here." Eventually it faced him, and their eyes met. The bear wandered over and Drew walked away, enticing the bear to follow. The tent zipper slowly slid open, and the man peeked out tentatively. The animal scurried deeper into the woods as if Drew's treasured pet.

Catastrophe averted, we settled back and awaited sunrise. The campsite packed in haste, our rescued camper booked it out of there and jumped into his car. Wheels spun and gravel flew.

I chuckled. Lucky for you, buddy, almost no more birthdays for you.

The beautiful morning energized me, and I marveled that the majesty of something as simple as a sunrise could still surprise me. We ambled past swing sets and birdfeeders, flags identifying team fans, allusions to the everyday lives of mortals. Drew had my hand in his and I wondered when we'd have some time alone. Kadie abruptly stopped, and I crashed right into her.

"Geez, Kadie. Put your brake lights on if you're going to—"

Kadie stared off into the woods, a hand clutching her chest. I followed her line of sight into the forested space. At first I thought it might be a small bear, but its gray fur didn't fit, its body more streamlined, built for speed, agility. A wolf...a huge one.

Nearby, a little girl kicked a soccer ball in the yard, and a golden retriever napped under the cool shade of the decking. A man stood behind the sliding glass door leading to the back deck, casually sipping from his mug as he watched his daughter happily engaged in play.

The sinister mongrel crouched low to the ground, ready to spring. The animal bounded out of the woods and lunged at the unsuspecting girl. Terror disfigured the man's face. The cup crashed to the floor. No way could he snatch his daughter away in time.

The family dog woke, jumped into action. It intercepted the ferocious predator seconds before its jaws could clamp down on the child's neck. The man bolted from the door, grabbed his daughter, and ran for the house.

The wolf's sharp teeth sliced through the family pet's fur. It ripped out the dog's throat. The mangled canine fell to the ground in a crumpled heap, blood pouring from the gaping hole in its neck.

I swiveled to Kadie, then Seth.
Where was Drew?

Our thoughts crashed into each other, stabbing me like a butcher's knife into my skull.

The dog was dead.

Drew was inside.

"Drew!" My shrill, terror-laden voice shattered the ether. Panic ripped through me. Seth and Kadie gasped.

Oh Drew, what have you done?

The terrified sobs behind the glass door pained my soul. The grief-stricken father waited behind the barricade of the porch doors, the child clutching him in a strangled hug.

My attention remained on the lifeless animal. A giant pool of blood soaked the grass, a puddle of reddish-black slime. I flashed to the animal's side and knelt. The Kiss of Light! Placing my hand on its head, I leaned forward and blew my divine breath into the dog's mouth. I prayed I could reach Drew.

Was I too late?

I couldn't lose Drew!

I'd sell my soul first.

But the dog didn't move, its dark eyes frozen in a vacant stare.

I peered into the forest. The wolf hadn't retreated. It hovered near the edge of the woods and I assumed it didn't see me, but wasn't sure. A violent rage boiled in my gut, a seismic explosion, unbridling my true strength. I clenched my hands, fingernails bit into flesh. I gritted my teeth, and a low, feral growl vibrated.

I charged at the predator, releasing liquid-fire screams. Canine eyes locked onto me. Without warning, it turned and escaped into the brush. Or was it trying to lure me? I didn't care. I wouldn't allow the creature to live.

Deep into the woods, the wolf stopped and spun. We faced off. It hunkered down, then leapt. I seized it by the throat, and we soared above the tree line. Fury fueled me, quickly replaced by panic. This wasn't the same as flashing, and I didn't know how I could remain airborne and still fight. A sudden realization zapped me. This was no earthly creature.

It had black magic.

I didn't.

In over my head.

The demon's mouth lurched toward my throat. I ducked to evade its fangs and a primal shriek escaped me as we wrestled in midair.

The rabid cur lunged a second time, claws swiping. The wolf growled and sank its razor-sharp teeth into my shoulder. I growled back. Pain surged through me, throbbing into my chest and down my arm. Black fluid oozed from my wound.

I needed to flash. Escape. *Focus!* Too weak to will my atoms into dispersing.

The predator's fangs dripped with my black blood. Numbness pervaded my human form, fear sapping what was left of my strength.

Yet I couldn't let this evil devil live, not after it had taken the life of my friend, my love. New anger ignited inside me. I let it soar and my aura went with it. The air crackled, lightning sparked. Lightning?

I gave a hard wrench to the animal's neck as my body's electricity flowed through the sinewy mass of beastly flesh. The sickening stench of burning fur assaulted my nostrils, the creature's neck snapped. I plummeted, in a lethal embrace with my canine combatant. Someone emitted a terrible ear-splitting scream.

Me.

The ground rose too fast. I fell hard on my injured shoulder, a crunch resonating. I swallowed back the pain threatening to paralyze me, my consciousness fading. The wolf's charred carcass straddled my body, the two of us frozen. With a final burst of disgust, I kicked the animal aside. Its red sticky blood dripped onto my face and chest. The smell of sulfur made me retch. Struggling to sit up, I tried to wipe the blood from my nose and mouth, but my arm wouldn't move, and I collapsed, surrendering to agony, defeat.

Kadie and Seth rushed to my side and fell to their knees. "Livy!" Kadie said. Seth held my hand.

"What the hell's going on?" A woman, a voice I didn't recognize.

Kadie shrieked, "Couldn't you have helped?"

"I'm here to guard the kid. We're forbidden to intervene, remember?"

"Yeah," another unfamiliar male voice said. "We didn't receive a death notice for either the father or the kid."

"We weren't sent here to intervene," Seth said. "We just happened to be walking by…"

"Then back to my original question," the female guardian said. "What the hell happened?"

"I…I don't know," Kadie whispered.

I gazed up briefly at the two confused guardians, but then my eyes drifted to the golden retriever sprawled across the blood-soaked grass. I stretched out my good arm, stroking the soft fur. "Drew…" I moaned. "Come back to me…Nothing makes sense without you…"

The lifeless carcass of the dog alongside the wolf completed the repulsive landscape of death, even as my consciousness continued to fade and I drowned in despair.

"Livy, are you in pain?" Seth said. The terror in his voice sped up the numbness cascading across my body. I couldn't speak. I wanted to die. Drew's face appeared in my mind's eye, and I longed for his touch, his smile, to gaze into those beautiful brown eyes. I didn't need a heart for it to feel like it was breaking.

"I don't know if she can hear us," Kadie said, her voice cracked. She took my hand in hers and gently stroked. "Livy, Livy, can you hear me?"

I ignored her.

"What's that black stuff coming out of her shoulder?" Seth asked, in a higher-pitched panicked tone.

"Blood," the female guardian explained. "Not a good sign."

"We have blood? How come I didn't know this?" Seth said, his voice harsh.

Kadie's voice saddened me. "I don't know, it's so black, I've never seen blood like this. It's rare to see it anyway. It's almost never spilled. We don't like to talk about it. We're squeamish about blood."

"No excuse! We should know about this! It's vital information."

The male guardian said, "Save the biology lesson for later. Right now getting her out of here is priority number one."

Seth said, "Shit, we're going to be in so much trouble. Aidan warned us about this."

"But everything happened so fast," Kadie said, her

voice high-pitched. "We didn't have time to restrain Drew."

"I know, I know," Seth said. "It was reckless. I don't understand why he did it."

Kadie settled in cross-legged alongside me and rubbed my good shoulder. "I guess it seemed easy when Livy did it, so he thought he could pull it off, too."

Kadie's words pounded me. This was my fault. Just like Aidan warned me.

"Liv, can you hear me?" Kadie implored. She shook my arm violently. Pain roared through me again, torrid molten rivers. "Liv, we have to leave, now!" But the urgency in Kadie's voice was lost on me. I didn't care any more. I was finished.

Seth said to Kadie, "We'll have to tandem flash with her, like you guys did when we made our first trips to Earth. I've never done it. Do you think we can manage?"

The male guardian interrupted, "She's pretty messed up. You can't be sure she'll come back together. Call for backup."

I lay sprawled across the lawn, my mind dull and begging for unconsciousness, when a familiar voice pricked at me. I opened my eyes for a second, my vision blurry.

"I'll carry her home," Johnny said.

Kadie and Seth faced the tall stately guardian.

"Oh, John, we're so sorry!" Kadie cried. "We couldn't stop Drew. Then, everything spiraled out of control."

"I know," Johnny said. "Nothing could be done. Do not blame yourself."

Johnny knelt on the grass next to me. He took off

his flannel shirt and used it to wipe the blood from my face, whispering, "Hey, sunshine."

I ignored him.

"Olivia," he said louder. "Look. At. Me."

Yet I rolled away as a groan escaped me. I simply wanted to die.

Johnny scooped me up into his strong arms and tried to push thoughts into my head, but I refused to let him enter my waning consciousness. Nothing he could say.

"Hurry," Johnny said to Kadie and Seth. "And whatever you do, keep up."

"Yes, of course," they readily agreed.

Following Johnny's lead, our sad little posse set out to return to the City of the Sun.

Too late…too late to save me.

Chapter 31

The icy wind kissed my skin, and I prayed it was a death kiss. The stratosphere's cosmic vibrations coursed through my body. I always hated this part.

Johnny marched up the steps to Eccli with me cradled in his arms. I wasn't dead. Yet. The alert guardians threw open the doors, allowing us to pass, where Bath Qol awaited, unsettled. Aidan flanked her.

"Take her to the infirmary," the director ordered Johnny. I didn't know such a place existed.

Johnny kicked open the back doors with his boot and carried me into the Ministration Building with its four imposing smokestacks. Our sad parade filed down the white-tiled hallway and entered a small room. Johnny laid me on a cot and stepped back to allow Bath Qol to assess the extent of my injuries.

"Olivia," Bath Qol said. "Can you hear me?" I ignored her, staring into space. "Look at me!" she said louder, pinching my cheeks between her strong fingers. She forced my face in her direction, but I closed my eyes tightly and bit my lips.

A few seconds later someone turned me over to examine my injured shoulder. Pain continued to pervade my aura, but it was nothing compared to the agony of losing Drew. A warm cloth covered my face, washing away the remnants of clotted, sulfurous blood. Numbness caressed my mind, encasing it in a suffocating fog. Voices drifted into my head, speaking in a language I didn't understand. Willing myself to vanish, I whispered, "Please, just let me go."

A commotion near my cot stirred me. I'd no idea how long I'd been there, and I didn't care. I closed my ears to the din in the room, but then one voice in particular penetrated the shadowy corners of my mind. At first, I couldn't place it. It wasn't Johnny, or Seth, but the voice of a man I knew, and the window of my soul cracked open.

"Olivia." Bath Qol, again. Why wouldn't she let me fragment into pieces, fade into oblivion? I was a danger to everyone I cared about.

"Olivia," Bath Qol repeated. "I've called Raphael to minister to you."

Was he furious with me? I welcomed his wrath. And I didn't need healing. I needed a firing squad…no, an otherworldly electric chair. That would finally blow my aura to smithereens, a fitting end to my pathetic existence.

Revived by anger, I raised my head and blinked in an attempt to focus my blurry vision. Seth and Kadie stood plastered against the back wall with Johnny wedged between them. Dark circles surrounded their eyes, their pinched faces just adding to my pain. I was so sorry they'd ever met me. Bath Qol stood at my side with her usual perfect posture, Raphael's statuesque form alongside her. His warrior-like body, clad in the white toga, knee-high leather boots, and gleaming metal cuffs around his wrists, made it look like he was heading off to a war.

"I've come to help you heal," Raphael said with authority.

Defiant, I said, "I need to be destroyed. For everyone's sake."

"I must disagree, Olivia." He crossed his arms over his chest, his massive arms reinforcing his warrior status.

"I don't care any more. Please. I'm done."

"Listen," Raphael said. "The animal you encountered, the one in the form of the wolf, wasn't an earthly creature."

This confirmed my suspicions. Black magic controlled that giant canine. So? Drew was still dead, and I couldn't do a damn thing to save him. My mind swam in a river of bloody sludge. Once more, I tried to shut out the mighty Scepter's words.

"This was a trial from the Underworld to gauge your strength."

Horror struck again, like hundreds of hot pokers piercing my skin. Drew died because of me? They came to test me, and he got sacrificed in the process!

Raphael continued, "There was no way for us to intervene. Andrew presumed it was a simple animation like the one you previously encountered. He was merely collateral damage. I'm sorry. But we need you."

I spat my anger. "Collateral damage! What the hell does that mean? We aren't at war."

Raphael's gaze unnerved me. I might have pushed him too far. Slowly, deliberately, he seemed to choose his words, his voice dangerously low. "We are most assuredly at war, Olivia, and we have been since time began."

"Well, I quit!"

"*I* will not. You're too highly evolved, and regardless of what you think, you handled yourself expertly. Your strength and skill are as impressive as those highly experienced in warfare."

"Then I'll drag myself down to the Fountain of Lost Souls and throw myself into the baby blender," I said, like a child having a tantrum.

"The fountain won't accept you. Your aura is too powerful."

Both rage and despair wrenched my soul.

Raphael leaned over and pressed his huge hand against my injured shoulder. I winced. Pain roared inside me again. Streams of liquid fire seared my skin, and I stifled a moan. He reached down and lifted me from the cot. I lay like a rag doll across his arms. His nose only inches from mine, he growled. "It's taken a millennium for us to get you here, and I've no intention of letting you give up."

More mysteries. Cryptic words. Nonsense. I'd had enough.

The mighty warrior marched me from the tiny room and out into the hallway. We entered a dimly lit passageway and up a spiral staircase I'd never traversed. Higher and higher. Where was he taking me?

The narrow staircase ended in a circular room. The chilly air smelled old and stale. Paintings of fierce warriors battling hideous horned creatures lined the walls. Bodies with bulging biceps, huge chests, and muscular thighs. Travelers on steroids. They wore golden breastplates and metal cuffs surrounded their wrists. Gleaming swords dripped with the black blood of fallen demons. Blood like mine.

The painted domed ceiling depicted the night sky, stars sparkled, and the brilliant white crescent moon hung low on the horizon. Giant stained glass windows alternated with the paintings on the walls. The mosaic of light hitting the panes turned the room's aura into an ocean of sparkling rubies, sapphires, and emeralds.

Raphael rested me on one bare knee and kicked a window open with the heel of his shiny leather boot. A black wrought-iron railing served as a protective barrier at the base of the windowsill. Odd. Was there a risk of someone falling?

His huge hand ripped off the rail and cast it aside. It clanged on the floor. Cradling my body in his arms, he stepped onto the window ledge then dropped my legs between his so I teetered. One massive arm gripped my waist, while the other circled my neck, his enormous biceps wedged under my chin. The heat of his skin against mine made my aura rush. I expected sparks to fly.

The vast sky stretched out before us, the ground nowhere in sight. The end had come and I was ready. Instantly, darkness stole away the sunlight, erasing the limitless blue sky. Great mountains of black and white smoke swirled around us and wind gusts transformed strands of my hair into tiny punishing whips. My face stung from the lashing.

What was happening? It never stormed here.

I stared into the bottomless sky abyss and decided I wasn't afraid. I welcomed the end of my existence. Raphael bent his head, his lips touching my ear, his breath hot on my cheek. "You're the champion of free will," he said, "so, Olivia, *choose*. Do you want to give up or do you wish to continue, no matter how difficult?"

Rage strangled my throat, compounding the effect of his arm around my neck. I struggled to speak, "G—

go ahead. Throw me out the window! Exactly what I deserve. I'll become one of the Fallen. Merge with the fog and float away."

"I'm disappointed, Olivia. You want to be a warrior. Warriors do not give up the fight when a comrade gets killed in battle. A true soldier continues the fight, to avenge the soul of her fellow warrior."

"I'm no warrior."

"Not yet, but you will become the stuff of legends, unless you take the coward's way out."

The stuff of legends...?

"We've been waiting for you a very long time. But now you must decide. This wormhole will shoot you to Earth's surface in a twinkling. Choose to fall to Earth, and you will never again be welcomed in the City of the Sun. It will be as if you never existed."

Raphael released his grip and rested his rough hands on my shoulders. He hesitated, and then shoved me out the window. I tumbled downward, head over heels. Finally. I'd will myself to die, let my aura diffuse. Shatter that imaginary lake. Explode like an atomic bomb.

Drew's face appeared behind my closed eyelids. If I gave up now, he'd truly have died in vain. I couldn't let that happen. My thoughts triggered a tornado in my head.

And then I saw her. The original feminine divine. Lilith. We lingered mid-air.

A sinister, cackling laugh spewed from her perfect pink lips. "You tried to intimidate me at the mountain summit. And now I have my revenge!" A guttural scream escaped my throat. The Princess of the Night had sent a demon after me. Lilith held sway over earthly beasts and she'd used her black magic. Now I wanted justice for Drew, vowing vengeance.

"You've surrendered your will to live, so now you're mine!" she said, her laughter maniacal.

"*Noooo....!* I screamed. Bolts of lightning flew from my body. Heavy dark clouds roiled the blackening sky, the roar of thunder threatening to shatter my aura. My body trembled cruelly, the atoms inside me about to blast to the farthest corners of the universe, the venom trapped in my soul erupting into furious light energy.

Instantly, the storm clouds vanished and Lilith too. The sky brightened, and the winds calmed. And that's when I understood it had been my doing. *I* was the storm that had stolen the eternal sunshine from the City of the Sun.

Embarrassed by my violent display, I found myself on the ground behind the Ministration Building, its smokestacks huffing fumes. My form shimmered and trembled, my molecules crashing into each other, resisting the bonds that normally held them together.

Michael stood alongside Raphael. Crap! How long had he been there? How much of my tantrum had he witnessed? I put my head down and focused on the fog nipping at my ankles.

With his index finger, Raphael chucked my chin up, forcing me to meet his stare. "Free will," he proclaimed. "I knew you'd choose the right pathway."

Michael took Raphael's place. "I warned you, did I not?"

"I guess so," I muttered.

"You've had your first true test."

I didn't say anything. I should've taken Michael's warnings more seriously.

In a grim tone, Michael said, "I'd hoped it would be many more years before you had to endure such a challenge. This portends your future."

His dark eyes unsettled me and my thoughts drifted to Raphael's declaration that they had been anticipating me, waiting a long time. What would I be asked to do?

Michael interrupted, "Are you beginning to understand that you're different from the others? Your path will be thorny. Do you accept this challenge?"

"Yes." I didn't know what else to say. Would I be capable of meeting the mighty Scepter's expectations?

"You must understand that every time you're weakened, Lilith and Ravana become bolder. It's imperative you guard against this. You're not ready yet. Your energy is raw, unfocused. You must master it."

"I understand," I said with newfound commitment.

"But I say this with a warning. Dark magic feeds on hate and anger. Be careful how you use it. The line between good and evil is easily blurred."

Michael's expression softened. "That was a risky display of power. I'm surprised you regained the ability to pull yourself back together. I'm sure it has taken a toll on your aura. You will need time to restore it."

The King of the Scepters addressed Bath Qol. "She's out of rotation until you decide she's sufficiently healed. I want her confined to premises until you deem her ready. I require assurance she'll be protected."

"I'm grounded!" I blurted before the director could answer.

"Careful," Michael warned.

I clenched my jaw and swallowed my words, realizing I'd probably pushed both Raphael and Michael nearly to their limits.

"I'll see to it immediately," the director said.

Michael sighed, his expression shifted to uncomfortable. "I'm sorry," he said quietly, as if he and I were alone.

"For what?"

"The pain in your eyes. I'm well aware you were rather…fond…of Andrew."

What did he know about Drew and me? How much had he actually witnessed? I recalled him telling me he watched me, often, but…the thought made me cringe.

"We'll take our leave now," announced the Lord High Commander.

The two glorious Scepters exploded in blinding white light, a flurry of wind and fog in their wake. Thankfully, Michael hadn't touched me…and, yet, I sort of wished he had. As I stared at the space where the two mighty warriors had stood, a painful longing engulfed me. I wanted to go with them.

Chapter 32

I sat on my bed and speculated over what assignment Kadie and Seth had been given. I walked to the bookcase and picked up *The Discovery of Witches,* a novel Kadie had *borrowed* from an earthly library, hoping to distract myself for a few hours. Time crept slower than a kid waiting for Santa to arrive.

Finally...dinner bells.

I entered the dining hall alone and tried to ignore the painful glances thrown my way. I couldn't decide what overwhelmed me more, humiliation or sadness...and eventually concluded they shared equal billing. I poured enough for two drinks, figuring extra fuel couldn't hurt. Throwing a handful of cookies on my plate, I made believe things might be normal again some day, whatever the hell that meant. Suddenly, I hated cookies. Give me a goddamned cheeseburger!

I sat at our usual table, and Kadie and Seth arrived shortly. The stares of the other recruits proved lead sinkers weighing me down. The ache in my chest gnawed at me as I realized only three of us would ever be sitting together. *Drew, Drew, Drew*. My appetite for this pathetic excuse for food vanished, swallowed by emotion. Drew was gone, yet everywhere in these familiar surroundings...the sound of his laughter and the adorable way he tilted his head when he listened to me make a serious point.

"How are you holding up?" Seth asked, as he and Kadie slid into seats, food and drink in hand. The pain in his voice added to the unbearable heaviness in my chest.

"I'm not. I'm about to lose my mind."

Kadie and Seth exchanged awkward glances.

Rachel appeared out of nowhere, holding her fizzy drink. She took a bite out of her super-cookie and chewed. "Nice work getting your partner killed." She swallowed, then smirked.

Kadie jumped up and shoved Rachel with both hands. "Get the fuck out of here!"

"Whatever," Rachel said. "I told you she'd be trouble on the very first day, didn't I?"

"Go! Get!" Kadie stood her ground and Rachel retreated, all eyes fixed on us. "What are you looking at?" screamed Kadie to the crowd. Slowly, people returned to their meal, and Kadie sat back down. She sighed, letting out a long slow breath, then ran her fingers through her hair. "How long are you grounded?" she asked.

"Thanks for sticking up for me, but Rachel's right…" I began.

"*I said*, how long are you grounded?"

Apparently, we weren't going to talk about this. "Until the boss decides I'm back to full strength." I realized they were truly concerned about me, and I was being a total bitch. I sighed. "Sorry, I'm just miserable sitting here alone all day while you guys are out saving the world." I squeezed both their hands and smiled weakly, thankful for their friendship. "And I'm mad at Michael because he grounded me again."

They tried to console me, telling me Michael and

Bath Qol cared about me and that this wasn't a punishment, but I just wallowed in my misery, unable to shake my foul mood.

We sat and talked a while longer, but I couldn't focus and half-listened to their tale of stopping a kidnapping. The shock over Drew's death cast an obvious pall over Eccli Hall too. Drew's face materialized in front of me again, a series of blurred contours, and the ache in my chest deepened. My heart was broken, not in two, but shredded, unidentifiable. Would it ever mend? Could the pieces be sewn back together?

I squeezed my eyes shut for a second. A needle pierced my fragile heart, blood soaked the white thread as it made little stitches in a futile attempt to make me whole again. Yet the stitches wouldn't hold, and I knew my heart was beyond repair.

The smell of fear permeated the room, terror of our own demise. It hung in the air around us, a sulfur-laden cloud, noxious. I'd never thought much about this before. Now I understood being immortal didn't guarantee you'd live forever.

Utterly exhausted, I got up to leave. Seth headed for the stairs to his room when I realized he'd be alone, forced to stare at Drew's empty bed. Up until now, I'd only been thinking of myself. I called after him.

"Need some company?"

He turned. "Nah…"

"Promise you'll call if you need me."

"I will. You too."

The recent tragedy played over and over again in my mind, making the night seem endless. I endured this maddening routine for nearly a week and didn't think I could tolerate one more minute of confinement. Should I throw myself at Bath Qol's feet and beg for mercy?

A beautiful morning heralded the day, as usual. Everyone else had already gone off to tackle assignments, and Eccli Hall became a haunted mansion to me. Sick of sitting in the garden and walking around the back yard, I threw myself on a couch in the Commons Room, wallowing in the quagmire of self-pity. *Tick, tock. Tick, tick, tock.* Did I hear a clock? But the room had no clock. The rustling of Bath Qol's gown turned my head.

"I've decided you're no longer grounded," the director said, gazing down at my prone form, her hands laced in front of her. "You're back in rotation tomorrow."

I jumped up. "Really? Oh thank you, thank you!" I threw my arms around her. She stood as stiff as a tree under my arms. I pulled back. Wide eyes told me I'd startled her. "I don't know what came over me."

She cleared her throat. "You are rather impetuous, Olivia. I should be used to it by now." An awkwardness hung between us until: "Try to stay out of trouble, only a few weeks left in the term and I don't want a repeat performance of your inability to keep yourself under control. Am I clear?"

"Yes ma'am, absolutely. Promise. No more mishaps for me."

After one firm nod, she turned on her heels and swished out of there.

I took the stairs two at a time and ran into my room. As I heaved my jeans and T-shirt into the laundry chute, an unexpected breeze caressed my skin. I went over to shut the open window. Hmm. A note on my bed. From who?

The crisp parchment lay atop a large book bound in black leather. A five-pointed star, forged in metal, decorated the top half, the pages gold-leafed. I sat down and placed the heavy book on my lap and read the note.
Dearest Olivia,

Please accept my gift to you. This is for your eyes only and will be vital to your future survival. Be careful. Those you trust may not be trustworthy.

—A Friend

Bold gilt letters spelled out the title: *The Book of Shadows*. I opened it carefully. Someone had written my name on the inside cover in the same handwriting as the note. At the bottom were the words: *Upon the death of this witch, this book must be destroyed to ensure the magic dies along with the body.*

The words appeared to be part of the standard print and would apply generically to anyone who owned the book. The first few pages depicted unfamiliar symbols for the sun, the moon, all the planets, and the phases of the moon. A page titled *Credo for Witches* outlined a statement of belief.

Be careful what you do.

Be careful whom you trust.

Be careful how you use The Power, for what is sent comes back.

Never use The Power against someone who has The Power, for you draw from the same well.

To use The Power you must feel it in your heart and know it in your mind.

Thumbing through the tissue-thin pages, I noted prayers and what looked to be instructions for religious rites and incantations. A chill shivered through me and I realized I still hadn't shut the window, clad only in my underwear. Clutching the strange book to my chest, I gazed out the open frame and wondered if I should report this.

Deciding I didn't need to call any more attention to myself, I tucked the note inside the book and hid both in the bookcase. My eyes only, for now.

Showered and dressed in clean jeans and a white button-down shirt, I wandered downstairs feeling entirely alone. It would probably be at least another hour before anyone got home.

I stopped in front of the stairs leading to the guys' dorms. I hated being here with nothing to do. Taking a seat on the bottom stair with my back pressed against the railing, I stretched my legs out across the step. My eyes drifted upward, Drew's room my target. I'd spoken to Seth once from outside his window. I could find their room.

Here I go again. Barely off in-house suspension and already doing something I shouldn't.

Up the staircase, down several hallways, I passed many open doors, unable to ignore the messiness of the rooms. Typical guys. Coming upon the door to Seth's room, I found it slightly ajar and pushed it open wider. Both beds were in disarray, clothes scattered on the floor. How come men never seemed able to get those clothes the last few feet into the hamper or in this case, the laundry chute?

And why had no one come to remove the remnants of Drew's short life? I thought of his parents, then thought of my last mom and dad. An unspeakable trauma for all.

The bed called to me and I snuggled into the

pillows and curled up, inhaling the lingering traces of Drew's scent...

A minute or hour later, someone whispered, "Livy?" Seth's tall frame loomed over me. Lost in memories of Drew, I hadn't heard him enter. I leapt up and nearly knocked him over. Seth clutched my arm to steady me.

I lurched for the door, but his grip prevented me from escaping.

"Wait!" he said, yanking me back.

"*Leave me alone.*"

"No." He dragged me backward and forcibly sat me on Drew's bed, his hands landed on his hips. "What happened to Drew was horrible, I get it. But we face death every goddamned day of this new life. And you can't keep holding yourself responsible every time something terrible happens. We're not going to get it right all the time. That's why we're in training."

I slumped and leaned back, banging my head against the wall three times. "Yeah, but if I hadn't performed that stupid stunt with the dog, Drew never would have tried this. You know it's true. It's my fault he's dead."

"*No. It. Is. Not.* What will it take to convince you? Nobody thinks that. No one."

"Rachel does."

"She's an asshole. Everybody seems to know it but Jesse."

I arose, like an old woman struggling for footing and threw my arms around Seth's neck. "I love you," I whispered, holding him tight for a long minute, and then I ran from the room.

Chapter 33

I was heading for a crisis, like when you collect all negative aspects of your life, put them in a huge imaginary bag, and strap it to your back. Carrying bad energy all day made you tired, cranky, and sometimes just plain mean. An entire term had passed, and what did I have to show for it? Guilty of some serious mistakes, I harbored grave doubts about my contributions, my supposed good deeds. I had no right to call myself a Traveler.

The last official day of briefings had arrived, and we waited for a rare evening meeting. There'd be a few more days of menial tasks before everyone left for break, and I needed to decide exactly what my plan would be for the time off. I figured I'd help out at Chrism Center, and Kadie invited me home to meet her family. A celebration to mark the term's end would take place tonight, yet I was in no mood for a party and planned to skip it.

The Commons Room proved nearly full, alive with chatter, and Kadie, Seth, and I took a seat on a couch. The chimes started ringing, startling me. Odd. We still had another hour before our final briefing. The clanging continued, and I thought it might be a drill. What could be wrong?

Others from outside started filing in, and everyone got to their feet, waiting for someone to alert us. A large contingent of Eccli personnel rushed in. I'd crossed paths with many during the term, but never seen them all together like this. They ushered us into the assembly ballroom where we'd first been welcomed to Eccli Hall. The chimes abruptly ceased.

Bath Qol, followed by the entire staff, entered at the front and stood before us. Anticipation electrified the air.

"I've called all the first term apprentices together because we have an enormous task to undertake. There's a malevolent force at work on Earth that needs to be banished immediately. The Scepters will be here momentarily to provide assignment details."

Was this a final exam, a last challenge to determine if we passed or failed? I pushed this crazy thought to Kadie and Seth. They gave matching shrugs.

The director stepped back in line with the rest of the staff. A cloud of blinding gold erupted onstage. The Scepters stood four abreast. The fidgeting crowd of apprentices gasped. Their warrior-like bodies sported full battle gear—the short white toga, knee-high leather boots, golden breastplates shielding massive chests, and gleaming iron cuffs surrounding their thick wrists. My imaginary heart skipped a beat as Michael came forward to address us. His booming voice shattered the stillness.

"I've called you together because an evil destructive force on Earth is taking a great many souls from us. It's manifesting itself as a rash of suicides, and mortals can't seem to understand why so many individuals have been taking their own lives. I needn't remind you that when a soul takes its own life, it is forever lost."

The Lord High Commander went on, his tone stretched thin. "We've determined the force behind this suicide cluster is *Shadow*, a demon summoned at Lucifer's will. Shadow has the ability to emit a high-pitched screech that can shatter souls already weakened by extreme sadness, anger, or loneliness. In essence these souls have surrendered their free will and capturing them doesn't violate the Covenant."

The mercury-like soul shards from Chrism Center immediately came to mind. I could understand how the soul of a child might be weak, but a fully-grown adult? So sad. Although, I *had* come seriously close to surrendering mine to Lilith…

"We've not seen this demon in nearly a millennium. We're sending all the first-year recruits to scout its location until we marshal sufficient forces to send it back into hiding. On Earth, it appears as a dark shadow passing over a soul, infusing it with a deep sense of despair and unworthiness. Shortly after, the soul destroys its mortal body."

Kadie reached over and took my hand, a sign of solidarity. I found Seth's. Thoughts traveled among us rapidly as the Lord High Commander levied the remainder of his directive.

"Be forewarned, Shadow can manifest as a dragon. None of you are capable of defending against such a formidable creature. So, I emphasize this is a scouting mission only. If one of your groups locates the force, you're to relay the information to the others and send a message back to inform us. Then return home immediately. We will summon our most elite legions to fight."

Wait a minute, did he say *dragon?*

The Lord High Commander paused, perhaps to allow time for his words to sink in. Many sideways glances skittered across the aisles mirroring the gravity of the situation. Familiar words from Aidan's lecture on demons echoed in my head: *Be careful what you hunt, lest you catch it.*

Michael didn't issue the standard, Peace be with you, but instead said, "Go now and search in the waves of the sea, in the whole of the continents, and in every people and city until you find this evil."

Dismissed, everyone crowded toward the exits. A hand grabbed my shoulder, the director. "You are to remain here," she said.

"What? Why?"

"The Lord High Commander's orders. You are not fully restored."

"I'm fine! Really, I am!"

"Absolutely not. You are confined to your room until this mission is completed."

"But…"

"Enough," she said. "The Lord High Commander is insistent and you will follow orders." She pirouetted and left me standing there with my mouth open.

"Goddammit!" I kicked the wall.

"It's for your own good," Seth said.

"They're just trying to keep you safe," Kadie added.

"I am sick and tired of this bullshit from Michael! Who the hell does he think he is anyway?" Kadie and Seth raised eyebrows at my ridiculous comment. I bit my lip instead of continuing my tirade. "I know, I know, don't say it…"

Seth put his hand on my arm. "We'll see you when

we get back. It probably won't be very exciting anyway. Just wandering around looking for a black cloud."

I stomped up the stairs to my room and threw open the window. Two hundred shooting stars swarmed the night sky. Unprecedented. Usually we just evaporated into thin air and reappeared at our destination. But this time I could see everyone, sparkling arrays of shimmering molecular clouds streaking across the firmament like a horde of cosmic fireflies. I desperately wanted to be part of this fledgling army...comrades in arms, fighting shoulder to shoulder in the name of the City of the Sun.

"Screw it!" I said aloud. "I'm going!" I flashed out the window and quickly homed in on Kadie and Seth's location.

The sun kissed the horizon good night, painting the sky as a kaleidoscope of oranges, purples, and reds, the slumbering towns blanketed in cool air while the heat of day rose from emptying streets. Kadie and Seth stood in an open field with white lines drawn at regular intervals on the turf. I gazed at the sprawling building and frowned. "This is my high school. The house I grew up in is a block away."

They wheeled on me. "What the hell are you doing here?" screamed Kadie.

"I couldn't just sit in my room while you guys were out on the most exciting mission to date!"

Kadie yelled again. "Michael will be furious!"

"He won't find out. Like you said, this will probably be boring, and no one will be the wiser. It's not like they had guards on my door."

"They should." Seth shook his head.

"Listen, guys, did you hear what I said before? We're only a block from my house."

"Coincidence," Kadie said.

Unlikely. My thoughts zeroed in on Lilith and Ravana. Could this be another attempt to test me? Or was I just unnecessarily impressed with my own importance?

"Something's wrong," I said. "Let's go." I flashed and Kadie and Seth landed beside me. We stood in front of a three-story brick house surrounded by a neatly manicured lawn. *My family's house.* No lights illuminated the inside. About fifty feet above the peaked roof, a dark menacing cloud lingered. A young boy of about twelve stood near the edge, his dark silhouette contrasted against the purple night sky.

Kadie gasped. "What's that kid doing on the roof? And that black fog, that's gotta be the demon. Do you think it can see us?"

"I don't know," I whispered. "I think that's my brother...Keith...he looks so much older and...holy shit, he's got a rope around his neck!"

Some of my classmates arrived on the scene. Rachel stood front and center, without Jesse. "Don't even think about doing something."

"Get out of my face," I said.

She grabbed my arm and forced me to look at her. "You're reckless. You'll get us all in trouble."

"I'll do whatever I think is right. You're either with me or not. I don't give a shit."

"You already got Drew killed!" Spittle flew from her lips landing on my face. I wiped it away with the back of my hand, then pushed her away from me. Anger strangled my throat, and yet I paused to consider her words of warning. This was different. I could save my brother, I couldn't save Drew.

An earsplitting screech pierced the quiet night and the shadowy cloud descended toward the rooftop. It inched toward my brother, a slithering wraithlike viper ready to strike.

I flashed to the roof, and untied the rope around the chimney, unaware that Kadie and Seth had followed. Kadie grabbed my arm and yanked me up. "Livy, no intervention without permission."

"No way I'm letting that thing take my brother!" I screamed, wrenching my arm free from Kadie's strong grip.

"Livy!" Seth yelled. "We're only on a scouting mission with direct orders to not get near the demon. Too dangerous!"

I paused, my eyes on my brother, who appeared totally unaware of the scene unfolding.

Seeing a rope around my brother's neck sickened me. I wanted it off him. His hands were clasped behind his back, his toes inching toward the gutter clogged with dead leaves. Tears trickled down his cheeks and his sad gaze focused on the gravel driveway below. It looked as if he'd spent the last week sick in bed, his dark hair a mass of tangled curls, his clothing wrinkled. I wanted to pull him into a protective hug. Make everything all right.

The monstrous demon had driven him to despair. If I could spirit the evil fog away from him the urge to kill himself might pass. Because if he jumped…I'd save him, no doubt. Hell! I'd face Michael's wrath with pleasure.

But I knew. The monster hadn't inadvertently

stumbled on my family. My eyes narrowed. I focused on the dark cloud circling my brother, then quickly freed him and flashed him to the ground. "Besides," I said to the crowd of my brethren forming around me, "it's me it wants."

"What?" Kadie said.

"The demon isn't after my brother, it's after me, and you can be sure Lilith and Ravana are behind this." My voice stayed low as I twirled, searching for signs of the wives. They had to be here. My anger ignited. "Leave him alone!" I screamed into the abyss of dark sky, "You can't have him. I'm the one you want!"

Chapter 34

Furious lightning and loud booms shattered the nighttime stillness. The darkness crackled. The ominous mist rose, morphing into a colossal crimson tornado. I shielded my eyes. *Breathe, one thousand, breathe.* Opening my eyelids, I gasped. Backlit by the eerily large crescent moon, the horrifying form of Shadow, the elusive dragon of long-forgotten fables, threatened. Its scaly sides swelled with each breath, making the bones of its rib cage stand out in relief, its muscles warping and stretching underneath crocodile-like hide. My brother didn't budge, somehow oblivious to the shocking apparition.

Oh my god. Flash. Now.

But I couldn't leave my brother defenseless, my family.

The shimmering army of my fellow recruits encircled me, their otherworldly radar homing in on this chaos. Dread and alarm ricocheted through us as the dragon's bulging eyes blazed red. It seemed to only see me, a tiny gnat in a swarm easily incinerated by a single breath.

The dragon hung midair, high over the roof, flaring its nostrils and spewing fire that fouled the atmosphere. Its roar rippled the space around us. Jerking its head upward, it flailed its wings. Gale-force winds blasted me against a tree trunk, stunning me as chunks of bark dispersed far and wide. My classmates lay littered on the ground like writhing autumn leaves.

Why didn't the dragon attack? Was it toying with us, a predator savoring its victims?

A low-pitched hum reverberated throughout my body, a drumbeat calling me to battle. My classmates' consciousness fused with mine, a collective—a mind-hive funneling one plea: Lead, Olivia, we will follow.

My eyes rolled into the back of my head. The vision shook me to the core—an enormous snow-white lion, not an earthly lion, but a mythical chimera with the wings of an eagle. Its white fur shone like a beacon.

Convulsions wracked my body, energy surged, bursting into a spectacular light show. The legion of apprentices sped toward me like iron filings to a magnet. Violently, we mutated into a monstrous entity. The winged, white lion. *Oh. My. God.*

We'd *shapeshifted.* All of us, yet—

I was the force behind the lion. *Me*, the ferocious attacker.

The dragon glided across treetops, setting the meager forest near my home aflame. My house would burn, my family dragged even deeper into this demonic fray.

Crazed with the need to kill the beast, I bared my lips, brandishing razor-sharp fangs. I dug my claws into the driveway gravel. Muscular hindquarters launched me above the flaming canopy, glorious wings transporting me higher and higher.

A rumble signaled the dragon's assault. It somersaulted and spiraled toward us...*me?*

We faced off, suspended mid-flight. The dragon's talons protracted. It snorted, gushing fire like two gargantuan blowtorches. An inferno in the sky. I swerved right to avoid the flames scorching my flank. The smell of charred fur knotted my gut. I growled; not in pain, anger ruled now.

This was not some ancient lumbering dinosaur, but a demon with preternatural prowess. And who was I kidding? I had no idea what I was doing.

I zoomed toward the stars, luring the dragon into the stratosphere, hoping the lack of oxygen might slow the beast. No such luck. Its mighty jaws lunged for my throat. Shining, blade-like talons ripped at my face, slashed at my eyes. Its snarl landed spittle on my nose, the rotting-flesh smell repulsive. My wings carried me backward, retreating, barely escaping the dragon's deadly incisors.

Too close. Way too close.

Guilt seized me. I'd already gotten Drew killed. Now I'd seduced my entire class into engaging a monster with no regard for the consequences. We could all be massacred. My fault. *Focus,* I commanded myself. Even as doubts whispered from within our mind-hive.

Banshee-like screams turned my head. Jet engines? A squadron of F-22 Raptors came in hot. I recognized these warplanes. My stepsister Carrie, a USAF test pilot, flew one.

Missiles launched. Executing a precise hairpin pivot, the dragon couldn't evade the mortal rockets, taking a hit to its hindquarters. In retaliation dragon-fire hailed down on the elite squadron. The planes maneuvered an escape at the last second, putting me in line for a head-on crash with them.

I saw one of the pilot's faces, the whites of her

eyes huge, and my heightened animal hearing picked up: "What the hell? Charlie delta, red alert! Copy home base, you getting this?"

Even with the helmet and oxygen mask I knew those hazel eyes. Carrie. This had turned into a clusterfuck of epic proportions. But...do something, act...lead the dragon away, save my stepsister.

I careened away from the jets in search of my foe, consumed by an urge to protect these unsuspecting heroes. The dragon feinted, a meteor skyrocketing to Earth and mysteriously...*vanished.*

Hunt! I raced through a veil of clouds, emerging on the other side. Streaming gusts stung my eyes. I swallowed giant gulps of air, the cool vapor soothing my seared lungs. I veered right, then left, traveling at supersonic speed, but the vast sky seemed endless. Where could it be?

I spied a mountainous cloudbank and barreled forward. Frantic, breathless, clueless. I'd lie in wait, convinced the dragon would return. Or was I being a coward? No. Lilith and Ravana still had me in their sights and would never give up this easily.

The pilots circled back, jet wash whisking away a chunk of my cloud cover. Save for the Raptors, the sky remained calm. No evidence of otherworldly beings or astronomical phenomena. After several passes, the planes ventured onward, leaving me alone. What report would be logged? Could they admit they saw a dragon? A crazed, gigantic lion in the sky?

I lingered amid thinning clouds. Where was the goddamned thing? Did I dare hope the dragon had returned to its lair? Or maybe it had taken a mortal hit? Silence. A desperate impulse rattled me, perhaps a wormhole would appear and we could escape? And yet I couldn't abandon the fight, must eliminate this ungodly threat to my family and perhaps the wide world. Hovering, panting, impatience plagued me. Seconds ticked by like hours.

Lava erupted across the sky, momentarily turning night into day. Son of a bitch! And yet lucent clouds exposed me, hiding, afraid. *Come on, Olivia. Get your shit together.*

My heart thumped like an IED about to explode. On me in a nanosecond, the dragon didn't appear incapacitated in the slightest. Damn. It hissed, and the hairs on my neck bristled. Mammoth claws pierced my leg, twirling me around like a cowman with an unbreakable lasso. A wild craving to tear the beast apart ignited an angry, murderous rage. I snapped my teeth together, anticipating the reptile's meat trapped in my jaws. It felt ugly, yet right.

I pictured myself in the jungle—primal, top carnivore in the food chain, fearlessly attacking my prey. Tearing its throat out mercilessly, hungrily, viciously.

I twisted and went for its jugular my leg still in its clutches. We tore at each other, claws slashing as blood oozed from shredded flesh.

Slicing, dicing. I flayed its snout, carving two nostrils into one. Dragon blood spurted into my mouth, sizzling black acid, agonizing. Seizing a leathery wing in my teeth, the bones made a sweet cracking noise. The dragon chomped down on my chest and shook me as if he'd scored a meal. My paws batted its face, strategically scratching. Its jaws held me fast.

I didn't know how much longer I could keep our

collective consciousness united. Panic throbbed, despair fracturing my resolve. This is where I'd get everyone killed.

Now or never. Never or now.

Summoning all my strength, I beat my wings and thrust my hind feet into the dragon's gut. My powerful haunches propelled me backward, leaving flesh and fur behind but taking a chunk out of its wing with me. I spat it out.

I fought to keep the vibrations of the dragon's shrill howl from scattering our atoms.

Side-by-side, neck and neck, the demon jerked its head and stared. Black blood poured from its mangled nostrils, its wing, my own blood smeared on its mouth. An unnatural hush ensued, a brutal interlude, the fiend's scarlet irises shivering terror though me. Huffing and puffing, I rallied a final burst of energy and sprung forward, then wheeled and attacked. The throat, that throat.

My claws pierced its neck. Its beady eyes flicked left and right in disbelief. My incisors ripped away soft tissue. I bit down on bone, snapping the dragon's upper vertebrae. Caustic blood burned my tongue. I ignored the pain. The winged lizard shrieked, more of a keening, resounding like the cries of a thousand dying harpies.

The dragon sputtered, yet only a meager spark discharged from its gashed nostrils. It whimpered, contorting, thrashing, until a torrid gasp signaled its last exhalation. The lifeless behemoth sagged, its heavy weight bearing down on my clenched teeth. I opened my blistered mouth and watched the carcass plunge earthward in a flaming trail.

My chest heaving, I roared triumphantly. Had we really vanquished the beast? Would I be praised, or punished?

Shock undulated through our mind-hive as a seismic blast below confirmed Shadow's demise. A mushroom cloud expanded, boulders detonating and fissures skittering along the desert floor, gushing hellfire.

Dragon slayer, is that what they'd call me centuries from now?

I coasted through the storm of black snowflakes, soaring up-up-upward. Elated!

Alive.

Chapter 35

Our specter fragmented. Silver sparks cavorted in the atmosphere as the mass of shocked apprentices transformed back into their former selves, all of us obscured in black soot. Kadie punched her fist in the air. "We killed it! We slayed a goddamned dragon!"

Everyone hooted and hollered, the sky a frenzied ballet of twirling auras.

But time to head home and give our reports. My fellow apprentices vanished in a display of dazzling stars shooting across the ebony sky. Yet I lingered, suspended in mid-air, my thoughts jumbled. I'd never experienced such rage, an irrepressible desire to destroy. Where had it come from?

Except I *had* done this before, the day I killed the demonic wolf that took Drew.

I wondered if Drew had given me the vision of the white lion. Had he helped me in some way? Or was it someone, or some*thing*, else?

In my heart of hearts I knew the culpability was mine and mine alone, and—

The barren ground rushed up at me, my body in uncontrollable free-fall. Sulfurous flames licked my face, threatening to consume me. Confusion intensified to artery-throbbing panic, my atoms chaotic, disintegration a certainty.

Seth and Kadie zoomed toward me like guardian

angels, flanking my sides. They tandem flashed with me. Their frantic panting, my wheezes, echoed as our three-headed comet rocketed away from the plumes of molten rock and soared into the night. Their energy refueled me, my atoms bonding according to the laws of physics.

We landed on the crusty desert floor. I said, "Holy shit! You saved my ass." Getting wrapped up in my own thoughts and not concentrating on staying airborne had almost finished me. I guess Bath Qol and Michael had been accurate in their assessment of my battle-readiness.

"No problem," Kadie said.

"We've got your back," Seth added. "Always. We're a team."

Yeah. A team of three, I thought, reflecting on Drew's absence. Would a new teammate be assigned to us next term? I hoped not. The idea of replacing Drew made my chest ache.

Catching our collective breath, I told them I needed to check on my brother before I headed back to Eccli. Of course they insisted on accompanying me. About to flash, extreme coldness hit me, like a block of ice to the solar plexus. I grabbed Kadie's arm. "Wait. *Please*."

"I'm here," Kadie said.

Dirt quivered under my feet. The shaking intensified and a geyser of crimson and gray smoke formed. Lilith emerged, standing among the dragon's ashes dressed in a red leather jacket and matching pants. Fists balled at her sides, her spikes of auburn hair heaved in rhythm with her ribcage. In an ominously pitched tone, she said, "*You*, Olivia, are in *my* way."

A beat later, Kadie whispered, "Any chance there's

a frog around?"

"Doubtful," Seth said.

"I don't need a frog, trust me." I awaited Lilith's next move.

"You always were so full of pride," she said. "Original sin. I'm about to silence you. Into Nihility."

"The Covenant?" Seth stepped closer to Lilith. He was right. We weren't allowed to kill each other.

Lilith confronted Seth, barely a foot separating them. "Damn the Covenant! I'm more than capable of starting a war across the universe over this." She swept her hand in a dramatic half circle.

I pushed Seth aside and stood in his place. "I should have known you were behind the demon-dragon, which, as I'm sure you witnessed, our army soundly defeated."

She huffed. "Army? Where is your army now?"

My aura prickling, I felt almost a shiver. I braced for the attack.

Her hand shot forward and hurled sparks at my feet. A giant fissure formed beneath me and I plummeted into the widening pit, blinded by the brightness of a thousand klieg lights...strobing in my head. My vision turned further inward. A door chiseled from amethyst, the latch unlocking, the door screeching open. Endless tangled cobwebs prevented me from walking through. Feverishly I brushed them away and leapt across the threshold.

Recollections, cascading, unstoppable. Lilith and Ravana striding past me on Center Street during the first trip back to Earth...At my death, they'd challenged Thomas and Johnny. The cemetery behind Dan's house, when they'd dragged me into a crypt. Then posing as

Good Samaritans, they'd offered a ride the night I saved Peter. Behind that supermarket...And during our recent mission when we'd plucked a family from death's brink.

I understood. Or thought I did. They'd used an incantation to make me forget, hoping to lure me into their coven?

My temper seethed. Acrid fumes invaded my nostrils. I willed myself up and into the clean night air and faced my nemesis. Kadie and Seth appeared spellbound, frozen in place. Lilith's games.

She pointed her stubby finger in my face. "I can access the most ancient magic. I draw power directly from the Source. I'll pulverize your aura."

"Perhaps I'm pretty powerful too. And I know what you and Ravana are up to."

More lethal light flew from Lilith's hands, but I fortified myself, the rainbow of my aura expanded and deepened in color—more protective than shielding us. The beams deflected, hitting Lilith, stunning her. She recoiled, falling. Her clenched hands grabbed at the dirt, and she shrieked through gritted teeth. I readied myself for another attack. Instead she scrambled away, crawling on her belly along the dusty soil. Before I could advance, she shapeshifted into a serpent and slithered into a hole.

That's when I knew...Lucifer's wives would one day grow to fear *me*.

"Holy of holies," Seth said. "Insane!" Looked like someone was no longer enchanted. Seth clapped his hands before Kadie's face, and she was herself again too.

Good. My friends were okay. Exhaustion overtook

me. The battle over, my body trembled violently. I leaned over, hands on my knees and blew out the longest breath.

Kadie rubbed my back lovingly. "Geez, that was amazing, Olivia."

"Thanks, but don't count your chickens."

Kadie shook her head at me, like she always did when I said something so human. She'd stopped asking me to explain. I straightened and scrubbed my face with my hands.

She said, "You look ridiculous. We're covered in black soot and now you've mushed it into war paint."

I contemplated the starry skies, honing in on the Orion constellation. "If a war is what they want, a war is what we'll give them."

****

Back at my family's house, the fire department had the forest blaze under control. My parents stood agape, bookending my brother, their arms wrapped around his shoulders.

I couldn't stop thinking: Because of me, they'd all been targeted. Yet…because of me, they'd also survived. All's well that ends well? And had my stepsister, Carrie, revealed the outrageous sighting she'd just experienced? Surely the military would designate it Eyes Only.

Watching the people I loved, pondering these things, unable to take it all in, I heard my little brother Keith say, "The whole time, I-I had the strangest feeling Olivia was here, watching over me…"

My parents hugged him closer. I wanted to join them so badly. Haltingly, Mom and Dad gazed left and right, their eyes somehow locking onto my direction. A sob escaped me. They could feel me too.

****

The detour resulted in our threesome being the last to return to Eccli Hall. A crowd lingered on the grounds. The heads of the Scepters loomed large in the background and I frowned. The task had been to search and report, not search and destroy. I'd disobeyed a direct order. Again. Damn.

The Lord High Commander led the band of four as they approached. I reflected on how we'd killed the monster without authorization and remembered the vision of the mighty winged, white lion. Was I the only one who had the vision? Would I be held responsible?

"Olivia, you're quite the sight covered in soot," Michael said. It seemed as if he struggled to keep from smiling. I didn't find this amusing at all, my lips shut tight.

Michael cleared his throat, squared his shoulders, and that hint of amusement dissipated. He clasped his hands behind his back. "We've reached a consensus that you were the one with this incredible vision and pushed it to your fellow apprentices. Quite a feat. Shapeshifting isn't an ability we've ever seen here."

His thoughts pressed down on me, my mind buried in wet sand. We both knew what his words meant. Travelers couldn't shapeshift. Only demons could. Neither of us pushed what we were really thinking, so it remained understood, but unsaid. Could Michael feel what I did? The sickening disgust at the bloodlust I'd experienced twisted my gut. The urge to kill, even something so evil, seemed wrong. A murderous rage I never wanted to experience again. Did this tie me even more securely to the Underworld? Did I enjoy killing? I hated it and yet loved it. Maybe Ravana spoke truth about who I'd become.

Michael's deep voice towed me from these musings. "It's one thing to shapeshift as an individual, but to pull it off with an army is quite astonishing, Olivia. Apparently you served as a catalyst for merging everyone's aura. What possessed you to do such a thing?"

Possessed was an appropriate word, what did possess me? Drew? Something more sinister? Or was it…just me? "I'm sorry, sir, I don't have an answer. I'm not exactly sure what happened."

"We are sure about one thing. You triggered it." Michael's jaw flexed as he waited.

"Uh…as we got close, I had this vision of an enormous winged, white lion pursuing the dragon, kind of like a dream. And then somehow that dream came true."

His eyes narrowed, probing me, which always made me think he purposely kept facts from me. "You do know where it came from? You do remember?"

"I get flashes," I said, "but then nothing." Aside from the spells cast by the wives, did other reasons exist for my memory fading?

"The winged, white lion was once your totem," Michael said, matter-of-factly. "Your first mortal life."

My eyes glazed over. I couldn't remember two lives ago, much less that far back. And how come I could never remember much about my past lives when others had no problem recalling even the most minuscule details?

Michael smiled, confusing me again. "The first time I saw you…the spring of '54." When I didn't respond he continued. "That would be 1054...But no matter."

What the...?

Michael continued as if he hadn't just made an incredible revelation. "You realize by pushing this vision to all your companions, you somehow forced the synergy of the entire two hundred to transform into a unified force." He paused. "However, I'm not happy about the risk you took. Not only with yourself but also with others. Did you consider the ramifications before you once again disregarded my orders?"

I thought I'd escaped a reprimand, but now...Perhaps a pattern was developing?

He continued, "Not to mention the spectacle this created. Fighter jets? A forest fire? What part of being invisible and inconspicuous do you not understand?"

"I..."

He stopped me. "Never mind. It will require some cleanup, however." He turned and addressed the group, commending everyone on the defeat of the powerful demon that had threatened the world for many millennia. He instructed them to enjoy the end of term celebration, which had now turned into more of a victory dance.

Everyone but the four Scepters headed inside, when Michael said. "Not you, Olivia."

Crap, here it comes.

"I confined you to the premises for a reason. You were not fully recovered, and you put yourself and others in grave risk. I am not happy."

Gabriel said, "Lord, Olivia should be praised not reprimanded for her actions. We've discussed this at length with you."

The Lord High Commander's voice deepened. "Stay out of this, all of you."

"My lord…" began Raphael.

"*Enough*! Go inside with the others. I will deal with Olivia on my own terms."

Slowly, one by one, they flashed, leaving me alone with the Lord High Commander.

"Why so angry?" I asked. "We did something good."

"I'm not angry, I'm furious!" He paused and sighed. "When I sent your class on patrol I fully intended for this to be a scouting mission. I'd no idea why Shadow had been unleashed at this time. I fear dark and difficult times lie ahead." Michael's jaw tightened. "I believe that—"

I put my hands up. "I know. Lilith and Ravana sent it. They used my brother as bait." I had no idea if he knew my stepsister had also been involved in the fray.

"Exactly," he said. "I'm trying very hard to keep you safe, Olivia. However, you continue to do what whatever you choose with total disregard for my orders. What if you'd lost this battle? What if you'd gotten everyone killed?"

"I…don't have an answer. It's like some other force takes over and I have no choice."

"That answer is totally unacceptable. And aren't you always telling me that you don't believe in fate or destiny?"

Well, he had me there. My mind collapsed, unable to come up with anything intelligent. I didn't answer him.

"You're irresponsible and impulsive. This has to stop or I'm taking you out of commission. I'll put you to work as a gardener or something equally menial."

He had to be kidding me. I'd just pulled off a spectacular feat! Why couldn't he see that? I was in no hurry to kill anything again, yet if I had to defend myself, or others, I'd do it. I still owed Lilith retribution for murdering Drew.

Placing his huge hands on my shoulders, Michael said, "I'm deadly serious about this, Olivia. I want total compliance with my orders. Understood?"

His touch jolted me. The familiar electric current emanated, running into my shoulders and traveling to my extremities. Sparks threatened to escape my fingertips, and as always we both acted as if nothing unusual happened. I pushed the force back in his direction, resisting the urge to merge our auras. I noticed I wasn't admiring him as much as I had. I seemed taller…older.

"Yes, sir," I said through my clenched jaw. "You're the boss."

"Good. You're excused. Go and prepare for the celebration." Michael's hands fell from my shoulders, and he sauntered away and vanished in brilliant white light. The electricity dissipated. I felt like I'd experienced a heat wave. And I could no longer deny his effect on me. Though I wasn't sure what to make of it.

Yet, I'd made him mad. Again. Why couldn't I just follow his orders? I shook my head. How had all this happened? A nagging uneasiness stabbed me, one I couldn't identify. It was as if I sought my way home, except, I just wasn't sure where that was. Dorothy knew where home was, she just had to find a way out of Oz. But I couldn't interpret the universe's signals, and nobody seemed inclined to help. Sometimes I thought I'd only scratched the surface of the universe's complexity. A universe that maybe could never be understood.

****

Kadie and I arrived at the end-of-term celebration late. I gasped as I entered the Great Hall. Alight with the glow of a thousand candles, the shimmering luminosity transformed it into a fantasy ballroom. Starched white linens adorned long banquet tables where baskets of golden and silver-hued fruits and gilded trays stacked with iced confections sat artfully arranged. I savored the thought of the feast. Silvery fountains spewed forth a bubbly drink that looked like champagne, although I doubted it was, and shiny goblets emblazoned with the Eccli Hall crest were stacked in tall, precarious, pyramids. The center of each table held a flaming candelabrum of tall white candles.

Kadie and I entered to the sounds of ovation, clapping. I lowered my head and stared at my feet, secretly elated at the levied praise. I dug my hands in my back pockets, unsure of how to handle this adulation. The applause grew louder when once again the Scepters approached me.

Gabriel stood before me. "Olivia," he said in his booming voice, "we commemorate your act of initiative and bravery on this day. You have removed a great weapon from the Underworld's army." He placed a pin on my vestment: a triplet of golden stars with the image of a winged lion forged in silver suspended from the center. Utterly uncomfortable at being singled out in front of peers, I simply said, "Thank you, sir." I bowed my head again and waited for release.

Gabriel lifted my chin with his knuckle. "This is only the beginning of your journey, Olivia." His eyes hinted at something...mischief or...*danger?* Yet I was weary fretting over the future and who I might, or might not, become. No more talk of destiny.

I gazed past his massive shoulder, where Michael's frown didn't seem compliant with Gabriel's words and actions. Gabriel ended the awkward moment and invited everyone to partake in the sumptuous feast, officially ending the term.

Kadie came up behind me, whispering, "Okay, this is getting too intense. Let's party!" I smiled. The Scepters left and the mood escalated into joy, the satisfaction of a job well done. I suffered through the shaking of hands and excessive back patting. I was a bona fide celebrity, which didn't help me stay humble. I'd have to keep working on that.

"Well done," came a male voice beside me. I turned to see Jesse, Rachel at his elbow.

"Thanks," I said. "But I'm just as shocked as everyone."

"You should be," Rachel said. "This could've been a funeral gathering."

As much as I despised Rachel, she was right. I didn't respond and focused on my feet. Jesse cleared his throat in an attempt to lighten the mood. "Well," he said. "I think the whole thing was abso-fucking-lutely awesome." He smiled, then ushered Rachel away.

The ethereal light of the waxing moon danced on tree leaves in the garden as I reflected on my new reality. I had people who cared for me and a calling to serve the souls of Earth. I would do everything and anything I could to be the best at what I did, to take care of the people who needed me.

I faced the window to the beckoning night, the silver crescent suspended oddly above the horizon. The moon lay on its side, the two pointy ends facing upward like demon horns.

I pushed open the French doors and strolled toward the garden, Kadie and Seth trailing me. Maybe the best of times were yet to come. An owl screeched. I jumped. Then scrutinized the treetops. Had the sound come from inside my head?

"What's wrong?" Kadie asked.

I scanned the foliage in search of the owl. "Did you hear that?"

Her eyebrows knit together. "What?"

Seth said, "What did you hear?"

I hesitated. "Never mind."

In some ways, my existence grew darker day by day. Who had sent me *The Book of Shadows*? Who was this so-called *friend*? I'd escaped from evil that incessantly followed me and now that I'd used my newfound abilities, I hoped Lucifer's wives stayed underground. Did destiny have me in its sights? I wasn't a fan of fate.

My chest tightened and I inhaled deeply, bolstering my shoulders against the demonic moon. A warrior I would become, I silently vowed. Yeah, the stuff of legends.

Epilogue

The flickering red flames welcomed Ravana home. She snapped her fingers and the purchases from the exclusive boutique she frequented appeared on the large wooden table. After the horrid debacle with the Shadow Demon she decided to indulge herself in earthly pleasures. Shopping, dining at an elegant restaurant, soothed her nerves. She needed to regroup.

Tugging on each finger, she removed her plum-colored cashmere gloves and scanned the room for her servants. She frowned. Where were they? She threw the gloves on the floor.

Two tall men stepped out from the shadows. Lucifer's chief guards. Her aura raced. *Damn, he already knew.*

"The boss requires your presence," Mason said. Ravana wanted to knock that big fat nose right off his swarthy face.

Ravana planted her hands on her hips. "And he sent you goons to retrieve me?" She sneered. "I think not."

"He doesn't like to be kept waiting," Mason said. Jason, built like a twig Ravana could snap with a twitch of her index finger, stepped nearer. She thought these two amusing, Jason and Mason...sounded totally ridiculous.

With a wave of her hand, she said, "If he wants me,

he should come get me himself."

The guards glanced at each other. Ravana knew they wouldn't manhandle her. She had infinitely more power than they did.

She felt him before she saw him. His words instantly sent her aura into pure red. "I'll take it from here," he said, his voice raspy, sultry.

Lucifer stepped into the scarlet fire glow, his blue eyes ablaze. With a nod, the guards fled from Ravana's lair. His longish blond hair nipped at the crisp white collar of his dress shirt, which contrasted beautifully against his bronze skin; a well-tailored black suit, crimson satin tie with matching pocket scarf and initialed gold cufflinks declared his regal status.

"Don't disobey me," he said.

"Don't put me in a cage, and I won't seek autonomy."

Lucifer roared with laughter but not because he found her amusing. He mocked her. For him, the line between anger and pleasure easily blurred. The challenge of walking that line excited Ravana.

"I do find your defiance entertaining," he said. Closing in on her, his shiny black shoes clicked on the stone floor. He still wore those stupid metal taps on the heels. The sound irked her. When were they in style? Sometime back in the 1930s or 40s. He was still so ridiculously old-fashioned in some ways. She wondered what devious business dealings he'd been involved in of late. It must be crucial, if he'd ventured out himself instead of sending one of his lackeys. Perhaps cheating some VIP financier out of enormous amounts of capital. Greed was definitely his favorite sin.

Grasping her left hand, he brought her wrist to his

mouth and kissed the red crescent mark. "Mine," he said, making her blood surge in torrents of passion. "Don't ever forget to whom you belong."

"Never, husband." His possessiveness chafed at her, a burlap swath on her skin, and she struggled to keep the annoyance off her face.

"I've always enjoyed your feisty nature, my sweet, your reluctance to be submissive. You're like a spirited little filly that needs to be broken…over and over and over again." Standing so close, the heat of his aura seared Ravana's skin. He chucked her chin up to gaze into her eyes. "You always provide a challenge."

"I'm always here to serve you, husband," Ravana said, careful to hide the sarcasm from her voice.

"I seriously doubt that, and I fear I've been too lax with you lately, my love. Perhaps you need to be reminded of your place." He grasped the laces around her neck, pulling the bow loose, and the black velvet cape drifted to the ground. He pushed her dress off her shoulders and ran his hands over her bare flesh, kissing her on the forehead. She shuddered.

"I know my place, and it's at your side," she muttered.

Lucifer's wild blue eyes sliced through her façade of steel and her skin prickled. She couldn't assess his mood. Anger or…lust? Perhaps both. The perfect pairing in Ravana's opinion.

Taking a step back, he clasped his hands behind him. "I'll get right to the point. Did you know or not?"

"Know what?" She batted her long dark lashes, feigned innocence.

"Don't be coy, little pet, you know what I'm referring to. I've already had a meeting of the minds with Lilith…"

And bodies…

"…She took her punishment well, perhaps a little too well. Although being shackled to the wall in my private dungeon for a few weeks should convince her that I won't tolerate her untoward actions. So, tell me, did you know about Shadow or not?"

Ravana hesitated. She needed to craft her answer carefully to avoid involvement in the unsuccessful assault on Olivia, and she wasn't sure what Lilith had already admitted to. "Yes, and no."

Lucifer backhanded her across the face, his gold wedding ring cutting her lip. She gritted her teeth, then wiped away the trickle of black blood from her chin. The searing pain awakened a yearning inside her. Inwardly, she smiled.

His eyes seemed to search her, poking at the mask she'd affixed to her face. He lunged for her and wrapped his massive hand around her throat, pushing her against the wall. He huffed. "Don't play games with me, Ravana. I asked you a direct question."

Ravana struggled to spit out the words. "I didn't know! Lilith acted on her own. She mentioned something about Shadow, but I thought it was just a joke. She's always saying crazy things. I never thought she'd act on it!"

His fingers tightened on her throat, and she waited for his reaction. Ravana felt her anger escalating. Lucifer remained silent for too long, and Ravana squirmed. "Let me go," she whispered. "Please, y-you're choking me."

Relaxing his hand, he ran his fingers across her reddened skin in a soothing motion. Ravana kept her mouth shut. His fury quickly faded, and he placed his palm on her cheek and rubbed his thumb over her bloodied mouth, as if applying ebony lip gloss.

He licked the blood from his thumb and growled. "You do worship me, do you not, my dear?"

Ravana kept her voice low and tried to sound reverential. "Always and forever," she whispered.

"Well, then I'd like some respect from my wife."

She knew what he meant and hesitated, she hated this stupid game. Her fury began to rise again. She despised it when he demanded she act subservient. Ravana put her hands behind her back and grasped her elbows. Her gaze fell to the floor as she spread her feet to shoulder width.

"Better," he said. "And have you forgotten how to address me, little pet?"

Ravana lifted her eyes. "No, sir."

"Lower your eyes. Now! You will not look upon me unless I allow it."

"Yes, sir," Ravana muttered. "Please, sir, you have to believe that I would never willfully disobey. And I'd never do something to displease you. Besides, I had no access to Shadow. Surely you know that. Only Lilith had the power to use him, *sir*."

"Eyes on me," he allowed.

Ravana glared at him.

"You will leave Olivia alone. Is that clear?"

"Yes, perfectly, sir."

"When I am ready to declare my intentions for Olivia, then I might allow your help. Until such time, you will not touch one hair on her lovely head. Do you understand?"

"Yes, sir."

"Good girl." Again he made her wait, and Ravana contemplated what he would mete out as punishment. Although he couldn't prove any wrongdoing, she fully expected him to take this opportunity to reinforce his dominance.

"Turn around," he commanded. Ravana slowly pivoted on her tiptoes like a tiny ballerina inside a jeweled music box. The anticipation of what he planned to do spread warmth between her legs.

Lucifer lowered her arms to her sides, pressed his muscular chest into her back. He wrapped one arm around her waist and pulled her into him. Grabbing her long locks into a tight spiral, he yanked her head back, exposing her nape. Passion erupted inside her like a seismic surge. "You have the most exquisite skin, my love," he murmured, his hot breath behind her ear. "So soft, the color of moonlight."

Nipping at her earlobe, his mouth traveled downward and he took her shoulder into his mouth. He bit down. Hard. Ravana closed her eyes and swooned, pulsating pain shimmering across her skin. His hand moved from her waist to her neck, his fingers squeezing, choking. A moan escaped her, and she could feel his wicked smile against her neck.

Ravana knew this charade would have to continue a while longer. Her plans to destroy Olivia needed revamping. She'd continue to manipulate Lilith, aiming her at the Little Lightning Girl like a lethal weapon. If she played her cards right, she could eliminate both Lilith and Olivia and then claim her rightful place as the one and only Queen of the Underworld.

In many ways Ravana's power exceeded her husband's. He knew nothing of witchcraft. True, he could summon divine lightning, something that only he, and now Olivia, could do. That made him dangerous, so she'd have to be careful. Plus, he had legions of demonic soldiers loyal to him. Yet if she could distract him long enough to put a new plan in place? Then she would seize the power...all of it...before he knew what hit him.

Lucifer seized her upper arm and turned her to face him. Ravana continued to display mock humility.

"Eyes on me," he ordered again.

Slowly, Ravana stared into his sumptuous face. His lips glistened invitingly, and his long blond hair reflected the crimson flames. The heat from his aura threatened to ignite her own, and she longed to satisfy her lustful hunger, a titanic craving never sated.

Lucifer moved his face to within inches of hers. "I'm not convinced you are being truthful with me, my darling. And so I intend to punish you simply as a reminder of who is in control. The lash of the bullwhip should serve to convince you. Of course, I also know how much pleasure you take from the pain. So perhaps this will be more of a reward for *not* disobeying. Either way, I will enjoy this." He smiled in his sinful way and then licked at the tiny speck of blood that lingered on her lip.

"Come, little pet. I want you naked." He wrapped his hand tightly around her neck and shoved her toward the chamber's back exit and down the long hallway to his private dungeon.

Ravana's aura surged in anticipation, and yet her mind began to drift. Vengeance streamed madly in her veins. She silently vowed, *Sister mine, I will set you on the bare rock and shed your blood, that it may never be recovered, spilled on the ground and covered by the dust of mortals.*

A word about the author...

Caryn McGill has immersed herself in a lifelong study of religion, astrology, reincarnation, and past-life regressions. This otherworldly journey coupled with her decades spent teaching science has produced her debut novel, *The Wives of Lucifer*.

Born on New York's Long Island, Caryn McGill resided on its bucolic East End until a recent move to Richmond, Virginia, where she's currently finishing her next novel.

Find Caryn McGill online:
Facebook at caryn.mcgillwrites,
Twitter @carynmcgill, and
www.writeonsisters.com where she occasionally blogs.

Thank you for purchasing
this publication of The Wild Rose Press, Inc.

If you enjoyed the story, we would appreciate your
letting others know by leaving a review.

For other wonderful stories,
please visit our on-line bookstore at
www.thewildrosepress.com.

For questions or more information
contact us at
info@thewildrosepress.com.

The Wild Rose Press, Inc.
www.thewildrosepress.com

Stay current with The Wild Rose Press, Inc.

Like us on Facebook

https://www.facebook.com/TheWildRosePress

And Follow us on Twitter
https://twitter.com/WildRosePress

Made in the USA
Middletown, DE
30 March 2016